I Want
You More

I Want
You More

Also by Swan Huntley

*You're Grounded: An Anti-Self-Help Book
to Calm You the F*ck Down*

The Bad Mood Book

Getting Clean With Stevie Green

The Goddesses

We Could Be Beautiful

I Want You More

Swan Huntley

ZIBBY PUBLISHING
New York

Library of Congress Control Number: 2023946567
Paperback ISBN: 978-1-958506-70-7
Hardcover ISBN: 978-1-958506-71-4
eBook ISBN: 978-1-958506-72-1

Book design by Neuwirth & Associates
Cover design by Danielle Christopher

www.zibbymedia.com

Printed in the United States of America
10 9 8 7 6 5 4 3 2 1

Luck is the residue of design.
—Branch Rickey

1

The story of me and Jane Bailey doesn't start with us. It starts with the death of my father.

After he was diagnosed with pancreatic cancer, I moved back into the drafty house of my childhood to take care of him. As I sliced his bananas and refilled his water and chatted with the hospice nurse about morphine and socks, I was thinking, *I'm about to inherit a beachfront property.*

While dreaming of a shinier future, I was also trying to be present. When somebody's dying, every moment is heavy with the threat that it could be the last, so you're scared to even take a shower. What if he died while I was washing my hair? The whole thing was exhausting.

In the movies, the dying person often imparts a great piece of wisdom to whoever's sitting by their bed. If I was waiting for that to happen, then how stupid of me, because of course it didn't. What my dad talked about were the sculptures he'd made recently ("Has anyone inquired?"), his relentless hatred of my mother ("Self-serving narcissist"), and his feelings about his diagnosis ("I'm still hoping it's a clerical error"). Then the morphine made him nonsensical ("Grass-fed beef!") and after that, he became silent, with the exception of some animalistic groaning that was hard to listen to.

In seven weeks, he aged thirty years. He went from being a grape to being a raisin, and his skin turned the color of ashes. I think the only parts of him that never changed were his feet. I sat with him for so many hours that I had plenty of time to notice this. I also had plenty of time to come up with what I thought were the correct parting words.

"I love you. Thanks for being my dad."

I said this at the very end when he was deep in his morphine cloud, so I'm not sure if he heard it or not.

On that same day, he closed his lips against a blueberry I was trying to feed him.

"Come on, Dad," I said, "blueberries are your favorite."

"His body's trying to die," the hospice nurse told me, and I was grateful for that, because I'm not sure I would have figured it out on my own.

I ate the blueberry myself.

A few hours later, my dad stopped breathing.

A good word for my childhood might be *desolate*.

When I was two years old, my mom left us in the most cinematic way. It was the middle of the night, and she carried only one suitcase. In my imagination, the suitcase had brown and tan checks on it and my mom was braced against the furious winds of Bolinas, hurrying to the cab that must have picked her up. Half a day later, she walked out of the airport in Rome and was blinded by the happiness of the sun. She promptly started a new life with her lover, who happened to be a woman. Like my dad, the woman was a sculptor, but unlike my dad, she was successful, which meant that she didn't have to teach at a community college to make money.

My dad never forgave my mom for leaving us. "I'm not

surprised she's a lesbian!" he said once. "She had sex like a corpse."

Five years after my mom moved to Rome, she became a corpse. Her plane to Mallorca crashed into the ocean. Her lover died, too.

In our drafty house on the beach, which Dad bought in 1972 for basically nothing, he raised me on microwaveable meals and haughty ideas. Even now, I can hear him saying, "The number of stupid people in America is astonishing." He thought that art was more important than food. And love. Or no, art *was* love. And anyone who didn't consider *making things* as necessary to their survival was an automaton.

When I was twelve, after it became clear that I sucked at drawing, painting, and sculpting, he said, "You'll be a writer. And you'll go to Stanford."

I did everything he wanted me to do. Straight As. Extracurriculars. No drugs. I hated him more than anyone, and I loved him more than anyone, too. I resented him for being so controlling while wanting him to control me. When I went off to Stanford, I called him almost every day to tell him about a problem and then ask, "What should I do?"

It was a confusing relationship. In a way, we were best friends.

According to an early version of a will that I found in one of his file cabinets, my dad had written that he wanted to be cremated and thrown into the Pacific "on a stormy day when the seas are wild and thrashing."

When I read that, I thought, *What a drama queen.* Then I carried out his wishes. The next time it rained, I went to the beach, opened the wooden box, turned it upside down, and watched the tiny pieces of my dad get sucked up by the tide.

A few days later, the lawyer called and said, "I have some news." She went on to tell me that no, I would not be inheriting the house. "Your dad left you five thousand dollars," she said. "Total."

He'd donated everything else to the community college where he taught as an adjunct in the hope that they'd name something tangible after him, even if it was only a bench.

2

I'd been so sure about my incoming inheritance that I didn't even bother getting a subletter while I watched my dad die. Even as my balance got dangerously low, I kept spending money. One day, I went to the Corte Madera mall and bought a nine-hundred-dollar fake-mink coat with a matching fedora, because why not? I was about to become a homeowner.

In my head, I had it all planned out. I'd repaint the walls, renovate the studio, and burn enough candles to eradicate my dad's smell. I imagined myself wrapped up in fog and grief and color swatches while cry-laughing about the futility of life. I'd get rid of my apartment in San Anselmo and ignore everyone for a while. In short, I would do nothing.

But now I couldn't afford to do nothing. I needed a job. So I sat down on the ugly denim pouf I had in my apartment and called my agent, Kim, who always answered the phone by yelling my name.

"Zara!"

At four foot eleven, Kim couldn't afford *not* to be loud, she'd told me once. I liked her a lot. She was sharky, boisterous, and apparently thrilled to be alive. I'd been observing Kim for a decade, and her electric personality had never dimmed, not even a little. Back when we were both twenty-three years old, Kim had read a short story I'd published in an obscure lit mag and sent me an email with a lot of exclamation marks in it. Then she'd signed me to her agency. The plan was for me to write more short stories and eventually sell a collection.

That never happened.

For a few years, I tried to write while working at a restaurant, but I mostly just slept. "I'm trying," I'd whine to Kim every time we had a check-in. "Serving food to people is draining."

I complained about restaurant life a lot, and one day Kim presented me with a solution. "I have a client who needs a ghostwriter," she said. "Do that."

At first, I assumed that ghostwriting would be a tangent in the story of my life. I imagined myself at a cocktail party in the future saying, "Oh yeah, I did that once." But then years passed, and when I looked up, the tangent had become the story. Somehow, I'd gone from "on the brink of meeting her potential" to "decidedly veering away from greatness."

That was my dad's version of the story, though. According to many other people, I was killing it. Somehow, the first book I ghostwrote ended up becoming a bestseller. Which meant that I could charge a lot more for the next book. Which also became a bestseller. Which meant that my fee rose again. The people who could afford me were the ones with the biggest book deals, and the ones with the biggest book deals were generally household names, and household names sold books whether the book was good or not. It was a loop that fed itself.

The only problem was that I hated ghostwriting. I mean, I really hated it. It just reminded me of all the books I wasn't writing for myself. The bigger problem was that I got used to living with my fear of success, which spoke to me in many voices. Usually, it was masquerading as something else, like practicality.

"Just work for money," my fear said. "That's what people do."

Maybe the biggest problem was that I didn't know who I was, or who I wanted to become. What does someone with only the vaguest sense of herself write about? I guess in the back of my head I was thinking, *When I find my story, I'll write my book.*

"You only call me when you need a gig," Kim said, "so I assume that's why you're calling."

I chose that as the moment to throw my tragedy grenade into the conversation. "My dad just died."

"Fuuuuuuuuck," Kim said. "You guys were so close."

"I don't know why I just told you that, because I don't really want to talk about it."

"Didn't you go to his house like every day?"

Yes, I'd been living there for months. But to Kim I said, "Ish."

"Well, I hope you're not spending too much time alone."

Not only was I spending all my time alone, I'd also stopped talking to everyone except for my oldest friend, Diego. I couldn't handle any more condolences.

"I'm fine," I told Kim. "Don't worry."

She considered that. "Are you still in your pajamas right now?"

"No," I lied.

"So if I asked you to send me a picture of yourself in real clothes, you'd do it?"

"Of course." I put the phone on speaker, quickly found a photo from weeks earlier, and sent it.

"Cute jeans," Kim said.

"Thanks." If I'd had more energy, I would have tried to think of a graceful segue, but instead I just took a blunt statement and softened it by adding a question mark at the end. "Let's talk about ghostwriting?"

"You know," Kim said, "this is perfect timing, because guess what? Jane Bailey's rep just asked me for a ghostwriter this morning."

"Who's that?"

"Girl, are you living in a cave?"

"Yes."

"Okay, let me give you the bullet points. Jane Bailey is definitely the most stylish person on Food TV. She kind of dresses like a cowgirl, but she's edgy, too. And she has this amazing, super-blond hair. Like if Debbie Harry used leave-in conditioner? That's it."

"Great," I said, imagining Debbie Harry as an edgy cowgirl.

"And her story would be easy to write. It's rags to riches, basically. She grew up poor somewhere in the South. Georgia? Tennessee? Who cares. Her family was on food stamps, and as a kid she started buying groceries and cooking. And now she has a show called *30 Bucks Tops*, which Food TV *loves* because it hits the 'real people' demographic. It's healthy meals on a budget, but she surprises you. Like she paired peanut-butter toast with a quail egg, for example. Which makes her kind of controversial, because who on a strict budget would buy a fucking quail egg?"

"Eccentric people."

"People who understand the concept of quality over quantity, according to Jane Bailey. Oh, and they're calling the book *I Want You More*. Which is a line from her show that went viral. It's actually hilarious. She was trying to decide between two cucumbers, and she was like, 'I want you more. No, I want *you* more. No, I want *you* more!'"

Given my financial situation, the only possibility was to lie. "I'd love to write her book," I said.

"Are you sure you want a job right now, Zara? You seem—"

"I'm positive."

Kim inhaled sharply. "Okay, I'll set up a call."

3

The call happened early the next day and lasted five minutes.

Jane's agent, Bryce, was *so* excited, and Jane was *so* excited, and I said I was *so* excited to learn more. I also said I was a big fan, even though I hadn't bothered to google Jane yet.

"We're thinking it's going to have, like, a ton of great advice," Bryce explained, "since Jane has so much wisdom. Especially for women. Women are definitely our target audience for this book. Even though, obviously, it'll also be for *all* people. Including Jane's bevvy of gay male fans! Holla! I want to be the president of your fan club, Jane."

"You're elected, Bryce," Jane said dryly.

Most of the call was me listening to Bryce and Jane talk about how totally relatable and also, like, *fun* the book was going to be. Jane's voice was deep, melodic, and faintly southern, and Bryce sounded like he worked at Disneyland.

"We're talking to some other candidates," he said at the end, "and we'll be in touch soon."

After we hung up, I googled her for the first time.

Pretty, but not too pretty was my initial reaction. Her nose rode the fine line between dignified and beakish, and her eyes were almond-shaped and chestnut-colored, which was a ridiculously nut-based description, but whatever, it was true.

In a photo taken at some restaurant opening, Jane wore pink-tinted aviators, a bag that was a cross between a purse and a fanny pack strapped across her chest, and a mysterious smile. Ripped jeans. Furry Birks. She looked comfortable and slightly boyish, and I liked the way her chin jutted out as if to say, *Yo.*

In another photo, I found Jane on a red carpet in a silvery gown, her arm wrapped around the waist of a man who was possibly younger than she was and equally stylish. A classic tuxedo. A crisp white shirt. Leather shoes. He stood at least a foot over Jane, and he looked down at her, grinning, as if she'd just said something funny.

I scanned through the accompanying text and learned the man's name was Julian Wright. He was the chef of a trendy Manhattan restaurant called Little Bear. We were the same age: thirty-three. Jane was forty. They'd been dating for a year.

Before Julian, Jane had been married to a hedge fund guy named Mark, who'd left her boatloads of money, which meant, as she once told the host of a morning talk show, that she could loaf for the rest of her life if she wanted to. But that wasn't Jane's style. While she credited some of her success to her husband's seed money, she knew she probably would have succeeded anyway, because she was, in her own words, "as scrappy as a hyena."

After looking at twelve million photos of Jane—and starting to feel like I really knew her, because that's what the repetition of seeing a face does to you—I watched the famous "I want you more" clip.

"I want you more," Jane said to one cucumber. Then she held up a second cucumber. "No, I want *you* more."

Her delivery was deadpan. Her timing was perfect. I could see why people adored her.

"But *adore* isn't a strong enough word," Diego said. "It's more like *worship*."

Diego, it turned out, was part of Jane's bevvy of gay male fans. When I told him about the interview, he was shocked.

"Jane *Bailey*? As in *Jane Bailey*? As in the goddess who told me to sprinkle gourmet potato chips on my heirloom tomatoes?"

"I had no idea she was such a big part of your life."

"Zara, you *need* to get this job."

I could hear Diego take a sip of something, probably coffee, and I imagined him at his desk in Lower Manhattan, staring at the ant-sized people on the street while contemplating his latest case. Diego worked as a DA because he was much more selfless than I was, which I'd known from the very first night I met him freshman year of college. A mutual friend set us up on a date. We went to a bad Chinese restaurant, ate soggy wontons, had the worst kiss ever, and decided to be friends. Nobody understood why we weren't dating since we loved each other so much. Then, about six months later, the riddle was solved.

We were both gay.

For a while after college, our lives were mostly the same, and then they became different. Diego moved to New York, married an investment banker named Luis, and bought a Volvo station wagon because they were thinking of possibly having a child and possibly naming her Victoria or Guinevere or something really pretty and antique like that.

I, meanwhile, was mentally taking stock of which microwaveable meals I had in the freezer, because my stomach was begging me for food. I'd had no appetite since my dad died, but I knew I had to force myself to eat. After that, I planned to go back to sleep. I'd barely left my apartment in two weeks.

"I feel like I'm slipping into the ether," I told Diego.

"I think it would be good if you saw some other humans throughout the day."

"I wish I had a Luis to take care of me."

"So sign up for a dating app."

As the days ticked by, I started to feel more shapeless. My sense of self had already been faint, and now it was disappearing. I drank more coffee to try to change how I felt, which sort of worked. I couldn't stop thinking about my dad. A second before he died, he'd squeezed my hand so hard. What had that meant? Was it an apology?

I'm sorry for leaving you nothing.

Or was it an explanation?

If I'd left you more, you would have divorced the civilized world and slept for years.

Knowing my dad, he probably believed both of these statements, but he would have said only the second one. It wasn't in his nature to apologize.

The dating app was a nice distraction at first. It buoyed my mood. But then, when none of the sane-looking women wrote back to me, I felt worse. It didn't take me long to go through all my available options within a five-mile radius, and then I kind of gave up.

Well, more accurately, I gave up while continuing to want somebody great to appear. Maybe she'd love horseback riding or something. Or she'd be a doctor?

Or a shy poet who presses flowers into books, I wrote in my journal.

Since I was a kid, I'd been obsessed with recording the details of my life. My journal was the only place where I could be completely honest, and the only place that didn't include my overbearing dad—well, until the day he admitted that he'd "leafed through" a few of my entries. I was thirteen years old, humiliated, and didn't speak to him for a week, and during that week I mummified all my journals in masking tape so he could never trespass again.

I took a sip of coffee and wrote, *Is there enough coffee in the world to keep me from vanishing into nothing?*

About a minute later, a thirty-five-year-old producer named Andie wrote to me on the dating app.

Dinner sometime?

Just these two words immediately reinforced my existence. It was the world saying to me, *You are someone.*

4

Andie and I met the very next night.

The restaurant she chose was full of plants and strings of lights and menu items that were farm-raised and organic and sustainable. It felt like the backyard of a friend, one who was equal parts glamorous and earthy.

When Andie saw me walk in, she stood up from the table and smiled. I thought that was nice. We said "Great to meet you" and hugged, and I liked her smell. There was something woodsy about it, maybe vetiver.

"I can't believe I've never been here before," I said.

"Yeah, isn't it so cool? I love the plants in here."

She was wearing a white button-down shirt with the top few buttons undone and a necklace with a crescent moon pendant that kept catching the light. Her hair was red and curly, her eyes were either hazel or green—I couldn't figure it out—and her movements were deliberate and unrushed. Her hand floated peacefully toward her water glass with the attitude of a jellyfish. I kept expecting her to look away from me, because most people don't sustain eye contact for very long, but Andie didn't do that. She gazed at me without discomfort. It was disarming, and I knew what it meant, too. Unlike me, Andie wasn't lost. She had a firm identity.

These were the things I decided about her as she told me that actually, the restaurant had been here only a year, so it wasn't surprising that I'd never been, and that, yeah, asking women out for dinner immediately on the app was what she always did.

"I don't want a pen pal. I want a relationship." She blinked slowly, like an animal in the sun. "What about you?"

I cleared my throat. I wanted to look away from her, but I couldn't. Were her eyes green or hazel? I thought of all the things I could say to protect myself, or to make myself sound smarter and more easygoing and generally just better than I actually was. I opened my mouth, prepared to be impressive. I left it open for a pause that was a beat too long. And then I said, "I want a relationship, too." The "too" came out like a squeak. And then I started crying.

"What's wrong?"

It was hard to get the words out. "My dad just died."

"Oh, I'm so sorry." Andie got out of her seat and wrapped me in her arms and didn't let go until I was done crying. Everything about her seemed to say, *I am a rock. You can be the unpredictable water, and I'll still be the rock, no problem.*

"I'm glad you told me," she said. "I don't like small talk. I'd rather talk about what's real."

So we ordered white wine and halibut and talked about what was real for two hours. Andie's parents were still alive and still together, which I thought was amazing, and she had a close group of friends she wanted me to meet. I said I would love to. I told her about how my mom left us in the middle of the night carrying a checked suitcase, braced against the harsh winds of Bolinas, and then flew to Rome, where she was blinded by the happiness of the sun.

After dinner, we went to Andie's picturesque A-frame in Mill

Valley and stayed up until four o'clock in the morning making out and talking more. We went through our likes and dislikes. She liked the *New York Times* in bed on Sundays and matcha lattes, and she disliked football, cats, and scented candles.

When it was my turn, I said, "I like walking. And I hate microwaveable meals. And death."

I ended up telling her a lot about my dad. I was thinking about how without him, I felt like a lost balloon floating into outer space, but instead of saying that, I described his sculptures and his tirelessness and his affinity for berries. I wasn't going to mention the financial situation, but then I did.

"He didn't leave me much," I said, "but I wasn't counting on a big inheritance, so it's fine."

In the morning, Andie made us coffee.

"Cream?" she asked as she poured a healthy dose into her cup.

"Yes, please."

We drank the coffee sprawled on the couch with our legs in a tangle until noon, then moved to the jacuzzi, where we fumbled around for each other's body parts like teenagers. At dusk, we went hiking in the Marin Headlands. For dinner, we ordered a Hawaiian pizza. That night, we had hot, fun sex on her bed with the sturdy walnut frame.

Less than twenty-four hours after meeting Andie, I felt like I was living a life beyond my wildest dreams—or I felt like her life was a life beyond my wildest dreams, and I wanted to be a part of it. When I woke up in her bed the next day, she said, "Please stay while I'm at work. I like knowing you're here." Then she kissed me and walked out the door with a briefcase in her hand, and it felt like we were in a sitcom or something.

A few minutes later, while I was washing one of her mugs in

the kitchen, I thought, *Soon, this might be my mug.* I looked out the window at her yard. *Soon, that might be my yard.*

Andie's style was a lot more bohemian than mine—layered rugs, antique mirrors, pink velvet pillows on a dark green couch—but the beauty of being shapeless is that at any moment, you can become something new.

I spent the next few hours staring at nothing, wondering what would happen in the future, and checking my email too many times. It had been four days since the interview with Jane, and I needed money. What was taking her so long?

Then, that afternoon, as if I'd willed it, she wrote:

> *Hey, Zara,*
> *If you still want the job, you're hired. I do have one*
> *request. Come to East Hampton for a few weeks*
> *and interview me in person? You can stay at my*
> *house.*

I called Kim. "I don't want to *live* with her!"

"Are you sure?" Kim asked. "They're offering fifty K more than you got for your last book."

That amount of money meant that after Jane's book, I could stop working for a while.

"Fuck," I said. "East Hampton?"

"You're going to love it," Kim said.

I called Diego, who was overjoyed. "I'll pick you up at the airport and drive you there myself!"

I looked out at our yard. "What about Andie, though?"

"Who you've known for five minutes?"

My eyes fell on our barbecue—*the* barbecue, *our* barbecue, whatever—and I imagined Andie having friends over for veggie kebabs while I was gone. I could see her saying something like, *Zara's so special. I can't wait for you guys to meet her.*

"I know it's been five minutes," I said to Diego, "but I can tell already that she's special."

That night, Andie came home with a baguette and plans to make bruschetta. When I told her the news, she showed me her disappointment for only a flash, and then she said, "Awesome!"

For the next two days, we had sex and went hiking and laughed a lot. The more time I spent with her, the more I didn't want to leave. I wanted her to beg me to stay. But she didn't. And it would have been illogical anyway. What was I going to do? Stress-swim back and forth across her pool while she was at the office?

The morning of my flight, she took off work to drive me to the airport. We promised to text and call each other constantly. We said "It's only a few weeks" seven hundred times. When I kissed her outside by the car, I thought I was doing the right thing.

5

I rolled my suitcase into the muggy New York afternoon and there was Diego, springing out of his brand-new red station wagon, which had the same shine as a Luden's cough drop. We hugged for longer than usual—a sorry-your-dad-just-died length of time—and got into the car. I told him Jane's address. After looking it up, he exclaimed, "Cottage Ave. Of course she lives right near the beach!"

Diego and I are on our way, I texted Jane.

Perfect, she wrote back.

He can't wait to meet you.

She didn't respond, but she should have, so I said it for her.

"Jane says she can't wait to meet you," I told Diego.

"I'm *dying*," he said and did a little dance in his seat.

We arrived in East Hampton when the sun was low in the sky. Manicured lawns. Refurbished windmills. Newly painted black streets with bright yellow lines down the center. The small downtown area was clean and commercial with a rustic edge. Diego thought we should probably show up *not* empty-handed, so we stopped at Citarella and bought Jane some flowers.

"I feel like she's a daisy person?" Diego said. "Cute and cost-effective."

As we followed the pristine winding roads to her house, I took a picture of the daisies in my lap and sent it to Andie.

I wish I were giving these to you tonight.

Me, too :(she texted back.

The pristine roads led us down to the ocean, and then we drove south along the beach. Or at least I thought it was south. The ocean should have made the answer obvious, but I'd never had a good sense of direction. I got easily confused and easily lost outside of cities, because there was too much nature, and nature was too big, and it was all the same. A tree. A tree. A house. A tree. That was one side of the road. On the other side was the ocean, appearing and then disappearing behind a series of sand dunes like an extended shot in an independent film about heartache.

"This is it," Diego said, turning right onto Cottage Ave. It was a thin road with very tall hedges on either side. At the end was Jane's modern wooden gate, which was framed in metal and almost comically tall. The top was lined in decorative pointy spires that might have seemed menacing if they weren't so beautiful.

"I bet we're on camera right now," Diego whispered as he pulled up to the call box and hit the button. While we listened to the ring, I looked around for cameras but didn't see any.

Then Jane picked up. "Hey, handsome!"

Diego was flustered, not knowing where to look. "Me?" he asked, smiling in various directions.

"Yes, you, with your pearly whites. Hello! And where's my Zara?"

"Hi, Jane." I waved at the call box, assuming that's where the camera was, although I didn't really know.

"My Zara!" she said. "Now, listen, when I open this gate,

follow the driveway all the way down and park in front of the house. It's impossible to fuck this up."

Diego laughed. "I think we can manage."

"No one else is in that car with you two, right?"

"No, ma'am," Diego said, becoming suddenly more southern in her presence.

"Okay, then."

A click. A long beep. As the gate slid open soundlessly, Diego whispered, "I cannot believe I'm about to meet Jane Bailey."

The driveway was flanked with trees spaced perfectly apart, and beyond them on both sides manicured grass sloped peacefully toward the hedged perimeter. The low light of dusk cast all the greens in a purplish, dreamlike haze, and the fireflies were just starting with their zippy glow patterns, which all looked like apostrophes to me.

Diego noticed the maze before I did. "Is that a *maze*?" He was in awe. "She lives in a fairytale."

"Yes," I said, but I wasn't really paying attention. I was imagining Andie in our kitchen, washing her pretty hands.

Jane's house came into view slowly. Dark wooden shingles, bright white trim, a roof that was the shape of a barn roof. Later I would google this and learn that the correct term was *gambrel*. A gambrel roof. It was an expansive house, two stories high, and the way it loomed over us made it seem more expansive than it was, and borderline celestial, too, as if it were nestled in the sky.

Jane, in comparison to her house, was tiny. When we saw her standing next to a fountain with a naked woman at its center, waving us closer with a fluttering hand, Diego said, "Oh my god." But he barely opened his mouth, so it came out sounding more like three commonly connected noises that together formed an expression than actual words.

Once we reached the end of the driveway, Jane motioned for us to circle the fountain. Then she held up her hand—*Stop!*—and Diego hit the brakes. I plastered a smile on my face and waved at Jane, who was wearing what I would later come to know as her signature outfit: a flannel top, ripped jeans, and furry Birks. I was keeping my face very pleasant, but I was thinking, *I do not want to be here.*

Then I got out of the car, and it was alarming how fast I was swallowed up by the atmosphere. There was the smell of freshly cut grass and the coolness of night approaching and then there was Jane approaching with her arms spread wide.

"It's so great to meet you!" She hugged me with what seemed like genuine excitement. Then she put her hands firmly on my shoulders and smiled, revealing teeth so white that they had to be veneers. "Aren't you just gorgeous," she said in a statement.

I handed her the daisies. "We got you these."

"That's so sweet!" She placed a hand over her heart. "You didn't have to do that."

"Oh, yes, we did," Diego said.

"You must be Diego! What a pleasure to meet you." Jane hugged Diego, who mouthed *Oh my god* over her shoulder as he tentatively patted her back.

"Please tell me you're staying for dinner, Diego," Jane said.

"Are you kidding?" he said. "Yes! Thank you so much!"

While Diego went to grab my suitcase, Jane took a step closer to me and I noticed she smelled like soap. "We're just about the same height, you and I," she said.

Diego slammed the trunk shut and pointed at me dramatically. "I want you more!" He pointed at Jane. "No, I want *you* more!" He laughed. "You two could almost be the same cucumber, get it?"

Jane smiled. "Shall we go inside? I'll show you your digs."

"That would be great," I said, and as we followed her toward the house, Diego turned to me and mouthed, *Digs!*

Jane's house and everything in it had the same vibe as downtown East Hampton: modern with a rustic edge. It was charming, but the cleanest version of charming, so clean that it was almost sterile. Wooden floors. Stark white walls. Ceilings that were impossibly high. There was a chandelier in the entryway with five protruding bulbs that reminded me of the bottom of an office chair.

The house smelled like her soap and cedar and—"Corn bread!" Diego inhaled, basking. "*Please* tell me we're eating your famous corn bread for dinner, Jane."

"And my famous roast chicken," she said, closing the door behind me.

"This is already the best night of my life," Diego gushed.

Jane smiled sweetly. "You're not a vegetarian, are you, hon?"

She was looking right at me when she said that, but for some reason, it still took me a beat to realize that I was *hon*. "No," I said. "I'm not."

"Thank *god*, because I hate vegetarians." She laughed. "That's off the record, of course."

"Of course," Diego said.

"And no pictures, either," she said more seriously. "Of anything. Okay? Not unless I approve them first. You can't be too careful these days. You know what I mean?"

"Absolutely," Diego said.

The smell of corn bread and chicken intensified as we followed her down a long hallway, which was decorated with framed pictures of Jane during various stages of her life. A headshot of Jane as a teenager. A black-and-white photo of Jane as a child in front of a dilapidated house. Jane on the cover of *Food TV Magazine*. Jane on the cover of *Women's Health*, wearing a neon-pink sports bra and flexing a seriously defined bicep, her skin lathered in something coppery. This was when I realized that although we had the same slight frame, Jane was much stronger than I was.

"I like to work out," she said, because apparently I'd stalled in front of the photo long enough for her to turn around.

When I noticed her looking at me, I smiled and crossed my arms over my chest, and she winked at me and went on with the spiel.

"We have a gym at the end of the hall there. It gets nice light during the day. We also have my office down here and an extra bedroom. Can you believe that? If you'd have told me as a girl that I would live in a house with *seven* bedrooms, I would have called you a nutter."

Jane laughed and kept walking, and we kept following as she turned through a wide arched opening in the hall. She motioned right. "Here we have the kitchen." Then left. "And the living room."

But what I saw first was the bright blue pool outside, and the perfectly set table just next to it. Again, Jane noticed what I was noticing.

"I thought we'd dine al fresco tonight," she said. "Speaking of which, I'm going to check on our chicken." Then she was hustling across the large room to the kitchen, where copper pots and pans dangled above the stove like jewels and the white marble countertops gleamed with the same intensity as her veneers.

In the living room, there was a white couch with very wide seats that reminded me of a cloud, and a woven basket full of cozy blankets. The fireplace was lit, and the shadows of irreverent flames cast confused but lovely pulses of light on everything around it.

"Chicken's almost ready," Jane called, and then she was walking toward us and slinging a blue-and-white striped towel over her shoulder with a smile. "I like to curl up here and read," she said. Then she took me by the hand, which surprised me. "Come on. Let's go upstairs."

I thought about taking my hand back, but she let go before I could. At the top of the staircase, she said, "And here we have my bedroom, your bedroom, another guest room, and an office, which you're welcome to use anytime."

"Thanks," I said, although really I was thinking, *No, thanks*. My plan was that we'd do the interviews and then I'd go back to California to write the book.

The hallway upstairs, like the one below it, was decorated with photos. One—which featured Jane and Julian at a garden party—had been taken down and was leaning against the wall. If Jane saw me notice this, she didn't make it obvious.

She showed us her bedroom first. White linen bedding. French doors. A Juliet balcony. And then there was her bathroom, which, she told us, was her favorite part of the whole entire house.

"I just love a soak at the end of a long day," she said with a sigh.

Did I think, in that moment, *Why am I in my client's bathroom right now listening to her tell me about her baths?*

Yes, I did, but the feeling was quickly replaced by curiosity. Why was Jane's bathroom so immaculate? There were no water droplets near the sink, no badly hung towels, and no toothpaste flecks on the mirror. On one side of the tub was a row of candles that stood like perfect soldiers. They'd never been lit.

"Jane, you know how to *live*," Diego said.

"It took me a while to learn, believe me." She laughed. "Now, come. Let's go to Zara's room!"

We followed her back down the hallway. In front of the first room on the left, the one that was closest to hers, she stopped. "Here we are," she said, inviting us in with an open palm.

"Oh my god, Zara," Diego said as he wheeled my suitcase in. "This is *to die*."

"It's gorgeous," I said, and it really was. The room was basically a replica of Jane's—same white linen bedding, same Juliet balcony—but smaller.

"You don't have a tub in here," she was saying, "just a shower. But don't worry, you're welcome to use my tub anytime."

"Thank you," I said, although I was absolutely never going to use her tub.

That's what I was thinking when she touched my back and said, "Why don't you take about ten minutes to settle in and then we can all meet downstairs for dinner. Sound good?"

"Sounds great!" Diego said.

We waited until the sound of her footsteps disappeared down the stairs, and then Diego asked me what I thought of her. "So?"

"She has no boundaries," I said as I flopped onto the bed.

"I think it's a southern-hospitality thing. They're overly friendly down there."

"That's not an excuse. Why is she touching me? It's like after people hire you, they think it's okay to pet you."

"Girl, I would let JB pet me all day long."

"You're calling her JB now?"

"No, that would be ridiculous. Plus, I don't think she'd like it. She's very particular. And *so* pretty. I can't believe how pretty she is in person. And magnetic, right? And her skin . . ."

While Diego continued to list Jane's positive attributes, I texted Andie.

We just got here. How was your day?

She didn't respond immediately, which probably meant that she was still at work.

Then Diego said, "Hey," and when I looked over, he took a picture of me.

"No pictures, hon," I whispered in her voice.

Diego scooted closer and took a selfie of us and whispered back, "She'll never know."

6

"My famous roast chicken, my famous corn bread, my famous fingerling potatoes." Jane stood over the table, pointing to all the dishes. "And a wedge salad with freshly cut radishes I picked this morning that isn't famous yet, but one day it very well could be!" She laughed at herself as she plucked the bottle of red from the center of the table. "Wine?"

"Please," Diego said, scooting his chair in with the energy of a boy who was about to ride his first roller coaster.

Instead of pouring for him, she looked at me. "Hon?"

"Oh, sure, I'll have some, thanks."

"Ladies first," she said, and filled my glass and then Diego's, but not her own.

"You're not having any?" I asked.

"Nah." She repositioned one of the candles on the table. "It doesn't bring out the best in me."

"Should we toast?" Diego asked.

"Absolutely." Jane lifted her glass of water. "A toast to new friends. And to a *New York Times* bestselling memoir. My cookbook made it there, so I think we have a good shot."

"Definitely," Diego said.

"Yes, definitely," I echoed, and then we started eating.

I wasn't that excited about Jane's food at first. I didn't like

chicken that much. Or wedge salad. As I scooped a small portion of fingerling potatoes onto my plate, I was thinking about
how I wanted to be eating Andie's bruschetta again tonight,
and every night for the rest of the summer.

Then I took a bite of Jane's chicken and—why was it so
good? I felt like I'd been transported to a better place, and without warning.

"How is it, hon?" Jane asked.

"It's *really* good," I said.

"It's *so* good, Jane," Diego agreed.

Jane's eyes remained on me. "I think you respect me more
now," she said, and raised one eyebrow.

"Massive respect," Diego said. "I could eat everything on
this table twice."

"Why, thank you, Diego," she said. "This is a *30 Bucks
Tops*–approved meal, of course."

"Amazing," Diego said. "I've watched every single episode,
by the way. Helping people make nourishing, healthy meals for
thirty bucks tops? It's brilliant, Jane."

She smiled and said, "I know."

"My favorite episode is the 'I want you more' one. Epic. But
I also love the one where you use tiny bits of steak as a salad
topping. What a shockingly sound idea that was!"

"My producer didn't get it at first, but I stood my ground. As
I always do." Her eyes fell on me just as I'd plunged a too-big
chunk of corn bread into my mouth. "What's your favorite episode, hon?" she asked.

It took me an embarrassing amount of time to chew and
swallow, and then I finally said, "The 'I want you more' one.
For sure."

She widened her eyes and smiled. "Are you lying to me?"

"No."

"You haven't watched any of them, have you?"

I cleared my throat. I took a sip of wine. I sat up taller. "I like to know as little about the client as possible before writing their book," I said. "That way, everything's fresh."

"Fresh." She licked the grease off her lips. "Ha."

The night got darker. The candles flickered. The ocean breeze was gentle. Diego gave Jane more compliments. Jane continued to thank him. I finished everything on my plate and then I ate more. I ate until my stomach hurt. Jane brought out strawberry shortcake for dessert, and I kept eating, despite my physical distress. I'd been seduced by her food. I couldn't stop, and this pleased her immensely.

"You've got a big appetite!" she said at one point. "It's bigger than you!" Later, she asked, "How's that shortcake, hon? You've got a little"—she motioned to her upper lip—"right there."

I wiped my mouth with her good napkin. "Thanks."

During the main course, Jane didn't say much about herself, but as we ate dessert, she said a lot. She talked mostly about how she was so glad to be away from the city. "Too much work," she said. "And too much drama." She had a tendency to work herself to the *bone*, which she felt was both her greatest strength and her greatest weakness. Her job, in the last few months, had become particularly distressing to her because Food TV had just hired a new personality, Bree Jones, and Bree Jones was now making a show that was basically a rip-off of Jane's show.

"*Little Money, Lotta Love*," she said. "It's the same idea as *30 Bucks Tops*, but they're conveniently pretending that it's not. Bree is from the South, like me. She's likable in that cookie-cutter way, you know what I mean?"

"Ugh," Diego said with a flick of the wrist. "She sounds terrible."

"She's the reason we're writing this book right now, Zara. We need to cast a *fat* shadow on Bree Jones."

"She's going down!" Diego pounded his fist on the table, but lightly.

"Food TV still hasn't renewed my contract for the upcoming season, and my lawyer says it has nothing to do with Bree Jones, but, you know, I worry. How could I not? Normally, I'd call my boyfriend for comfort, but . . ." Jane sighed, and then her hand was descending over the candle and she was trailing her finger through the flame, back and forth and back and forth. Diego and I were watching intently, neither of us speaking—and then suddenly Jane was shaking herself to a more alert state and refocusing her eyes and pulling her shoulders back and delivering the news in one flat sentence: "We broke up."

"No!" Diego couldn't believe it.

"Yes."

"What *happened*?"

"Honey, his drinking happened."

"Oh my god, that photo of him vomiting into his hand is tragic," Diego said.

"Have you seen it, Zara?" Jane asked.

"No."

"Here," she said, and then she was holding up her phone to show me a photo of Julian on a New York City street at night, trying to catch his vomit in his hand.

Jane sighed. "Dating is just a bear." She looked up at her house. "Not that I'm complaining. I have *seven* bedrooms."

"And you deserve each and every one of them," Diego said.

"I really do. I've been through hell." She laughed, then tossed her napkin onto her plate and sat back. "Well, that was nice. And you, Diego, are welcome back here anytime. Please feel free to come use the pool whenever you like."

"Really? Thank you!"

"You're welcome." Jane stood. "Should we all take a photo together before you go, Diego? Something for you to post on your Instagram?"

"Yes!" Diego pushed his chair back with force, and then the three of us gathered. Jane put her arm around me and gave the side of my stomach a little squeeze, which I assumed meant something about how I'd eaten so much, but I wasn't sure. Then Diego held up his phone. We smiled. The camera flashed. And Jane said, "Let me see that. I need to approve."

"Of course." Diego handed her the phone.

"Approved," she said quickly. Then she swiped back and saw the two other photos that Diego had taken upstairs. "Not approved," she said. "Not approved." She smiled at him. "But you can keep those since I'm a wonderful person."

"I'm *so* sorry." Diego took his phone back with great hesitation, almost as though it no longer belonged to him.

"You're forgiven." She patted his shoulder. "Now, listen, when you get to the end of the driveway, the gate will open automatically. It was so nice to meet you, sweetheart," she said, then kissed him on the cheek.

"It was *so* nice to meet you, too, Jane!"

"I'll walk you to the car," I said.

"Don't take any photos on the way out, you hear?" She laughed.

"No, ma'am," Diego said seriously.

We walked outside without speaking. At the car, Diego whispered, "I'm *humiliated*."

"Don't worry about it," I said. "She forgave you."

"Okay," Diego said. "Yeah, you're right. I should just let it go."

"Definitely let it go. Who cares." I set my hand on my stomach and stuck my tongue out. "I'm so full."

"Oh my god, same. Her food is borderline life-changing."

Diego opened his car door and the reality of what was about to happen hit me. "I can't believe I'm going to be alone with her in this house. Don't you think it's weird?"

"No, she's a generous woman with a house that's too big. I think it makes total sense."

I sighed. "Please come back and use the pool."

"I will, don't worry."

The fireflies were mostly gone now, but over Diego's shoulder I saw just one, and I thought of my dad then, and of how all his life he'd wanted to be bathed in light, but instead he'd remained an obscure figure in a foggy town.

"Are you crying?" Diego asked.

I rubbed my eyes. "No."

"Oh, Zara."

"I'm fine."

"Well, if later you're not fine, just call me. I'll drop everything."

I felt heavy as I watched Diego get into his car, and heavier still as I stood there, my eyes locked on his red taillights, watching them get smaller and smaller and then disappear. The night was quiet except for the orchestral ring of crickets, which sounded like one high never-ending note. I looked up at the stars, and then at the house looming over me. I took a deep breath. I told my feet to start moving.

Back inside, I found Jane bringing in the last of the dishes. I said the requisite thing. "Can I help you clean up?"

"No, no." She set the dishes down on the kitchen island. "Bijou will take care of it in the morning. She's the housekeeper. And Tom, her husband, is the gardener. Cute, huh?"

"Cute," I repeated.

She pulled two glasses from the cabinet, filled them with water, and handed me one. "Let's go to bed."

I watched her turn off the fireplace with a remote control and then all the lights and followed her in the near dark up the stairs.

"Tomorrow," she said, "you can come down for breakfast whenever you wake up. I assume you'll be jet-lagged, and that's fine. I want to take you into town, show you around a little. And then we can get started on the book! Are you excited?"

"Very."

Jane turned. "You are not."

"No, I'm—"

"Listen, it's fine, I get it. A job is a job is a job. Am I right?"

I smiled but didn't answer.

We were upstairs now, standing near the photo of Julian that Jane had taken off the wall. She placed her hand on my arm and left it there for a moment that felt too long, and in her deep voice, she said, "Night, hon."

"Good night," I said, and then I watched her glide into her bedroom and close the door.

The space between my bedroom and Jane's seemed smaller now that we were the only ones in the house, and the quiet seemed quieter. The sound of crickets had been replaced with total silence, which is a rare thing. When you experience total silence, it makes you realize how accustomed you are to the constant noises of the world.

I walked to my bedroom gingerly. I closed the door gently. I unzipped my suitcase so slowly that it barely made a sound. I looked at the dresser that was right there and considered filling it with my clothes but didn't. As I took a shower, I imagined Jane in her bathroom doing the same thing. There was a box of Dove soap on the ledge. I washed myself with it while thinking, *This is her smell. I'm going to smell like her now.*

And then I got into bed and the sheets were so luxuriously soft that I decided I'd be buying them when I got back home. Soon, I'd have more money, better sheets, and Andie would be my girlfriend. I just had to get through the next few weeks, and a few weeks was nothing.

I think you'd like this bed, I wrote to Andie.

If you're in it, then yes.

We texted back and forth for a while, and then we said *Good night* and *Talk to you tomorrow* and *xoxoxo*, and I set the phone down and turned off the light. Before I closed my eyes, I took one last look at the bright stars out the window. I rubbed my still-too-full stomach. And then I heard a faint mechanical sound. It lasted for just a second and at the end was a short beep.

7

I woke up flooded in sunlight. As I looked out the window at the cloudless sky, it was hard not to feel grateful. I'd landed a job right when I desperately needed one. Jane's food was astounding, and her house was impressive. My first date with Andie was turning into a relationship. After months of crying about my dad, things were finally turning around.

I pushed the covers off me, opened the French doors, and stepped onto the balcony. The smell of the ocean was intoxicating. Below me, a gardener—had she said his name was Tom?—was mowing his way across the great expanse of grass. He waved cheerfully when he saw me, and I waved back, and it felt like we were at a resort.

In daylight and from this angle, I noticed several things that I hadn't noticed the night before: how the long driveway curved like a snake, and how the maze was much more extensive than I'd originally imagined. It was vast and trimmed with the same precision as Jane's hedged perimeter, which was so tall that nothing beyond it could be seen, even from the second story. I liked that. It gave the impression that we were tucked away from the outside world.

When I closed the doors, the smell of the ocean was replaced by the smell of bacon, and I knew I needed to get downstairs soon. As I took a quick shower and got dressed—jeans, a white T-shirt—I went through the list of questions that would need to be addressed. What would our daily schedule be like? Could I go to the beach? How were we defining "a few weeks"?

The best-case scenario would be that I'd interview Jane intensely for a short period and then leave. We'd probably need about forty hours of interview time, which equaled one full-time workweek, or two part-time workweeks. Of course, how much time we worked each day would depend on how much Jane felt like talking about herself. Normally, people got tired after about two hours.

I emerged from my room prepared to say hi in case she was standing right there. She wasn't. The hallway was empty and the photo of Julian that had been resting against the wall was now gone. Jane's morning voice was drifting up from downstairs, and its rhythm was pleasant and comforting. I heard the bang of a pan and the rush of the sink and then the sound of another woman's voice as I descended the stairs. When I got to the kitchen, Jane, her hair high up in a perky ponytail and her body swathed in head-to-toe spandex that amplified every one of her well-defined curves, said, "Morning, hon! This is Bijou."

Bijou was in her fifties maybe, with flawless skin, a stocky build, and a wide smile.

"Hello," she said in a thick French accent, and waved at me with her free hand. In her other hand was a vacuum cleaner and on her feet were shoes so white that I assumed they had to be brand-new.

"Hi," I said. "Nice to meet you."

"Bijou is our housekeeper from Senegal, and Tom is her industrious husband from Sweden. They met here in East Hampton! Isn't that adorable? The perfect romance." Jane, pink-cheeked and moving with bouncy energy, swung her arm around Bijou's shoulder, but for only a second. "Sorry, I'm going to get you all sweaty, Bij."

"Jane loves exercise," Bijou said. "That is why her body is like this."

"Thanks, Bij. I'll take that as a compliment! I like to meet my potential. Know what I mean?"

Bijou was now invested in untangling the cord of the vacuum cleaner, so she didn't respond.

"Anyway," Jane said to me, "I made you breakfast. It's a *30 Bucks Tops*–approved meal, of course. Well, except for the coffee. The coffee's crazy expensive. Bijou put everything outside for you." She motioned to the outdoor table, which had a massive amount of stuff on it for one person.

"Thank you," I said.

Jane smiled. "My pleasure."

Bijou untangled the final knot of the vacuum cord and looked at me. "I'm going to clean your room now," she said, and walked off.

"You go eat, and I'll go shower," Jane said. "And then I'll take you on a grand tour of East Hampton."

"Great," I said. "And I was thinking we could start interviews this afternoon? If we do two sessions every day, maybe one in the morning and one in the afternoon, we can get this done quickly."

Jane squinted at me. "You're *dying* to get out of here already, aren't you?"

"No," I said evenly. "I just want to maximize our time together."

"Two sessions every day sounds good to me," she said.

I felt relieved. Maybe Jane was going to be an easy client.

———

As I sat down for breakfast, I promised myself that I would not eat too much.

Then I ate too much.

Bacon, scrambled eggs with cheddar, grits, French toast dusted in powdered sugar. Again, the taste of Jane's food was transcendent. Again, I could not stop. Jane's coffee was better than Andie's, and her cream was better, too.

I inhaled the breakfast. All my senses were reveling. The sound of birds filled the air. The sun warmed my face just the right amount. The pool was still, reflecting the cloudless sky like a painting, and the lush greens of the grass and the high hedge were vivid almost to the point of being Technicolor. In a way, none of it seemed real, or all of it seemed too good to be true.

I wanted to finish all the food on the table, but I left just a little bit of each dish so that Jane wouldn't think I was gross. I told myself to ignore those little bits. But apparently, I couldn't. There was a square of French toast left, and I kept cutting off thin slivers of it while telling myself, *This is the* last *piece*. I'd just cut another one of these slivers when Tom appeared with a pair of shears in his hand and said, "You must be the ghostwriter."

"You must be Tom."

Up close, he was a Viking. Blond, blue eyes, extremely tall, shoulders so wide you could have sat a child on each one. Like his wife, Tom had a smile plastered on his face. Unlike his wife, he had no accent. He sounded American.

"It's wonderful you're here," he said. "Jane usually doesn't let people up to the house. Bijou and I are the only—"

"Are you talking about me, Tom?"

The sound of Jane's voice rising up from somewhere behind me was so startling that I gasped. And then she was right there, putting her hands on my shoulders and saying, "My *my*, you do know how to eat!"

"It was so good," I said. "Thank you."

"Of course," she said warmly, and her hands remained on my shoulders as she told Tom the lawn looked spectacular and then suggested it might be nice to add some more spinach to the garden beds, and maybe some more radishes, too. "But double-check with Bijou first," she said. "Carrots might be better."

Tom stood there smiling and nodding along as Jane spoke. At first, I just thought he was being dutiful, but then I realized that he was totally mesmerized by her. The longer I watched him, the more convinced I became that Tom wanted to rip Jane's clothes off and sink his teeth into her neck like a vampire.

Eventually, she let go of my shoulders and walked out onto the lawn to explain something to Tom about the sprinkler system, and that's when I noticed Bijou staring at them from inside the house. I was too far away to see her clenching her jaw, but I imagined that's what she was doing.

When she looked over at me, I gave her a consoling wave. She ignored it, then disappeared. I returned my attention to Jane, who was wearing a playful tie-dye blouse and faded jeans that I liked better than mine. She pointed at something across the property, her hand shielding her face from the sun.

"So maybe we could install three more of those," she said.

"Absolutely." Tom shifted his weight. I thought he was trying to make himself look more attractive for her. "I'll pick them up this afternoon."

"Perfect. You done for the day?"

"Yes," Tom said.

"All right, let's caravan out of here." Jane pointed a finger gun at me. "Zara? Get your crap. I'll meet you in the driveway in five."

Five minutes later, I walked outside to find Bijou and Tom sitting in a white truck with a bunch of gardening supplies in the back. They both smiled when they saw me, and I smiled back as I walked around the fountain with the naked woman at its center and toward Jane, who was standing in front of the garage.

"That's Aphrodite," she said about the naked woman, "the goddess of love."

"Nice," I said, just to say something.

"I got it after Mark died. My late husband. He would have hated it. He was very traditional."

She pressed a button on her phone and the garage door opened, revealing a dark gray Range Rover, which she explained like this: "I like to be bigger than everyone else on the road. Makes me feel powerful."

Inside, the car smelled new and, like everything else Jane owned, it was spotlessly clean. No dirt. No dust. No random pieces of gum in the cup holder. She backed us out smoothly into the sunny day, hit a button on her phone again, and the garage door began to slide shut. "And the alarm." She held her phone up and hit another button. "In case you haven't noticed, I'm all about security around here."

"And you do everything from your phone?"

"Yes, siree," Jane said. "I started using that facial-recognition thing now."

As we drove toward the gate, she motioned out the window. "Have you noticed my maze yet?"

"I have," I said.

"My daddy took me to a used bookstore when I was eight years old and told me I could choose *one* book and you know what I chose? A coffee-table book called *Mazes of the World*. I just loved it for some reason, and I decided that when I grew up, I would have my own maze. And now I do. You could call it a test of intelligence. I'll send you through sometime and we can test you."

"Great," I said, wondering how many activities I'd have to do with her.

While we waited for the gate to slide open, she said, "I'm surprised no one's out here waiting for me."

"Who would be waiting for you?"

"You wouldn't believe how many fans stop by here. I've got people coming from all over, pressing the button on the call box incessantly. Sometimes they leave me gifts, too. One woman came all the way from Dallas on the Greyhound to give me some oranges from her tree! Can you believe that? She said her orange tree had been blessed by God."

I couldn't imagine a life in which strangers left gifts outside my house. More, I couldn't imagine a life in which receiving them was normal. Jane had gotten used to a reality that most people would never experience. What was that like?

"Did you eat the oranges?" I asked her.

"Honey! I would rather eat a basket of McDonald's chicken nuggets than that lady's oranges. And I wouldn't touch a McDonald's nugget with a ten-foot pole, just to be clear."

I laughed.

"Zara," she said in a serious voice, "do you know why I invited you here?"

"Why?"

"To win you over."

"Win me over?"

"Yes," she said. "I need the writer of my book to fall in love with me."

8

Jane's grand tour of East Hampton was, in her own words, "not going to be very grand. So you should lower your expectations right now."

About the beach, she said, "Good sand here. Better than the West Coast." About a historic building, she said, "That's a historic building, but don't ask me anything about history because I know jack shit." About the downtown area, she said, "Isn't it just what you expected?"

"Yes," I said.

She pulled into a parking lot. "East Hampton used to be a quiet place. Now it's packed with tourists. See them?" She motioned to two teenagers with sunburnt legs and shopping bags dangling from their skinny wrists. "Tourists."

"Definitely," I said. If Jane was going to ignore the fact that I, too, was a tourist, then I would do the same.

"I've been coming to East Hampton for fifteen years. Can you believe that? Mark loved it out here. And then he died, that bastard."

"I'm sorry."

"Thanks," she said, and set her hand over her heart.

She continued to crawl the car through the crowded lot, looking for a space, and when she found one, she said, "See that? I'm blessed by the almighty parking gods. I *always* find a spot, because I'm lucky."

"Cool," I said.

"I mean, in general, my life has been defined largely by luck. When I was a girl, I used to wish upon pebbles instead of pennies. I'd throw them into an empty well near our house and ask for a beautiful life." She turned the engine off. "Do you consider yourself to be a lucky person, Zara?"

"I guess so."

"That's a no," she said. "But don't worry, you can become lucky at any time."

"Great," I said, and then I laughed like it meant nothing, but the truth was that I wanted to believe her.

"Now, listen, I'm taking you to my favorite bakery, which is not *30 Bucks Tops*–approved. There's the public life of Jane Bailey, and then there's the private life of Jane Bailey. I didn't get rich to keep eating like I'm poor." She raised a finger. "And that stays out of the memoir."

"Of course," I promised.

"All righty," she said, opening the door. "Let's go."

The main drag was bustling with people laughing and eating ice cream and window-shopping and petting their well-groomed dogs. Striped shirts. Loafers. White jeans. Wide-brimmed hats. It was a caricature of the Hamptons at full throttle. At first, I was too busy noticing everyone else to notice how some of them were gawking at Jane, and then someone called her name.

"Jane Bailey!"

It was an older man sitting on a bench.

"Hello!" Jane called back, and then she waved and smiled like a pageant queen.

"Who was that?" I asked her.

"No clue," she said.

It was after that that I became attuned to the gawking. Most people didn't say anything. They just stared, or they stared for a second and then started whispering to a friend, or a mother, or whoever they'd come to town with that day. Of course, I'd known Jane was famous, but it didn't seem real to me until that man called her name.

Jane seemed to love the attention. She smiled at everyone. She stopped to sign an autograph for a young woman who wanted to become a chef one day. "I believe in you," Jane told her as she scrawled her name on the pizza box the woman happened to be carrying, because it was the only thing she had to write on.

The young woman was thrilled. "Thank you so much! I'm framing this!"

"My pleasure," Jane answered, and then she draped her arm over my shoulders and ushered me down the busy street, and soon after that another fan spotted her and yelled, "I want you more!" And Jane, without missing a beat, yelled back, "I want *you* more!"

It was bizarre. And intrusive. And unnatural. The adulation poured onto Jane made me want to plant a tree with my bare hands or engage in some other grounding activity. As we walked on, I was having some philosophical thoughts about how, as a society, we were obsessed with all the wrong things. I was also thinking that walking alongside one of those wrong things was kind of fun.

Jane's favorite bakery was called Carissa's. When she walked in, the man behind the counter said, "Jane! You're back!" The man's name was Danny, and he had a thick Boston accent. Jane introduced me as her friend, and Danny said, "Any friend of

Jane's is a friend of mine." She proceeded to order a loaf of sourdough, a loaf of pickled rye, and some olive ciabatta with her hands on her waist, and by the time Danny was done bagging it, I noticed that I also had my hands on my waist.

Afterward, at the register, I picked up a bag of truffle potato chips so that my hands would have something to do, and Jane said, "We'll take those chips, too, Danny," and patted me on the back. Maybe her touchy-feely-ness made me feel guilty, because right after that, I texted Andie: *I wish you were here.*

"Who're you texting, hon?" Jane asked.

"Diego," I said.

When she turned around to pay, I texted Diego to reverse the fact that I'd just lied.

Hi.

Then I looked up at Jane, who was dropping her wallet into her bag. Her bag was huge and her wallet was small, and the way she let go of it made me think of her as a girl, dropping a pebble into a well. I thought, *I need to start writing everything down.*

On the walk back to the car, more fans shouted her name. They whispered. They stared. She threw her arm around my shoulders again, and I said, "Being famous seems like a full-time job."

"Honey," she said as she waved at some random person she didn't know, "it's a circus."

The idea to go to the Clam Bar was an afterthought, one that Jane would blame herself for later. We were on our way home when she said, "You know what? I don't feel like making lunch. Let's go pick up some lobster rolls."

"Great," I said. Somehow, despite my ample breakfast, I was starving.

Jane called in the order. "Tell Nick I'll come through the back," she said into the phone, and then we began the short drive to Napeague, which was just fifteen minutes away.

I smiled and sat back in the comfortable seat and enjoyed the feeling of being bigger than everyone else on the road. Jane turned on country music—"Dolly Parton is such a dame," she said and started humming along. I looked out the window and saw explosions of flowers and white picket fences, and the grass in every yard looked like a green shag carpet I wanted to roll around on.

Jane was a good driver. She had finesse. The Range Rover was humungous and smooth, and being inside of it felt like being inside of a whale. It felt like the encounter between ease and power. Those were my poetic thoughts. My more logistical thoughts were that I was trading in my 2010 Jetta as soon as I got home, and that I really enjoyed the relaxed feeling of being the passenger rather than the driver. I didn't need to make decisions. All I had to do was exist.

The Clam Bar was a picturesque seafood shack off 27 with outdoor tables under yellow umbrellas. Jane drove through the parking lot and pulled around to the back, where there were a bunch of trash cans and a cook sitting on an upside-down bucket smoking a cigarette.

"I'll go in," she said. "You sit tight." Then she got out of the car and walked through the kitchen door like it was her house.

Minutes passed. Then more minutes. The cook finished his cigarette and went back inside. The heat of the day wafting in through the open window had a softening effect. I felt like falling asleep. I closed my eyes and listened to the sound of cars driving by on the road and the clanging of metal coming from the kitchen. When I opened them again, I saw a man walking toward me. Sunglasses. Beachy blond hair. He was handsome and tall and moving closer, and then he was calling out, "Hey!"

I looked around, because I assumed he was talking to somebody else, but no one was there. I turned back toward the man, who'd picked up speed. He was almost at the car, barreling forward with a sense of desperation that made me think he might be a criminal, and out of instinct I tried to roll the window up, but Jane had taken the keys. I imagined what was about to happen—I had about forty dollars in my wallet, he could have that; hopefully he wouldn't hurt me—and then, just as the man grabbed the window ledge—thick fingers, he smelled like red sauce—Jane appeared in the kitchen doorway and screamed, "Julian!"

The tone of her voice made it sound like she was punishing a child. She seemed annoyed and exasperated, sighing loudly as she walked toward Julian, who'd already taken his hand off the car and was moving toward her.

"Jane." He still looked desperate, but in a heartbreaking way now, like he was about to collapse at her feet.

"What are you doing here?" Jane asked. "I thought you were in the city." In one swift motion, she placed her hand on Julian's chest and pushed. In her other hand was the bag of lobster rolls we'd be eating for lunch, and for whatever reason, that made me feel a little bit smug. I would be in Jane's future and Julian, most likely, would not.

Jane shot me a look, then walked farther away from me and motioned for Julian to follow her, and after that, I couldn't hear anything they said. For the rest of the conversation, I pretended to be uninterested while glancing up at them as often as possible.

Julian kept changing his posture, but in all of his postures, he seemed stressed. He stuffed his hands into his pockets, he folded his arms across his chest, he rubbed his face with both hands really hard.

Jane, meanwhile, appeared to be consoling him. At some point, she placed the take-out bag on the ground and gave him a hug. At first, he didn't hug her back, but then he did. She said things into his ear—I could see her mouth moving—and his body, which had been angrily running toward me only minutes earlier, became a rag doll in her arms.

Jane let go first. She took Julian's hands and said something that I assumed was encouraging.

Julian seemed to agree with whatever she'd said, and then he motioned to the car.

And Jane, in response, locked her eyes on me and smiled mischievously.

9

On the drive home, Jane explained it like this: Julian was the sweetest man alive, but when he got drunk, he got violent. No, he'd never *hit* Jane, but he had pushed her several times too hard—"much, *much* too hard"—and it was scary. Who wouldn't be scared by that?

"I was scared when he was running toward me," I said. "Before you came out."

She slapped the wheel. "See? He can be terrifying!"

In the beginning of their relationship, she told me, Julian had been a completely different man. First of all, he was sober. And successful. And if Jane was being honest, she thought that dating him would increase her relevance. Because, yeah, she *did* want to become Martha Stewart Junior, and it's not like she was getting any younger.

For a while, they were this golden couple. The press loved them. Jane started getting invitations to more important places with more important people, and more requests to promote quality brands. It even seemed, for a second, like Food TV might give her a spin-off travel show. And then?

Boom! The fantasy was shattered. Julian's drunken antics were the main culprit. "I started to fear for my life, and I'm not kidding," she said.

She went on to tell me that Julian had just been released from rehab a few days earlier, which she was well aware of because she'd *paid* for it! Not that she really cared, because she had more money than God and all his angels, but still!

She had no idea he'd come to East Hampton, or that he'd be working at the Clam Bar for the summer. Hell, she wouldn't have guessed that Julian would ever work at a roadside shack like that. It was such a step down from Little Bear. Julian had really squandered that opportunity when he threw a baked potato at the maître d's head, which Jane still could not believe.

"That's why he got fired. He was in a blackout." She let out a long sigh. "He wants to get back together. That's the real reason he's in East Hampton."

I waited for her to say more, and when she didn't, I offered a general consolation. "Seems like a tough situation."

"He thinks if he stays sober, I'll take him back."

"Will you?"

"Who knows." She took a contemplative breath. "Anyway, that was quite a scene for you to witness. My guess is that you might have some questions for me. So if there's anything you want to know, you just ask, hon."

We were passing the sand dunes now. Beyond them the beach was decorated in colorful umbrellas. Even though the windows were open, Jane's soapy smell was strong.

"Is it true you don't let a lot of people up to your house?" I asked.

Jane laughed. "Who told you that? Tom?"

"Maybe."

"Tom," Jane said, in a joke-admonishing way. "And yes, that's true. I don't let a lot of people up to my house. Because trust is overrated, in my opinion. My childhood taught me that, and becoming a public figure taught it to me even more. I don't need a large entourage. I need only a tiny army of trustworthy humans around me."

As a ghostwriter, I'd found that it was best to remain as ghost-like as possible. If clients asked me questions about myself, I was usually very careful to reveal only the bare minimum.

But somehow—was it because she'd called me her friend in town?—as we sat eating lobster rolls on the edge of her pool, our feet dangling in the water, I heard myself saying, "I used to be obsessed with lobster rolls."

She took a sip of the peach iced tea she'd brought out for us. "What ended the obsession?" she asked.

"I can't remember," I said, although of course I remembered. I'd dated a selfish drummer who *loved* lobster rolls, and I'd adopted her obsession while we were together.

"You can't remember?" Jane asked. "You're lying."

I couldn't tell if she was kidding or not. "What?"

"I'm good at reading people, hon," she said, "and I know you're lying to me right now."

I laughed. "I am not."

Her eyebrow arched up. "No?"

I kicked my legs in the water. I took a sip of iced tea. Then I admitted it. "Fine, I'm lying."

Playfully, she socked me in the arm. "Knew it!"

"My ex loved lobster rolls. But I stopped eating them when we broke up."

I told myself that I didn't need to come out to Jane. I hadn't come out to any of my other clients. But then, the next second, I was saying, "Her name was Cecilia."

Jane seemed zero percent surprised at the reveal of a woman's name, which I took to mean that she'd guessed I was gay.

"I've never met a Cecilia I didn't despise," she said.

"Me neither," I agreed, even though I'd never met another Cecilia.

"Tell me," she said. "Are you dating anyone now?"

"No," I said.

"Sure you're not," she said, but didn't push.

10

That afternoon, I interviewed Jane for the first time. We sat in the living room on the couch that reminded me of a cloud, which had seats so wide that it was really more like a bed than a couch. I curled my legs under me, and Jane did the same.

The sun was slanting in through the long row of sliding glass doors, casting a halo of light around her head. She seemed gentler and more reflective than she had earlier, and I thought, *Of course she does. People have layers. People are many different people throughout the course of a day.*

I decided that the relaxed version of Jane was probably the real Jane, and that the other version—the boisterous, productive one—was the show she put on for other people. She was, after all, a performer.

What I'm really trying to say is that this was the moment I realized she was beautiful. And when it hit me—*Oh, you're beautiful*—I looked away from her, because I worried that if she saw my eyes then she'd be able to see my thoughts.

I hit record and set the phone down between us, and she whispered, "I'm nervous." And just like that, she became softer to me, and vulnerable, a ladybug on its back.

"Don't worry," I said. "Everyone is nervous at first."

"Okay, captain." She tucked her hair behind her ear and looked up at me. "You lead the way."

I sat up straighter, and in my most polished tone, I explained the process in a way that was designed to make her feel safe. "I know it can seem daunting," I said. "You're going to tell me a lot about yourself, and you're not going to know how all the information will be organized until the end, when you read the book. I understand that it's an immense amount of faith you're placing in me, and I want you to know that I have your best interests at heart."

A slow smile spread across her face. "Oh, Zara, you've got another side to you."

My face flushed. "Yeah, well, people have layers. People are many different people throughout the course of a day."

She squinted at me. "In-ter-est-ing."

"So, the question of this book is 'How did Jane Bailey become Jane Bailey?' Let's start from the beginning."

"The ugly childhood."

"The ugly childhood."

"Okay." Jane took a deep breath. "Here I go."

For the next six hours, Jane talked and I listened. She told me her story in great detail. There were long asides about fields of corn and broken faucets and the special way young Jane used to tie her shoelaces, because what she really wanted to be all her life was special.

"I was born in a dinky hole of a place where everyone and their grandmother owned a rifle and a dirty baseball cap."

That's how she began.

Her dinky hole was called Arden, and it was just outside of

Asheville, North Carolina, and really, that had probably been her first stroke of luck: being born so close to a city with a good personality. Her mother didn't take her to Asheville very often, but going there every once in a while and getting a glimpse of some artsy folks who spoke educated English was enough to cause young Jane to realize that there was a better world beyond her own out there and that one day, she would escape to that better world.

"I was always trying to get out. From the second I could run, I was running away." She laughed. "I tried to run away about eighty times. Really, I was trying to run away from my mother."

Jane's mother's name was Honey, but she was the opposite of sweet. "Meanest woman I ever met," Jane said. "Sometimes she'd lock me in my room for days at a time. I just sat in there and cleaned for hours. My room was the only clean place in that house—until my mother had me start cleaning the whole thing. I actually liked it. Pushing a broom back and forth was soothing to me."

Jane's daddy's name was Edward. "And he was the opposite of my mother. Too sweet. And too mute. He said almost nothing. But when he did speak, it was always substantial. He had a knack for predicting the future, too. Just before my mother killed him, he said, 'Jane, I think my time here is waning thin.'"

For the most part, during interviews, I said nothing, but here I said, "What?"

"My mother killed my father," Jane said. "Then she killed herself out of guilt. It was the most heroic ending she could have chosen, I think. Or at least it was the most just. She punished herself before the law could punish her, you know what I mean? She wouldn't have done well in jail. She didn't like to be cooped up."

Jane was eleven years old when her parents died, but on a soul level, she felt she was more like sixty. "I grew up fast," she said. "Because both my parents were like children. Poor, messy children." Edward was a school janitor and Honey was constantly getting fired for her difficult attitude, so they didn't have much money. And they were lazy, too. When Jane was about nine, her mother parked in front of the grocery store and said, "I think you should do the shopping today. I'm going to sit here and read until you get back." One of Honey's favorite hobbies was to read mystery novels in the car while chain-smoking Newport 100s.

"I remember that first day in the supermarket vividly," Jane said. "I had about fifty bucks in food stamps, and as I walked the aisles, I was doing math. I was good at math, so it was easy for me. I remember thinking taco shells were a smart investment because they were cheap, and the package contained enough for two or three meals. Anyway, I did such a good job that my mother had me do the grocery shopping every time after that, and she had me start cooking, too. So there I was at nine years old, cooking our meals and cleaning our house. She used to say, 'Jane, you're just better at cooking and cleaning than I am.' That made me feel good about myself, you know? Like I had real skills and she was proud of me."

Obviously, this was where the idea for *30 Bucks Tops* came from—but it would take Jane quite a while to realize that cooking was her ticket. "For many years, I didn't know what my ticket was," she said. "I was confused as hell, just trying to figure out who to be. And I didn't know. So you know what I did, sweetheart? I became a chameleon."

It was a relief to hear that. Once, Jane had been as confused about who to become as I was now.

———

At dinnertime, we took a break and Jane made us thick ham sandwiches on the pickled rye we'd bought at Carissa's. I ate mine quickly. Jane ate half of hers and said, "I'm full."

When she got up to put the dishes in the sink, I skimmed through Andie's latest string of texts. She'd asked me several questions, the last of which was *What's your address there?*

I sent her Jane's address and wrote, *Still working, sweetheart. More soon!*

Andie wrote back, *Sweetheart! You've never called me that before. I love it. :)*

"Who's Andie?" Jane asked.

I flinched, then turned to find her standing over me with a sly smile on her face.

"Jane!" she yelled at herself. "Don't spy! How rude." She kept her eyes on me as she walked around the couch and sat down. "Is she your girlfriend?"

"We're talking about *you* right now, Jane, not me."

She arched an eyebrow.

"Unless you want to stop."

"No," she said. "I like talking to you, Zara." Then she placed her hand on my knee and squeezed. "Andie's why you're rushing to get home. Is it a new relationship?" She widened her eyes. "It must be."

I let a pause get fat and then fatter.

"Fine, keep your secrets." She took her hand off my knee and said, "I'm going supine for the rest of this," and then she lay back on the couch, with her head so close to me that I could have easily reached over and touched her hair.

I had the impulse to lie back with her, because it looked so comfortable, but of course I didn't. I stayed in my upright position as I pressed record and set the phone between us again.

"So what happened after your parents died?"

After her parents died, Jane left Arden. "I went up to Bay Shore, Long Island, to live with my sister, Claire, who was ten years older than me and liked to gamble. Claire had a boyfriend named Neil, and Neil liked to gamble, too. They smoked a lot of pot and owned an iguana named Iggy. What an uninspired name, am I right?"

One day Claire took Jane to the mall to get new sneakers—"only because the old ones were so tight that I cut holes in the front so my toes could dangle out and the school called home about it"—and while Jane was waiting for Claire to get her corn dog at the food court, she started doing dance moves just to keep herself entertained. "I was always singing and dancing," she said. "Camera-ready from the get."

Anyway, there in the food court, Jane was doing some type of pirouette and a woman with black hair and red lipstick approached her and said, "You should be an actress." When Claire returned with her corn dog, she started talking to the woman, who turned out to be a talent manager named Rosa Maria Brown.

"That was another major stroke of luck," she said. "Rosa Maria Brown."

Soon after the random encounter at the food court, Jane was signed to Rosa Maria Brown's management company. She started going on auditions. "Mostly commercials. I wasn't the prettiest girl, but my personality made up for what I lacked in appearance." Jane loved the auditions, because they brought her into the better world, the world she'd known was waiting for her. The other girls in the waiting rooms always had their

moms with them, and sometimes Jane hated their guts solely
for that reason. They wore nice shoes, and they had nice hair,
and most of them had nicer faces than Jane.

In the beginning, Claire would drive Jane to auditions, which
happened mostly in the city, but then she got bored so she put
her on the train instead. Jane used to lie and pretend that she
had more auditions booked than she really did, and during the
free time she created for herself, she'd walk up and down the
streets of Manhattan, smelling the foul smells and pushing her
way through the throngs of people and enjoying the suspense
of freedom.

I am going to live here one day, she thought to herself. *And
I am going to be rich.*

Back at school in Bay Shore, Jane told some of the kids about
her plans. Most of them didn't care. Or they said, "Cool." But
this one kid, Joey, told her she was an idiot.

"And he cackled in my face," Jane said. "I can still remember exactly. The hallway smelled like pepperoni pizza. Joey
was a redhead who had truly been touched by the ugly stick,
poor thing. Now I can see that he must have hated himself,
and he was just taking his hate out on me, but at the time, all
I could hear was the word *idiot.* So I punched him square in
the jaw."

Jane left a long silence here, and eventually I filled it. "Good
for you," I said.

"First and last punch I ever threw," she said. "I got kicked
out of that school and sent to a different school, which was
farther away from the house. That really pissed Claire off. She
used to drive me there while saying, 'Our shit parents didn't
leave us enough money to pay for all this gas!' Our parents
hadn't technically left us anything because they'd never thought

to write up a will. Plus, they didn't really have anything. Except for their puny house. Claire sold that fast and then gambled away all the proceeds even faster. She tried to work after that, but she couldn't keep a steady job and Neil was always bailing us out. Neil, bless his heart. He really loved Claire." Jane sighed. "And love does incredibly stupid things to people. As we saw with Julian earlier."

She grabbed her phone off the coffee table. "Speak of the devil. He texts me a novel even when he's *not* drunk!" She yawned. "You know what, hon? I'm falling asleep."

"Let's stop for tonight," I said. "You did a great job."

She sat up. "Did I really?"

"Really."

"Can I tell you something, Zara?"

"Sure."

She rolled her lips together. "Originally, I only cared if you liked me. But now I'm actually starting to like you."

I laughed. "You didn't like me before?"

"It's not that I *disliked* you," she said. "You were just a little bit cold when you got here."

"I was keeping a professional distance."

"And now I can feel that you want to be closer to me."

An anxious buzz shot up my spine, but I kept my face calm.

"As I told you, I want the writer of my book to fall in love with me. But I'm not sure you're falling for the right reasons."

My heartbeat moved into my ears and began to throb there. "What do you mean?" I asked.

"I noticed that you really warmed to me after we went to town," she said, "which leads me to believe that what you like about me is that other people like me."

"I didn't even know who you were until this job came up," I said.

"That's the whole point, doll. You haven't been truly aware of who I am until today." She raised one eyebrow. By this point, she'd done the singular eyebrow raise enough times that I considered it to be one of her signature moves.

I raised both of my eyebrows, because I was incapable of raising only one, and asked, "Who *are* you?"

"Who am *I*?" Jane laughed. "I'm nobody."

That night, I took my clothes out of my suitcase and put them in the dresser. In the shower, I washed myself with her Dove soap, and again I imagined her in her shower doing the same thing. I wondered if she sang in the shower, and I wondered if when she shaved her legs, she used shaving cream or not. I wondered, too, if she would have liked my pajamas. They were very plain: a pair of men's boxers and a men's undershirt, both white. I brushed my teeth, and when I looked in the mirror, for some reason I remembered that Jane and I were the same height. At first, this fact had seemed insignificant to me, but now it seemed to mean something, although I couldn't have explained why.

In bed, I checked my phone.

Kim had texted me to ask me how it was going, and I wrote back, *Great!*

I texted Diego: *I like Jane more now.*

And then Andie and I texted for a while. She was going to send me a package, she said, and I thanked her in advance. I took a picture of my legs on the bed and sent it to her, then deleted it. I didn't want to make the same mistake that Diego had made—or I did, but I didn't want to get caught for it.

After the strange mechanical sound interrupted the silence

of the house, followed by the single beep, I said good night to Andie with a bunch of *x*'s and *o*'s.

As I set my phone down on the bedside table, next to the glass of water that Jane had poured for me, I thought, *Only four people in the world know where I am right now: Kim, Diego, Andie, and Jane. Oh, and Bijou and Tom, so fine, technically six.*

It was a thought that might have made many people feel uneasy, but I found it comforting. I didn't need a large entourage. I needed only a tiny army of trustworthy humans around me.

11

Jane wasn't in the kitchen the next morning, but she'd left me a note:

Breakfast Outside! xx

Outside, the table was almost a replica of the day before. The same dishes rested in the same places like the pupils of a classroom with assigned seating, and the silver coffee carafe towered proudly in the center.

I felt myself smiling as I poured a cup and then added a heavy dose of cream. I had the same feeling I'd had less than twenty-four hours into meeting Andie. I was living a life beyond my wildest dreams—or Jane's life was a life beyond my wildest dreams, and I was glad to be a part of it.

As gracefully as possible, I ate roughly half the food on the table, because it was more than enough for one person, and maybe also because the image of Jane eating only half her ham sandwich the night before was fresh in my mind. It took me about fifteen minutes to recognize this second reason, and when I did, I thought it was funny.

She's rubbing off on me, I texted Diego.

"Let me guess," Jane said from somewhere behind me. "You're texting Diego."

"Stop scaring me like that, Jane!" I turned to find her sipping from a water bottle. Her head was craned back and her biceps glistened in the sun. Like the day before, her workout gear was skintight, and her aura was as perky as her ponytail.

"Maybe I like scaring you." She sat down in the chair next to mine and looked at the half-eaten dishes on the table. "Not as hungry today?"

"It's just so much food! Please, you finish the rest."

"Nah, a big breakfast isn't my thing. I suck down an energy bar and a cup of coffee at six and then I'm done."

"You know, you don't have to make me all this food every day. I'd be fine with an energy bar."

She cocked her head. "You sure, hon?"

"Positive."

"All righty, then," she said. "Your wish is my command." Her phone buzzed. She pulled it out of her waistband and looked at the screen. "Guess who it is?"

"Julian writing you another novel."

Jane grunted a laugh. "Yeah, about his sobriety." Then she narrated the text as she was typing it. "You're doing great!" She scrunched her face. "Should I add 'honey'?"

"Sure?"

"You're doing great, *honey*. That's a little sweeter."

When she was done, she grinned at me and said, "Before we start today, you wanna go to the beach?"

Fifteen minutes later, I descended the stairs in my beach gear—a white shirt and cut-offs with the one bathing suit I owned underneath—and found Jane in her pink-tinted aviators and a white linen dress with colorful embroidery striped down the front. She was checking her phone again. "This man just keeps texting me," she said and groaned, then picked her large straw bag up off the floor and grabbed two bottles of water from the fridge while saying, "I gotta stop it with the plastic. I'm going to get canceled."

Along with the two water bottles now in Jane's bag, there were also two rolled-up towels sticking out of it, and I thought, *How generous of her to pack everything up for us.* It seemed only natural for me to offer to do my fair share of the work, so I said, "Do you want me to carry your bag?"

"You want to *carry* my bag?" She placed her hand on my arm and smiled at me. "No, hon. I need your typing arms intact for when you sit down to write my book. I can't be fatiguing you with manual labor!" She slid the door closed and hit a button on her phone to turn the alarm on. "Now, come on," she said. "Let me show you my secret passageway to the beach. I built it so I can escape when necessary."

"Escape what?"

"Oh, honey, just wait until the fans come ringing."

Instead of going toward the gate, we moved diagonally across the peaceful slope. At the patch of peach trees, Jane twisted one off a branch and tossed it at me. "Think fast!"

I had to lunge to catch it, and when I did, she was impressed.

"Ooh, better reflexes than I thought!"

We walked all the way down to the bottom of the property, where a dark green door interrupted the hedged perimeter. Jane set her hand on the doorknob but didn't open it. On the other side of the hedge, I could hear cars swooshing by.

"Georgica's so goddamn busy this time of day," she said. "And of course I can't have anyone knowing about my door. What if the fans started parking outside of it?"

At a lull between cars, she turned the key and pushed the

door open with one forceful thrust. "Quick, quick!" she said, and I sprang forward.

By the time I'd turned around, Jane had already closed the door behind me, but it no longer looked like a door. The Georgica side of Jane's secret passageway was covered in leaves, making it indistinguishable from the rest of the hedge.

"I want a hidden door," I said.

Jane winked at me. "If you want it badly enough, you'll get it, don't worry."

There were no sidewalks, so we walked on the road, moving toward the edge every time a car drove by, which wasn't often. All the houses were surrounded by privacy hedges like Jane's and sepa-rated by large distances. Nothing about this atmosphere suggested chaos. It suggested ease. It suggested that whatever happened to you here would probably be good.

The beach was only three blocks away and Jane talked for most of the time it took to get there. I liked that. I found the sound of her voice comforting, both because it was constant, so I never had to guess what she was thinking, and because of its optimistic melody.

What she said on the short walk was all over the place, an unfiltered stream of consciousness, and what that told me was that Jane was choosing to trust me a little. Sure, she'd hired me to be her ghostwriter, so it was necessary that she open up to me, but she was opening up more than the necessary amount. She didn't need to show me her secret door. She didn't need to tell me what she was texting Julian. She didn't need to invite me here, into her home and into her life. But she was doing all of these things, and I felt flattered by that.

When we arrived at the beach, she walked definitively to a spot that she liked, dropped the bag, and said, "Here."

Our towels were sunflower yellow, and we laid them out side by side and touching, because Jane said that way it was like we'd have one great big towel, which was better than two little ones. She sat down on her side, and I sat down on mine. I slid my flip-flops off and looked out at the mellow waves. I watched a child kick a ball and chase after it. I kept my eyes on the child, but I could see Jane in my periphery pulling her dress over her head.

I glanced at her for a flash and saw that she was wearing a string bikini in the same neon-pink color as the sports bra she'd worn on the cover of *Women's Health*. It was impossible not to admire Jane's body, and it was impossible not to envy her complete lack of self-consciousness. I concentrated on the child, because I didn't want to stare at Jane, by which I meant I wanted to eat her with my eyes. Unlike with Andie, staring at Jane seemed forbidden, and that made me want to do it more.

I noticed an older woman in a straw hat gaping at Jane, which reminded me that I was one of many fans. It was only natural to want to look at beauty. Beauty was what we were all searching for all the time. Beauty was food for the eyes. Beauty was the opposite of death. These were the heady thoughts I was having when Jane handed me a tube of sunscreen and said, "Would you mind?"

Before I responded, she turned and gave me her back. She knew I wouldn't reject her, and of course I didn't. I said "No problem" with slightly too much chirp, and then I squirted a dollop of sunscreen into my palm and began to rub it onto her skin in a perfunctory way, a way that said *I don't find you sexy at all*.

"It's the worst when you have to do your own back," she said. "I can't tell you how many times I've ended up with a handprint on my spine. I call that the No Friends Tan."

I laughed. I was glad that she was talking, because silence in this moment would have been too intimate. I worked quickly. I tried to imagine her shoulders were the shoulders of an animal or a kid—some being that I didn't equate with sex at all.

Once I was done, she said, "Turn around. I'll do you."

I imagined saying, *No, it's fine,* but instead I turned around and pulled my T-shirt off with a forced air of confidence, which I hoped she would read as real.

"Let's lather you up," she said, and then she rubbed the lotion in with the same diligence I imagined she used to apply a marinade to a piece of meat. When she got to my neck, she lingered there to give it a brief massage.

"Because I'm nice," she said.

I responded with an obligatory, "Thanks."

Once she'd finished applying the sunscreen, I was disappointed and relieved at the same time. I realized I hadn't been breathing while her hands were on me.

We spent about an hour lying next to each other on our communal yellow towel. Sometimes, when Jane got excited about an idea, she grabbed my arm.

"We should have shrimp ceviche tonight!"

She spent some of the hour texting Julian, and I spent some of it texting Andie, and we shared tidbits of our respective conversations with each other.

"Julian's asking me what he should wear to his AA meeting," she said. "This man cannot live without me."

"Andie's ordering a Hawaiian pizza later," I told her. "Our favorite. Oh, and she sent me a package to your house."

"Ooh," Jane cooed. "I wonder what it is."

After the sun had baked us "to the state of crispy sweet potatoes," as Jane put it, we went swimming. As I followed her into the waves, I thought, *I wonder how long it would take me to get Jane's ass.* It wasn't that I was unhappy with my body. I'd always thought it was fine. But was "fine" the same thing as "mediocre"? I had a strong feeling that Jane's answer to that question would be yes.

The ocean was colder than I thought it would be, and the waves were less mellow up close. As I waded in, one almost knocked me over. I fought back after that, or I got smarter, ducking underneath the next one and emerging gracefully, my long, wet hair cascading down my back, my face calm despite the ongoing disruption of being pushed and pulled by the tide. Or at least this was what I imagined Jane was seeing, although when I looked at her, she was far ahead beyond the waves, her face turned away from me.

I swam out farther, but not toward Jane. I didn't need to follow her everywhere, and it didn't seem like she wanted to be followed. She was communing with nature, and therefore I would, too. I told myself to concentrate on the details: the salt in my mouth, the heat of the sun, the weightlessness of my body in water. When I looked at Jane again, she was even farther away.

After a little while, I decided I was done swimming and returned to our towel. I was very thirsty, and I knew there was a cold bottle of water in Jane's bag for me, but I wasn't sure if I should take it out or not.

If the bag had been open, it would have been easy, but Jane had zipped it up and stacked her shoes, her dress, and her hat on top of it. In order to take the water out, I'd need to remove and then restack these items. And she would know that I had done that. Which was maybe fine?

I decided to wait. Instead, I took a picture of the ocean and sent it to Andie.

Amazing! she wrote.

But I couldn't stop thinking about how thirsty I was.

Do you think it would be okay to take a bottle of water out of Jane's bag while she's swimming?

Probably?

So I carefully removed her hat, her dress, and her shoes, in that order, unzipped the bag, removed the water bottle, and then reassembled her tower so that it looked exactly the same as before.

Happy with my work, I downed half the water in a few gulps. It was delicious. I lay back on the towel and closed my eyes against the sun. And when I did that, the crashing waves sounded louder. I heard the child with the ball squealing.

Then a large cloud passed over the sun, but when I opened my eyes, I realized that it wasn't a cloud passing over the sun. It was Jane standing over me, her shadow casting its form on my body.

"Hey there," she said.

"Hey." I propped myself up on my elbows.

She glanced at my water bottle. "I see you found yourself a beverage."

My face flushed, and my entire body, which had been melting in the embrace of the hot day, was suddenly cold.

Jane looked away for a moment that seemed to last forever. I was about to say, *I'm so sorry,* or maybe defend myself, but then she plopped down on the towel and set her warm hand on my back and said in her sweet voice, which made everything sound as good as candy, "Zara? What's mine is yours."

On the way back up to the house, Jane outlined our day. We'd shower, then eat lunch. Was I okay with a salad? Yes, I loved salad, I told her. "Then we can curl up on the couch again and keep talking. Let's get 'er done so you can go home to your Andie!"

We were passing through the patch of peach trees when she said that, and every one of them sparkled like a rare gemstone, and the sun dappled Jane's toned shoulders, and the only message to be taken from all the lush green that surrounded us was a message about abundance. For the first time, I wondered how California was going to look to me after East Hampton. Would I still find it beautiful?

12

Freshly showered and wearing my white T-shirt and jeans again—a fashion choice that was as close to not making a choice as you could get—I walked into the kitchen to find Jane pulling a pair of polka-dot socks out of one of the many open cardboard boxes that had been neatly arranged on the counter-top. At the central island, Bijou was chopping a carrot. Next to her cutting board was a wooden bowl filled with greens.

"Goddess Bijou's making us lunch today," Jane said.

"Thanks, Bijou," I said.

Bijou didn't respond.

"Bij?" Jane asked sweetly.

Bijou, her eyes focused on her chopping, said, "Yes?"

"Zara just thanked you for making our lunch."

Bijou looked up at me and widened her perpetual smile. "You're welcome."

As Jane inspected the socks, I inspected her outfit: an over-sized button-down shirt and a pair of white shorts so tiny that I didn't even see them at first.

"When cooking's your job," she was saying, "you don't nec-essarily want to do it all the time. And Bijou likes taking care of me, don't you, Bij?"

Bijou gave Jane her full attention this time. "Yes," she said.

"Oh, and would you be a real doll and make us some ceviche before you go?" Jane asked. "I don't want to have to break to make dinner tonight."

"Yes," Bijou said again.

"You're the best, Bij," Jane said as she tucked the pair of socks back into the box and scooted it to the far end of the counter. "And guess what? You're getting some socks."

Bijou seemed glad. "Super," she said.

Offhandedly—she was already peering into the next box—Jane added, "Unless you want them, Zara."

Bijou looked up at me fast.

"No, no," I said. "You can have them, Bijou."

Bijou, happy with my response, went back to her chopping, and Jane pulled a bag full of plaid hand towels out of a box.

"And you're getting some hand towels," she said to Bijou, placing the box next to the one that contained the rejected socks.

"What is all this stuff?" I asked.

"The rich getting richer." Jane chuckled, then picked up a new box and turned it upside down. A tub of cream and a loofah fell out, followed by a note, which she read aloud. "'Dear Jane, We hope you enjoy our Yummy Yummy Foot Cream and Yummy Yummy Loofah! We want *you* more!'"

"Shouldn't it be shower gel and a loofah?"

"Good point." She turned the loofah around in the light. "Cheap," she muttered.

Then to Bijou: "Bij, you're getting a lot of stuff today."

"Thank you," Bijou said as she let the chopped carrots fall from her cupped hands into the bowl.

"If I posted all these products on my Instagram, you know how much money I'd make?" Jane asked me.

"How much?"

"A lot. But I can't cheapen my brand. I'm classy." She laughed. "Although really I'm more like a hillbilly cake with classy icing on top that's always threatening to melt off."

I sat on the barstool next to hers as she went through the rest of the boxes. She was decisive, so it didn't take long. Sometimes she asked for my opinion. Did I like the speckled phone case? What about the multicolored olives from Italy? My answers pleased her, because I said what I expected her to say and mostly I guessed correctly.

"We have the same taste," she said.

I agreed. "We really do."

We both thought the only item worth Instagramming was a gold bracelet adorned with a *J* charm. Jane deemed it "unhateable," and I concurred. She put it on and asked me to take a picture of her wearing it—and by "a picture," she meant twenty.

"That's how many you need to get one good shot," she said. "It's a twenty-to-one ratio."

She set her elbow on the counter and her hand against her face so the *J* dangled in full view. Every second, she gave me a new angle. Her chin dipped down, her chin rose up, her open palm became a fist, her fingers braided together.

Once I'd taken about twenty shots, we chose the best one— which we both knew was the best, no question—and Jane sent it to her PR gal, Candice.

"Candice," she narrated, "please get this company to pay me beaucoup bucks." Then, to me, she said, "Of course, I don't need the actual money. But it's important because it's a symbol of my worth."

"Right," I said.

She unclasped the bracelet. "Give me your wrist, Zara. I want you to have this."

As I gave her my wrist, I said, "But my name doesn't start with *J*."

Jane looped the thin metallic chain around me. "I know."

I didn't argue. Even though it didn't make sense for me to wear a *J* charm, I wanted the bracelet. "Thank you so much," I said.

As I lifted my arm to the light to admire my new gift, I could feel Bijou boring a hole into my head with her stare, so I made a point not to look at her.

We ate lunch at the outside table while Bijou stayed inside preparing the ceviche for later. Jane, as usual, explained to me what we would be eating before we ate it. "Green salad with garbanzo beans, carrots, avocado, pickled beets, and the real clincher: kettle-cooked potato chips on top." She sighed as she dropped her napkin onto her lap. "The potato-chip-instead-of-croutons idea is one of my best. Very popular, because everybody loves a chip."

She spent a lot of the meal checking her phone, which I didn't mind. She wrote to her lawyer to check on her contract again, and to the pool guy about the possibility of updating the tiles, and she responded to Julian.

As we ate, I kept looking through the sliding glass doors at Bijou: Bijou squeezing a lime into the ceviche, Bijou putting the last of her free stuff into her bag, Bijou flattening the empty boxes. The reason I kept looking was because Bijou, when she didn't know she was being watched, did not look very happy. She looked exhausted, her face slack in all the places it usually wasn't.

13

For our second interview, Jane didn't bother sitting up at all. She lay back on the cloudlike couch, covered her legs in a white cashmere blanket, closed her eyes, and said, "I'm ready for my psychoanalysis, Dr. Zara."

Like the last time, I sat right behind her, gazing over the tip of her nose as she spoke.

"Where'd we leave off?" she asked.

"You just threw a punch for the first and only time in your life."

"Oh, yes," she said. "Joey."

"And then you got sent to a new school and Claire was mad about gas."

"Claire," she scoffed. "And that new school was horrible. The entire building smelled like paint thinner and every other girl there was named Amber. I dropped out eventually. After I landed my first job."

Jane's first job was a laundry detergent commercial. "Which really went with my personality. I've always been very into cleanliness, as you can tell." The commercial featured a family and Jane played the daughter. She had two lines. The first was "Mom, have you seen my soccer jersey?" For that one she had to act concerned, like her young life depended on finding this jersey. The second line was an elated "Thanks, Mom!" after her fake mother had handed her the jersey from the dryer. When Jane saw the commercial later on TV, she died. "I thought I was going to become a movie star, I truly did."

But unfortunately, Jane didn't become a movie star. And she didn't get to keep the money she made for the commercial, either, because Claire, her legal guardian, was in charge. "She gave me fifty bucks, and I bought a pleather skirt the next time I went to Manhattan." So, yes, the chance encounter with Rosa Maria Brown at the mall had been a stroke of luck, but it was thwarted by the dollar signs in Claire's eyes.

Jane dropped out of high school her sophomore year. When she announced to Claire that she was done with her education, Claire didn't give a shit. She just wanted Jane to book more commercials so she could gamble the money away. But Jane was the one with the leverage. *She* was the talent. So she told Claire that she wanted 50 percent or she wouldn't go on auditions anymore. Claire, after some cajoling, agreed. What other choice did she have?

What happened next: Jane booked more commercials—for dog food, for a miniature trampoline, for a chewing gum brand that had just come out with a new mint-tangerine flavor, which tasted disgusting, by the way—and she got to keep half her earnings. She also got a small part in a TV pilot about kids in high school who discover a new dimension of the solar system. It didn't get picked up, though, probably because of that ridiculous plot.

Meanwhile, in her personal life, Jane had started drinking. And doing coke. And frequenting nightclubs that didn't care about her age. She wore four-inch stilettos and heavy eyeliner and little black dresses the size of napkins. The men in the nightclubs gave her lots of attention, which she loved, except for all the times she didn't.

Jane was a natural storyteller, and I was rapt. As she spoke, I watched her forehead tighten with lines and memorized their pattern: five lines right in the center, spaced not too far apart, and one line above all of those, way up near her hair. I thought of that top one as a stretched-out cloud and of the ones below it as the ocean. When Jane squeezed her eyes shut and rocked her head back and forth to the emotion of what she was saying, I imagined her as a child having a bad dream. Sometimes her eyes shot open. That was usually when she'd recovered a vivid memory she hadn't thought about in a while. Sometimes she licked her lips. Sometimes she asked for my approval.

"Zara, am I making sense?"

I always told her yes.

"At one of the nightclubs, I met a sleazeball named Jed who wouldn't leave me alone, so I paid the bouncer to lock him in the broom closet for an hour."

As I watched Jane's hand fall to her forehead, covering the cloud-and-ocean lines, I was not thinking about what it meant to lock someone in a broom closet, or about how this was related to Jane's mother locking her in her room for hours at a time when she was young.

I was thinking, *Her knees knocked together like that are cute.*

Then I was trying to remember what Andie's knees looked like.

Then I was looking at Jane's knees again.

Claire didn't give a shit that Jane would come home at five o'clock in the morning reeking of seedy behavior. Once in a while, Neil, that sweet moron, did give a shit. "Are you okay?"

he'd ask. And Jane would say, "I'm fine." Because she thought she *was* fine. She was still showing up to auditions. She was still booking commercials. Her sixteenth birthday came and went, and then her seventeenth, and she continued to book one job after the next—until the commercials stopped coming.

"Rosa Maria Brown asked me to lunch one day and I showed up so high on coke that I couldn't even pretend to eat my pasta. She called me 'a dangerous girl.'" Jane laughed. "What a diss." Anyway, Rosa Maria Brown dropped her after that, and she told Jane's agents to drop her, too. Jane was sure that she'd find new reps fast, but it wasn't that easy, "because the acting world, like any world, is tiny."

Flash forward to her eighteenth birthday: Jane left Claire and Neil in Bay Shore and moved into a run-down studio apartment in Brooklyn—this was back when Brooklyn was a dump—with the little money she had saved. "I'd become Claire in a way. My eight balls of coke were her gambling chips." The last thing Claire said to Jane was "You're not even pretty anymore," and Jane never forgot it. Much later, after Jane got rich, Claire would come begging for money, and Jane would tell her, "I'll buy you one corn dog. That's it."

Jane's eighteenth year was a depressing one. No more acting. No more future. A mattress on a floor shared with roaches. A drug-dealer boyfriend who started paying her rent. But then they had a nasty fight—"the kind you don't come back from"— and broke up, and Jane was forced to get a regular job. "I bought myself a newspaper and saw this fancy restaurant called Eduardo's was looking to hire a coat-check girl. It was the first interview I went to, and I didn't want to take the job, but I had no choice. So I became a coat-check girl. I thought my life was ending."

Jane continued to think her life was ending until one night, when a handsome older man asked her to hang his coat. "I knew from the moment I saw him that he would be mine."

What Jane noticed first were Mark's blue eyes, which sparkled like a thousand oceans. Mark was also a thousand years older than Jane—"twenty, to be accurate"—but Jane didn't care. Jane's closest friend at the time was a woman named Francine, who was a waitress at Eduardo's, and when Jane told Francine that she thought Mark was a catch, Francine said, "You're looking for a daddy." Jane didn't correct her. "How else am I going to get out of this coatroom? By winning the lotto?"

How do you move up from the station you were born into? How do you not become your parents? According to Jane, there was only one answer, and the answer was luck.

"Every time I saw an opportunity, I clawed at it. I chased it with all my might. That's what makes me lucky. Unlucky people don't see opportunity. They expect opportunity to bite them in the ass."

Even in her darkest days as a cokehead coat-check girl, even when she thought her life was ending, some little piece of Jane knew that unlike the kids she'd grown up with, she was destined for greatness.

Yes, Jane remembered the night she met Mark perfectly. He handed her his coat and she grinned at him and said, "This is a nice coat. But I think you can do better."

Mark was totally shocked that a coat-check girl would speak to him in that way, or that anyone would speak to him in that way, quite frankly. He was a very powerful man. Everybody catered to him. But nobody, deep down, wants to be catered to. People want to be treated like shit a little.

Mark asked Jane what kind of coat was better than his, and she told him she'd be happy to accompany him on a shopping trip.

"My schedule's very busy," she said, "but I happen to be free tomorrow at noon."

So the following day, Jane and her next big stroke of luck met up at Bergdorf Goodman.

At seven, we called it quits and ate the shrimp ceviche outside by the pool.

"Do you feel good about the book so far?" Jane asked me.

"Absolutely," I said. "You're in good hands."

She cocked her head. "I like being in your hands, Zara."

"Ha," I said, which I guess was my awkward invitation for her to laugh along with me or tell me she was kidding, but instead she just gazed at me coolly.

What was she thinking? Did she know what I was thinking? Were we thinking the same thing?

Later, as we were bringing the dishes back into the house, she yawned and said, "I need a bath."

"Sounds nice."

"Do you want to use my tub, hon?" she asked. "You can go first."

"No, no, it's fine. I'll take a shower."

"You sure? I'd be happy to wait."

"No, it's okay, but thank you."

"Okay," she said, "but one night, you should say yes, and I'll make you the best bath. With bubbles and salts and everything you could ever want."

On the way up the stairs, she explained her morning routine to me. "I wake up at six, pound a coffee and an energy bar, and then I work out. You're more than welcome to join me if you want."

I'd never been a gym person. I'd also never been a person who woke up at six o'clock in the morning. I was aware, as I said, "That sounds fun," that I wouldn't have said the same thing to Diego. I wasn't sure what I would have said to Andie.

"Great!" Jane said. We were at the top of the staircase now, next to the empty section of the wall where Julian's photo used to be. "Bright and early, then. I'll see you downstairs."

"Bright and early," I echoed.

I watched Jane glide down the hall and into her room and then I glided into mine. As I stood in the shower, I rolled my neck around under the hot stream of water and fell into all the random thoughts that arise during showers.

I replayed the moment my dad had squeezed my hand right before he died.

I imagined Tom and Bijou arguing at home. "I'm *not* flirting with Jane!" Tom would say, and Bijou, who'd be wearing her new polka-dot socks, would call him a liar and storm around the house.

I thought about how when I said "Bright and early" to Jane, it didn't really feel like me talking. It felt like I was rewriting myself as a new character now, a character my father would never meet.

After my shower, I texted Diego and Andie. I told them that it had been a good day with good food. And:

Really long interviews.

Shrimp ceviche.

She gave me a bracelet she got for free. With a J charm on it.

To that, Diego responded, *A J?*

Andie wrote, *Does she realize your name starts with a Z?*

I know, I wrote to each of them. *Isn't it funny?*

I didn't really like their negative reactions, so I signed off after that and opened my journal.

What I love about writing is that it's a way to create memories. I write down only the things I want to remember. After enough time passes, I forget all the things I left out, and whatever I wrote becomes the only truth.

14

Jane was drinking her coffee when I walked into the kitchen at six. An oversized cardigan hung gladly over her shoulders, and underneath it she wore her usual skintight workout gear. Her hair was down still, not yet in its perky ponytail, and this detail made her seem more unprotected than usual.

"Morning, hon." She looked up from her phone. "How'd you sleep?"

"Great," I said. "It's so quiet in here."

"I had this house soundproofed in the hope that it would help me sleep better. But no." She laughed. "I never sleep. I'm a vampire."

When she said that, I imagined Tom as a vampire pushing her cardigan off her shoulders and sinking his teeth into her neck.

She picked up the carafe of coffee and filled my mug. In front of me on a plate was one of her homemade energy bars. It was small, the size of my palm, and cut in the shape of a square.

"Made with walnuts, dates, protein powder, sesame seeds, and some other stuff. It's the first recipe in my cookbook." She turned to me and winked. "Which I assume you haven't read."

"Not yet."

"I'll give you a signed copy. How about that?"

"Awesome," I said, and I meant it.

Just as I was about to take my first sip of coffee, she asked, "Do you want some cream with that, hon?"

I glanced at her coffee. It was black, no cream.

"I don't take cream," I said, "but thanks."

For the next ten minutes or so, we sat at the kitchen counter, eating and drinking in the low light of morning. I told Jane that her energy bar was delicious, because of course it was, and that I liked her coffee better than the coffee I'd been drinking at home, and she promised to send me back with a boat full of it. We were speaking in softer voices than usual, as people tend to do early in the day, and the combination of that and the shadowy kitchen made everything we said seem more intimate than it possibly was.

Jane told me that she'd felt happy after yesterday's interview, because it reminded her of how sweet Mark had been in the beginning.

"And I felt sadder, too," she continued, "thinking about my cokehead days. What a waste, you know? But I suppose it was necessary. Nothing is for nothing."

"Nothing is for nothing," I repeated. "We should definitely put that line in the book."

A moment later, her phone vibrated on the counter. As she held the screen up to her face to unlock it, I prepared to listen to Julian's latest texts. But then she said, "The fans are here early today. Look at this."

She turned her phone around to show me the two middle-aged women standing in her driveway. They were both plump. One was wearing glasses.

"I've got a camera on the call box and another one on the top of the gate," she said.

I watched the woman wearing glasses press the button on the

call box. The vacant look in her eyes made me think that she was detached from reality. She said something to her friend, who seemed to agree, and then the two of them took a selfie in front of the gate and left.

"Now you understand why I'm security-obsessed," Jane said.

"Yeah," I said. "I would be, too."

Next, she confided in me that even though she'd set a Google alert, she still googled herself every morning, just in case the alert thing didn't work. As she typed her name into the search bar, she explained why. "I need to know if anything mean about me has been added to the internet overnight."

It only took her a second to see that nothing had been added.

"Phew," she said. "I still haven't been cancelled."

I was relieved for her. "Oh, good."

"The brand, you see, is the only thing that matters, Zara." She laughed. "Hell, the brand is more real than reality!"

Our first workout together was awkward, which is how most firsts are with most people.

As we walked down the hall, she said, "This gym gets great light during the day," and I said, "Right, you mentioned that on the tour."

She turned. "Look who's been paying attention."

I smiled, happy that she'd noticed my observational skills.

"Julian and I used to work out together down here," she said. "You're my new Julian."

I didn't know if I should laugh or say something clever, so I ended up making an odd sound that was basically two grunts in a row.

The gym contained a bunch of weights, a rowing machine,

and two elliptical machines that faced the garden. I watched her step onto one of them and put her earbuds in.

I'd left my phone and my earbuds upstairs because it had been so long since I'd entered a gym that I hadn't even considered adding music to the experience. But I didn't want to admit that to Jane, so when she asked me if I usually listened to music while I worked out, I said, "Not always."

I stepped onto the machine next to hers and started pedaling. As she tied her hair into its perky ponytail, she said, "I do forty-five minutes here, then I do arms and abs for fifteen."

I thought that sounded like a lot of time, but I said "Great" like it was normal.

"I'm pressing play now," she said. "Bye." Then she faced forward and pedaled harder.

It was a long forty-five minutes, and I knew that if Jane hadn't been next to me, I would have stopped. The other thing I'd forgotten to bring downstairs was a hair tie, so I had to keep brushing my hair out of my face in silence as Jane pedaled intensely to whatever great music she was listening to.

When she was done with the elliptical, she went to the weights area and I went to the rowing machine to prove—to myself or to her, I wasn't sure—that I was capable of independence. A few times, I looked over at her doing things I knew my body was too weak to do. The weights Jane lifted were far too heavy for me. The sit-ups Jane did were full of a power I did not possess. The determination on her face was what struck me most, because I knew that that determination was the difference between us. It was the reason that Jane lived in a house with seven bedrooms and I did not.

15

For the next few days, Jane and I did everything together. "Everything but bathe and sleep," she said at one point with a wink.

My body got used to waking up at five forty-five in the morning. My taste buds came to expect her energy bars. My workouts improved. Slowly, I was becoming as scrappy as a hyena, and I had Jane to thank for that. She sent me a playlist so we could listen to the same music while we worked out. She'd named it *Fuck Yeah!* We hit play at the exact same moment and sometimes when a good song came on, we'd exchange a look that meant *Fuck yeah!*

I didn't want Jane to know I'd only brought one pair of leggings with me—because then it would have been obvious that I was not a regular exerciser—so I washed them in my bathroom sink at night and then wore them again the following day. After a few days, she noticed.

"Why are your pants wet, hon?"

So I confessed.

"We have a washing machine, you know," she said. "But you should have more than one pair anyway. Borrow some of mine."

This was the first time Jane showed me her closet, which was the same size as Andie's bedroom. It looked like a boutique:

well organized, color-coded, every item screaming, *Own me!* Her hangers were spaced perfectly apart like the trees along her driveway, and every pair of her shoes was shining underneath its own spotlight.

In the center of the closet was a long wooden bench. She told me to sit down as she opened the drawers along the wall looking for workout clothes that I might like.

"This?" She held up a tight top with straps that crisscrossed in the back. It was not a top I would have chosen for myself, but since Jane had chosen it for me, I said, "Sure."

"With these crops?"

They were black like my leggings, but nicer. "Perfect."

She presented me with five workout outfits and I thanked her profusely.

"This is so much more fun than dressing Julian," she said. "Because you're a girl."

I never actually used the laundry machine because Bijou started doing my laundry. Every morning at seven thirty on the dot, she walked through the front door in her clean white shoes. I kept expecting them to get dirty, but they never did, because she was obsessed with keeping them clean. One day I saw her painting over a scuff with Wite-Out.

Another day we ran into each other in the hall and she said, "You are wearing Jane's clothes?" The smile was on her face, but her tone wasn't that pleasant.

Jane, who was coming around the corner just then, clapped her on the back and said, "Yes! But thanks for looking out for me, Bij."

Bijou came to the house every day, but Tom only came with her three times a week. On the days Tom didn't work, he dropped

Bijou off at the front gate. She always brought groceries with her, because Jane preferred to shop daily, like a French person.

"I would go to the store myself," she said, "but then I'd have to say hello to every other person. It takes a lot of energy to do that, you know what I mean?"

Sometimes, along with groceries, Bijou showed up carrying things that Jane's fans had left for her at the gate. They were mostly bouquets of flowers and notes of adoration, and sometimes containers filled with food. Apparently, Jane's fans wanted her to know they were also good at cooking.

"They're all hoping to get a shout-out on Instagram," she said. "As if that's ever going to happen."

Bijou always took the food home with her because she didn't like to waste anything. Most days, at noon, when she left, she carried gifts: the treats left by strangers and the free stuff companies sent to Jane in the hope that she'd promote it.

We settled into a routine, and that was incredibly comforting to me. To exist within a framework that I hadn't invented myself felt like a vacation.

After our workout, we went down to the beach for an hour. The art of moving through Jane's secret door became second nature to me. I knew to stay still as we listened to the cars driving by on Georgica, and I knew to move quickly when she said, "Go!"

My feet memorized the short walk to the beach. My body memorized the ocean. It also memorized Jane's hands as she rubbed sunscreen onto my back. My favorite part was the brief neck massage at the end.

I didn't return the favor for days, possibly because I didn't want her to think I was flirting with her, and then one day I had a new thought: *This isn't very nice of me*. So I reciprocated with a neck massage that was just as brief as the ones she'd given me.

"Ah, that feels so good, hon," she moaned, and I tried to ignore the thrill I felt.

Jane always swam out much farther than I did, and the way she bounded into the waves and spiraled her arms so fast made it clear that she didn't want me to follow. Her swims were the only time during the day when she put space between us, and even though it sort of hurt my feelings, I knew it was probably healthy.

Her food continued to be transcendent.

Even when Bijou made it instead of Jane, which, given our interview schedule, was most of the time, it was transcendent. Almost all of Jane's meal descriptions contained the phrase *from the garden*, which seemed like the perfect mix of decadence and earth-consciousness. We ate arugula from the garden on top of seared ahi, leeks from the garden with filet mignon, and peaches from the garden paired with yogurt from a nearby farm. Part of Bijou's daily routine was to go out to the garden beds and pick the food that Tom had planted.

"If I didn't delegate," Jane told me, "then I'd never get anything done."

One day during lunch, she told me that a person's attitude toward life is illustrated by their relationship to the food on their plate. "If you scarf your meal, then you're operating from a place of scarcity. If you eat slowly, then you're operating from a place of abundance."

I thought back to the first few days at her house when I'd scarfed everything in sight. Of course, I wasn't going to mention this. I wanted to erase it. But then Jane mentioned it.

"When you got here, you were operating from a place of scarcity," she said, "and now you're operating from a place of abundance."

I laughed. "That might be true."

"*Might* be?"

"Is," I said. "It is true."

Later that night, in my journal, I wrote, *Sometimes I think Jane sees me more clearly than I see myself.*

I knew that Jane's ability to read people was part of her success, because she told me that one morning at breakfast.

"The trick to becoming successful is to figure out what people want," she said. "Everybody wants something. If you can figure out what that something is, then you have the upper hand."

"What do you want?" I asked her.

"I want my fucking contract," she said without missing a beat. "What do you want?"

Suddenly and unexpectedly, a horrible sadness rose up into my throat, and it must have registered on my face, because Jane asked, "What's wrong, hon?"

I swallowed my uncried tears. "My dad just died."

"Oh, sweetheart." She got up off her stool and wrapped her arms around me. "I'm sorry," she said, and as she stroked my back, I started to sob.

The hug went on and on, and just as I'd gotten used to the taste of her coffee and the smell of her soap and the feel of her strong shoulders under my hands as I rubbed her sunscreen in, I got used to her body pressed against mine. It felt like she was protecting me in a way I hadn't even known I needed to be protected.

———

She gave me a copy of her cookbook, and inscribed it with this note:

> **Dearest Zara,**
> **I'd be toast without you.**
> **Love, Jane**

The cookbook was called—no surprise—*30 Bucks Tops* and Jane looked stunning on the cover. She wore her signature outfit—a flannel top and ripped jeans—which was designed to say to the women of America, *I'm down-home like you are.* In her hands was a steaming apple pie, and on her face was a smile that somehow managed to be lively and calm at once.

I stayed up late going through all the recipes and examining the pictures of Jane posing with various meals. The one of her standing behind her famous roast chicken was probably my favorite, because I thought she looked happiest in that one.

Every few pages, I'd flip back to the beginning and read her note to me again.

> **Dearest Zara,**
> **I'd be toast without you.**
> **Love, Jane**

She posted the pictures I'd taken of her wearing the *J* bracelet on Instagram and made a few thousand bucks.

"The Instagram racket," she said. "Otherwise known as highway robbery."

Throughout the week, I took more pictures of Jane for her Instagram page: Jane at the beach, Jane tossing the salad that Bijou had made, Jane holding up two pears. She stared at one, ignored the other, and captioned the photo *I want* you *more!*

Even though I never appeared in the photos, I began to feel like I was a part of them. I was the invisible helping hand. I was the woman behind the lens. I was half the team.

Julian kept texting incessantly.

I kept waiting for Jane to get annoyed, but she didn't seem to mind.

"I'd block his number," I said one day, to which she replied, "I like you like this."

"Like what?" I asked.

"Territorial."

One day at the beach, she asked to see a photo of Andie. We were lying facedown on the great big yellow towel, and she said, "Oh, come *on*. You're so secretive."

So I showed her Andie's profile on the dating app.

"Oooh," Jane said. "She's cute!"

Then she went through all of Andie's photos and made comments about them. "Nice eyes . . . Oh, she's a hiker . . . and she likes plants . . . and wears glasses at the computer, okay, that's sensible . . . Oh god, look at these cookies she made! She's too sweet!"

"Way too sweet," I said.

"You're the hotter one," Jane said. "No question."

I could feel myself blush, so I covered the cheek that was facing her with my hand and kept my eyes on the phone as I said "Ha."

———

My text exchanges with Andie were getting more interesting because I started asking her better questions.

Do you generally trust people?

Do you go to a gym?

Do you ever bake pies?

Andie trusted people, yes, until they gave her a reason not to.

No, she wasn't a fan of the gym. She liked hiking better.

And she loved baking pies! Her favorite was blueberry, and she promised to make it for me when I got home.

I told myself that it was normal to compare Andie to Jane. They were two women who'd entered my life recently, two new additions, roughly the same age, living very different lives. I found this intriguing, and I leaned in to the comparison. I think that's why I asked Andie the same questions that Jane had already answered. I wanted to see what they agreed on and what they disagreed on, and I guess I imagined their preferences laid out as the options on a multiple-choice test, and I imagined myself as the test taker, bubbling in my answers.

One afternoon during a bathroom break, Jane got an email about Bree Jones.

"That floozy is going to start filming tomorrow," she said. "And I still haven't gotten my contract."

We extended the bathroom break to talk about Jane's fears for half an hour. Was Bree prettier than Jane? What if Bree's show did so well that Food TV fired Jane? What the hell was everyone at Food TV thinking? Were they drunk?

I'd never seen Jane so upset. She paced across the living room with a nervousness that surprised me. I said reassuring things—"They're *not* going to fire you"—and when she asked for my opinion, I gave it to her.

"Do you think Bree Jones has a better nose than me, Zara? Be honest."

"No," I said. "Not even close."

"Okay," she said, rubbing her temples. "Okay."

At this point, I'd become very aware of how secluded Jane was on her property, veiled by hedges and gates. Besides me, the only people she saw were Bijou and Tom, and they worked for her. I technically might have been working for her, too, but it didn't feel like a job anymore. It felt fun. She'd mentioned the names of a few friends, but it didn't seem like she was very close to them. Now I understood what Tom had meant when he said that no one came up to the house.

When Jane got tired of pacing, she perched herself next to me on the couch and leaned her head on my shoulder and whispered, "Promise me I'm going to be fine."

"I promise," I said, and I gave her a long hug, just like she'd done for me when I was upset about my dad.

She thanked me and called me sweetheart, and then she grabbed the remote control off the coffee table and turned the fireplace on.

As I watched the flames burst to life, it became clear.

The only person Jane had right now was me.

Every night, I wrote in my journal. I quickly filled up the first journal, so I ordered several more to the house.

I wrote about all the funny things Jane said, and all the wise things. I wrote about how she looked softest early in the morning and late at night. I wrote about how my ass was becoming so firm that I'd be able to bounce a dime off it soon, thanks to the workouts in her gym. I wrote about the astonishing greens of East Hampton, and about the healing powers of its salty ocean air.

I wrote, *I hope I fall in love with Andie.*

I wrote about the shape of Jane's lips.

For the first time, Andie decided to call instead of text me. I didn't answer.

Sorry, I wrote, *it's hard to talk here. I don't really have my own space.*

No worries! Did you get the package I sent?

Not yet!

Bijou hadn't seen the package and neither had Jane. "Must be in transit still," she said.

Must be in transit still, I wrote to Andie.

Okay, let me know when it gets there, sweetheart. :(

Every morning and every night, Jane's alarm made its usual sounds. There was the short beep and then the mechanical rasp.

As the days went by, I became so accustomed to these sounds that I sort of stopped hearing them.

Not long after Jane had called me territorial, Julian demanded to see her in person.

"Do you think I should go?" she asked as we were walking through the patch of peach trees one morning on our way to the beach. I was carrying the big straw bag, because I'd insisted a few days earlier, and ever since then it had been understood that carrying the bag was my job, not hers.

"I don't know," I said. "Do you want to go?"

"I don't know." Jane tugged at a peach but didn't twist it off. "I'm suddenly confused about my love life."

When she said that, all the little hairs on my neck stood up and screamed.

Casually, I asked, "What do you mean?"

She said my name. "Zara."

"What?"

She bit her lip and shook her head just slightly. "You're funny," she said, and as we kept walking, I asked her why, but she wouldn't answer.

"You're just funny. That's all."

I smiled, and then we continued in silence, which felt more intimate than anything that had been said.

Later that day, after another five-hour interview, she decided that she wouldn't see Julian yet. She narrated the text as she was writing it.

"We need to focus on the book, babe. We're on a productivity streak and don't want to lose steam!"

I used the same line on Diego when he told me he was dying to come swim in the pool.

When I asked Jane if it would be okay, she said, "To be honest, hon, I like Diego, but he lied to me. And I have a rule about liars. One strike and you're out."

I thought it was severe. All Diego had done was take some benign photos.

But I also understood where Jane was coming from. She was entitled to privacy, especially inside her own home.

I wrote to Diego. *We're on a productivity streak and don't want to lose steam!*

No worries, he wrote.

Later, Jane asked me what I'd told Diego.

"That we need to focus on the book," I said.

She raised her eyebrow. "So you lied."

"I mean, we *are* focusing on the book, so technically it's not a lie."

"But it's not exactly the whole truth, either," she said. "So you lied."

I considered that. "But I didn't lie to *you.*"

Jane's eyes tightened at the corners for one split second, then widened as she lifted her chin just a bit higher and gazed down the length of her nose at me.

"If you ever do lie to me," she said, "I'll know."

16

Before I explain what happened during that second week in East Hampton, I'm going to tell the rest of Jane's story in one fell swoop. As usual, these are just the broad strokes. As usual, imagine me sitting behind her on the cloudlike couch as she talked. Imagine us soaked in the strong afternoon light that came in sideways through the long row of sliding glass doors. Imagine us glowing in purple shadows at dusk. Imagine us in front of the fireplace. Imagine how the flames cast flickering shadows on Jane's face, and imagine me watching her closely, because I really did. For all those hours, I never took my eyes off her.

Jane was only eighteen years old when she told Mark Bailey he needed a coat upgrade. Can you believe that? Just eighteen and she had the audacity to tell this powerful older man that his apparel was subpar.

"So I told him to meet me at Bergdorf Goodman," she said. The next day, Mark appeared in the men's section and he was right on time. What Jane wouldn't tell Mark until a few years later was that she'd arrived an hour early to pick out the perfect coat. She wanted to be sure that he was getting the best one they had, and she wanted it to seem like she'd chosen it quickly and effortlessly.

It was made of virgin wool, the coat, and dark gray. But the best part was the cut. Mark wasn't the tallest man, and this coat somehow made him look miles taller. He loved it. And he asked her out for dinner that night. And then it was on.

The thing Jane would never tell Mark was that she stopped doing drugs the night she met him. "Because I knew that a cokehead couldn't land a man like that. He was serious, and he made me want to take myself seriously. So I went home and flushed the coke. If you want a new life, then you better start living a new life."

It all happened very fast. A month after they met, Jane moved into Mark's SoHo loft, and that's where her new life really began. Goodbye, roach motel, hello, four stories of luxury real estate that Mark had just renovated. Jane didn't quit her job as a coat-check girl immediately, though. "I wanted to prove to him that it wasn't just about his money. Because it wasn't. I fell madly in love with Mark. He was sweet and he made me feel safe for the first time in my life. Unlike the other men I'd been with, I was positive that Mark loved me, and that he'd never leave."

For about six months, Jane kept trekking up to Midtown to hang coats at night. She finally quit when Mark proposed. "It was part of the proposal. He said, 'Marry me and quit that job so you can spend more time thinking about what you really want to do.'"

Mark knew that Jane wasn't a housewife type. She was too ambitious for that. Jane, too, knew she wasn't going to be happy buying things for their house forever, and becoming a mother was off the table from the start. "I never wanted kids and neither did Mark. That was a big thing we had in common."

But sometimes—or all the time, really—life doesn't go the

way you planned. After the wedding—a jam-packed affair at the Plaza—they bought the house in East Hampton, and suddenly Jane was spending all her time doing housewife things. Shopping. More shopping. Hiring a private Pilates instructor. Going to work dinners with Mark and to lunches with other housewives, none of whom Jane thought had any nuance or depth. "They were all like high school cheerleaders, just old."

At first, Jane started cooking out of necessity. She and Mark threw a lot of dinner parties, and she figured she might as well make the food herself, because she'd been good at it as a kid. "Remember, that and my ability to clean were the two things my mother had praised me for growing up."

Jane and Mark's dinner party guests praised her for her cooking, too. "And the old cheerleaders started asking me for my recipes. Sometimes I'd switch the amount of an ingredient on purpose just so they would fail."

Along with being bored, Jane was also anxious. Now she had all the time and money in the world, but she still didn't understand what her life's purpose was supposed to be. She started drinking too much. Which Mark didn't like. And she did shitty things when she was drunk. Sometimes, she . . . well, actually, no, there was no point in getting into all that, because she definitely didn't want it in the book.

"I can't sound like a boozehound, you understand, hon?"

"I understand," I said.

Anyway, back to the confusion about her life's purpose. Jane didn't want to be an actress anymore. The rejection was too dismal, and everyone in Hollywood had an eating disorder. She wasn't interested in getting her GED or going to college. "I've just never been the school type," she said. So, for many, many years—a whopping nine of them—Jane went from one profession to the next while cooking stayed in the background as a hobby.

She became a real estate agent. That was the pits. All those showings. And Jane was wearing high heels back in those days, which made all of her Sundays doubly uncomfortable. After she sold a few houses, she quit and became a decorator, because people were always telling her, "Jane! Your décor is spectacular!"

"But I couldn't do what I wanted. I had to do what the client wanted, and the client usually had bad taste, which was why they'd hired me in the first place. It was a dead end."

Eventually, at the age of twenty-six or twenty-seven, Jane did what any frustrated housewife with no kids and a lot of extra money did. She started volunteering. "Philanthropy with the old cheerleaders." And Jane loved it, minus the old cheerleaders. But it took her a while to find the right cause. "Just like the jobs, I went from one to the next for a while."

First Jane got into saving the nature preserves of Long Island. Then she got into endangered birds. "But it felt empty to me," she said. "Mostly I was just asking Mark's work friends for money."

Eventually, she found this great organization that offered life skills classes to underprivileged young people who'd managed to get off the streets and into a housing community in Harlem. The young people were mostly between the ages of fourteen and twenty-eight, and a lot of them had been drug addicts and sex workers. Now they were trying to reenter the workforce. And learn how to be functioning members of society. They'd all had the worst childhoods, which Jane could relate to. And they were all on food stamps.

Can you guess what happened next?

Jane started version oh-point-oh of *30 Bucks Tops*, a cooking class designed to teach these young people how to make good food with very little money.

"The elements started congealing," Jane said. "The cooking, the food stamps, my own history. That's how you know you're on the right track in life: when all the elements congeal. And I just loved it. I didn't even mind the drive to Harlem twice a week. I'd spend hours at the grocery store writing down the prices of all my potential ingredients. I got happy when I started teaching those classes. And I adored my students. There was this one guy Damien who used to say, 'This food *sucks*!' And he was usually right, too. My meals weren't all winners in the beginning. Oh, Damien. That's the thing about poor people. Poor people tell you the truth. Rich people just lie to your face. In a way, I had more in common with my students than I did with my rich friends. Because you can't change where you come from. You're never going to get a new hometown."

For a year, Jane was happy teaching her students in Harlem. And Mark was supportive—sort of. Sometimes he got annoyed about how much time the class was sucking up. Jane didn't like that. It made her wonder what had happened to the encouraging husband who wanted his wife to find her life's purpose. This was when the Mark fairy tale ended. They started arguing a lot.

"Suddenly, all my skirts were too short and my lipstick was too red and when he didn't think I was listening to him, he'd just wail on me. I had no idea he was violent until then."

I was shocked. "He was violent?" It seemed important to repeat the exact words.

"Yes, and it came out of nowhere."

I imagined Mark hitting Jane and the bruises she must have had to hide. "I'm so sorry," I said.

"Me, too," she said. "It was painful."

"Have you ever talked about this publicly?"

"No, we're revealing it in the book." The thought seemed to enliven her. "It's tidbits like this that are going to make me more relatable and enhance the brand."

"The brand is more real than reality."

She pointed a finger at me. "Damn, you have a great memory, don't you?"

In general, I thought my memory was probably average. But when it came to Jane, I remembered everything.

Anyway, Jane got used to Mark's beatings. He didn't hit her face, which was nice of him. Those kids in Harlem never saw her as a victim. And neither did anyone else, because, yes, of course she never let her wounds be seen. "When someone's wearing long sleeves all summer, they're either sun-phobic or trapped in a domestic violence situation."

If life had unfolded differently, Jane might have gone straight from the volunteer gig to Food TV, but that's not what happened. It would be four more years before *30 Bucks Tops* was born, because life threw Jane a curveball.

At the age of forty-nine, Mark died suddenly and unexpectedly in their home—this home, the home we were sitting in right now. He was in perfect health, doing better than ever at work, and one night he fell while getting out of the bath and hit his head on the edge of the sink. Jane heard the thud, came running, and found Mark on the bathroom floor, bleeding from the head.

"One gushing stream of blood," she said. "I'll never forget how fast that blood gushed out of his head."

She called 911. The paramedics tried to resuscitate Mark. But not for very long. There was so much blood that everyone in the bathroom knew he was dead. Mark was zippered into a body bag and carried out on a stretcher. That night, Jane scrubbed the floor clean and then she cried herself to sleep. In the weeks that followed, she had the bathroom redone.

The funeral was beautiful. Friends and family shared fond memories of Mark, and they weren't bullshit, either. Mark truly had been a great guy—except for all the times his anger got the best of him. Ultimately, Jane had compassion for Mark, because he was unhappy. "Only people who hate themselves are that hateful," she said. "I'm not sure if I ever stopped loving him, to be honest. It was complicated."

Widow seemed like the wrong term for a twenty-nine-year-old, and Jane thought Oxford or whoever did the dictionary should invent a new word for young women whose husbands had died. Although by "young," she supposed what she really meant was "young-ish." Because it's not like she was a spring chicken anymore. Her ass was no longer flawless and the skin underneath her eyes now had the texture of a fig that had been sitting in the sun. Sadness ruins a body, and Jane was devastated.

"I really thought Mark and I would grow old together. We used to have these rocking chairs outside on the patio . . . I assumed we'd be rocking in those chairs forever."

Jane got rid of those chairs after the funeral, and everything else that reminded her of Mark. His suits, his expired passports, all the shit in his office. Even the coat from their very first date at Bergdorf Goodman—she got rid of that, too.

After redoing the bathroom, she remodeled the kitchen, and then she got carried away and renovated the whole house.

"I threw myself into tiny details. I'd be up at three a.m. comparing finishes. It was obsessive. I just wanted some modicum of control." Round knobs versus square knobs. How dark to stain the wood. The faucets: fuckin' A, there were so many faucet heads to choose from. This was the minutia that consumed Jane's life after Mark died.

Once she was done with the house, she moved her control outside to the yard. This was when she installed the Aphrodite fountain, which Mark never would have approved of, because he was too proper for nudity.

"Mark never understood my love for women," she said. Then she gave me the slightest smile, a smile with many potential meanings behind it, and a fuzziness flooded my chest. As I watched her lie back down, I let go of my composed expression and let myself grin. I was glad she didn't turn around right then, because she might have asked me why I looked so giddy, and I wouldn't have been sure how to answer her.

"Anyway, we planted those trees along the driveway, and Tom replenished the abandoned garden beds with new veggies and herbs. Bijou, by this time, had already started cooking for me. I was just too tired, so I taught her some recipes."

The maze was the most ambitious addition to the yard. As Jane had mentioned earlier, she'd dreamed of having her very own maze as a child.

"When I'd go to that well and throw my pebbles in, I'd wish for a house with a maze and for my mom to be nicer to me." She laughed. "At least one of those wishes came true."

The maze had thirteen concentric corridors and therefore many incorrect possibilities. It took Jane about forty-five minutes to get through it the first time, and it took Bijou and Tom twice that long. And they were two people! Now Jane knew the way through like the back of her hand.

"Soon, you'll attempt it, Zara," she said with a wink. "And we'll see what you're made of."

Beyond the desire to create a new atmosphere for herself, one that didn't include the triggering memories of Mark, Jane also became house-focused because she didn't want that much human interaction.

"Most people are terrible at dealing with grief. Everybody tries to say the right thing, but everything they say sounds wrong. It's impossible." Her friends had also been Mark's friends, and they wanted to talk about Mark all the time, which Jane didn't want to do. For a few years, she just found it easier to not mention him.

"That was my way of grieving," she said. "I needed to do it alone." I told her that I totally understood, and when she replied, "I know you do, honey," I felt seen by her.

"Other things changed during this period," Jane continued. "Actually, everything changed."

She quit the volunteer gig in Harlem. "I just couldn't show up there anymore. I had nothing to give." She sold the SoHo loft and bought a new car and settled on a new look. The plaid flannels. The ripped jeans. The furry Birks. Wearing a uniform was convenient, because she no longer had to decide how to present herself every day. More important, she knew that if she wore the same items consistently enough, they would make her easily identifiable. She might not have been totally aware of it at the time, but she was already thinking of herself as a brand.

The most notable upgrade was Jane's hair. She cut it short and shaggy, with long bangs that fell to her eyebrows, and dyed it white blond. People treated her like she was younger and cooler after that.

Once she had her new look, she quit Pilates and started working out in the gym. "Here's a saying I like: 'When your insides are a mess, focus on making your ass look as young as possible.'"

Contrary to what some people thought, Jane was not transforming her body for any future man. She was doing it for herself. She saw no men in her near future, wasn't interested in dating at all. Every once in a while a friend would try to set her up and she always said no. Because Jane still didn't have a strong foothold on this earth. She still didn't know what she was supposed to be doing with her life. And she didn't want a man to tamper with her self-discovery process. With Mark, she'd sort of gotten swallowed up into his world, and she vowed to herself to never let that happen again.

Jane celebrated her thirtieth birthday by herself, and her thirty-first birthday by herself, and her thirty-second birthday by herself. For all those birthdays, she did the same thing, the thing that gave her the most comfort.

"I watched TV and ate my guiltiest pleasure: pork rinds on top of French vanilla ice cream." Yes, this recipe had made it into her cookbook, although using the word *recipe* was a stretch. "All you do is dump your cheap pork rinds on top of your expensive French vanilla ice cream and voilà! The perfect southern way to mar something nice. I call it Rinds 'n Cream."

Normally Jane liked to watch Lifetime Original Movies with her Rinds 'n Cream. Tales of bulimic babysitters? Yes, please. Tales of murdering babysitters? Yes, please. Tales of husbands cheating on their wives with murdering, bulimic babysitters? Oh yes.

On birthday thirty-three, she started channel-surfing for whatever reason and the television literally froze on the Food TV channel. The batteries in her remote had died. And she was so full of Rinds 'n Cream that she couldn't be bothered to get up. So even though she'd always flipped past Food TV, she kept watching. She had no choice. She was stuck there on the channel and stuck there on the couch.

It was the Barefoot Contessa on the screen. Jane recognized her, because she used to have a store in East Hampton, and she vaguely remembered going to an event years earlier at which Barefoot was present, although she couldn't recall the specifics.

Anyway, cut to Jane's epiphany. Barefoot was making some lasagna thing that was similar to a lasagna thing that Jane had made with her students in Harlem, and she thought, *Wait a minute. I should be on that TV screen! That is what I'm meant to be doing in this life!*

So she did some research. And found that there were a bunch of women with cooking shows, including Sandra Lee, who'd also had a rough childhood and who was also cooking with inexpensive ingredients—but Sandra's show was designed for people who wanted to cut corners. Jane wasn't interested in that. She didn't want to *semi*-make meals. She wanted to *make*-make them. And therefore, the conclusion of Jane's research study was that Food TV needed her to fill an obvious gap in their market. That was the logical truth. The emotional truth was that Jane just *knew* in her gut that she was meant to be on that goddamn screen.

It took her another year to get on the goddamn screen, though. She called up her old pal Rosa Maria Brown, apologized for the atrocious behavior she'd exhibited more than a decade earlier, and asked for help. Rosa Maria was kind enough to point Jane in the right direction. And one of Mark's friends knew the head of development at Food TV. That helped, too.

"You can't get anywhere in this world without connections," Jane said. "Connections and money. That truth, however, should in no way deflate anybody's tires. If you're not rich, then go out and make yourself some money. If you have no connections, then go out and make yourself some friends. You can spin shit into gold if you try hard enough, I promise you."

After she'd met the right executives, it wasn't hard to convince them to give her a show, which she filmed shortly thereafter. On her thirty-fourth birthday, she ate Rinds 'n Cream alone again, because why ruin a good thing? Then, about a month later, the show premiered. And ratings were high from the get. The viewers loved Jane. A writer for the *New York Times* called her "the real deal." Fashion bloggers started writing about her clothes. She created her Instagram page and got forty thousand followers overnight.

"I was being recognized, finally, for who I was. I'd found my purpose. And I'd found fame, which inflated my head to the size of a giant balloon for a time, if I'm honest. Then I received my first hateful email, and it pricked the balloon, and I deteriorated into a sad piece of plastic pulp."

The learning curve of the fame game, according to Jane, spares no one. "It's like the maze. You make mistakes at first. You just do."

The most popular mistake is to give too much away. In the beginning, if Jane got an invitation to a restaurant opening or some other event, she'd just go. But then she realized they were only inviting her to get a photo of her there, and those photos sold for money, and why wasn't she getting a cut? So she wised up and started charging for appearances. She wised up with Instagram, too, and started charging more for the products she chose to endorse.

Fame brought Jane some good stuff. "Endless swag bags, most of which I gave to Bijou."

And it brought her some bad stuff. "Strangers ripping me to shreds, unwell fans showing up at my house." One of those fans hopped her gate and jumped into her swimming pool. That's when she installed the taller gate and the improved security system and had Tom build the secret escape door in the hedge so she could get out undetected if necessary.

Two years into her life as a Food TV personality, Jane had mastered the fame game and *30 Bucks Tops* was still kicking ass in the ratings. She'd come up with a bunch of new recipes that spoke to her audience and solidified her brand. Jell-O 'n Fancy Berries. Cream Cheese Cabbage. Leftover Soup That Won't Make You Sad at All. Naturally, it was then time to write her cookbook, which became an instant bestseller that stayed on the list for twenty-nine weeks. "My Famous Roast Chicken" was the official title of her chicken recipe, because it was famous by then. Or, whatever, it was on the cusp of fame, and naming it "famous" made it official.

After the cookbook, the auxiliary rewards started to pour in. "Because money attracts money, power attracts power, hype attracts hype. In other words, the big fish get bigger, and they obscure all the little fishes who are struggling, and it's completely and utterly unfair, but when you used to be a struggling little fish, you kind of think, 'Yeah, I deserve this now. I suffered enough.'"

The auxiliary rewards included some shit that really had nothing to do with cooking, which is what *auxiliary* means: side-note shit, unrelated shit, the shit that eventually builds you an empire.

Did Jane want to appear on QVC?

Yes!

Did she want to be on the cover of *Women's Health*?

Absolutely!

Did she want to be the spokesperson for a company that sold weights?

Of course!

Jane felt especially proud of the *Women's Health* cover, because she'd spent all that time and effort transforming her body.

It was shortly after the commercial for the weights that Jane met Julian at his old restaurant, Little Bear. "We were perfect together. But then he fell into the bottle. And chucked that baked potato at the poor maître d's head. And after he got fired, he got aggressive with me. And verbally abusive. It was like one day I looked up and he'd become Mark."

But the main story wasn't men. It was that *30 Bucks Tops* had been running for four seasons now, and besides a very small—not even very small but *microscopic*!—dip in viewership, the show was still kicking ass.

Which was why it made no sense—no sense at all—for Food TV to hire that floozy Bree Jones.

Okay, fine, maybe Jane did worry that she was no longer at the apex, but we weren't going to put that in the book, because the book was going to be inspirational. Jane felt like it was her duty to be a positive voice in this big, bad world, which was crawling with toxic negativity.

So at the end of the book, it would be best to say that Jane was feeling better than ever now, and that she was more resilient than ever now, too. Considering where she'd come from, it was a miracle she'd gotten this far. Which meant that her readers also had the capacity to make their journeys miraculous.

"Last question," I said. "What is the single most important message you want to convey in this book?"

"Luck doesn't fall off trees. You have to shake the trunk of the tree until the luck falls from its branches. And if, for whatever reason, that doesn't work, here's what you do: you go buy yourself an axe at the Home Depot, and you chop the tree down."

17

The reasons why we warm to some people and not others are often obvious. But just as often, they can't be explained.

I had arrived at Jane's house with the desire to be nothing beyond polite. Not long after, I had new desires, and the desires had a new urgency behind them, and this urgency felt wild and irreverent and mysteriously sparked, like a forest fire with no distinguishable cause.

I knew that Jane was beautiful and charismatic, the light in any room. I knew that I was enchanted by her lifestyle and intrigued by her fame, and I knew that I felt special being so close to someone who many people wanted to be close to.

These were the explicable reasons I'd warmed to Jane.

But underneath these reasons there were others for which I had no language. It wasn't just that I thought she was sexy. It was that in her presence, I felt like I was drunk and full of adrenaline at the same time.

That was the scary part: how quickly she had rendered me powerless.

The second week in East Hampton was even more exhilarating than the first. I noticed several times that my face hurt from smiling so much.

On Monday, we went down to the maze and Jane said, "I'm timing you." Then she took out her phone. "Ready . . . set . . ."—and at "go," she started the clock.

Wanting to impress her, and hoping to beat her time of forty-five minutes, I moved quickly, running from one dead end to the next. Was I hitting the same dead ends? It was hard to know.

Eventually, I slowed down and made up a new plan, which was to leave a trail of leaves behind me so that I'd know where I had been. I wasn't sure if this counted as cheating or not, but it didn't matter, because I wasn't going to tell Jane about it. The hedges were high—eight feet, she'd said—and at first it felt sort of fun to be protected between them.

But as the minutes ticked by, the sense of protection morphed into a sense of entrapment. I was frustrated, sweating, stifled, stuck. And worried that if I didn't solve her maze fast enough, she would think less of me.

"Forty-seven!" she called when I finally stumbled out onto the lawn.

She was lying in the grass with a satisfied look on her face.

"I'm glad you didn't beat my time," she said. "Because then I would have had to kill you."

That night, and many nights that followed, my forty-seven minutes in the maze were compressed into this recurring nightmare: At first, I felt happy. As I walked the lush green corridors, I was surrounded by butterflies and washed in sunlight.

Then I got lost. And my anxiety rose. And rose. And rose. The high hedges got higher. I panicked. I couldn't breathe. The hedges kept growing until all I could see was a sliver of sky.

The dream always ended with me realizing that I would never escape. I was going to die in the maze.

———

On Tuesday, we watched an episode of her show together.

The name *30 BUCKS TOPS* appeared on the screen in thick yellow font, and then there was Jane in a blue flannel top rolled up to the elbows, saying, "Hey there, people, today on *30 Bucks Tops*, we're going to be making one of my very favorite things: maple bacon carrot avocado toast with a side of cheesy spinach!"

The real Jane said, "That cheesy spinach was a nightmare. I had to redo it thirty-nine times."

Jane's TV kitchen was very brightly lit. In the background was a bouquet of purple flowers in a white vase. Pots and pans dangled from a series of hooks, just like they did in her real kitchen right behind us. The kitchen on TV was a studio, real Jane explained, that was overly air-conditioned and quite frankly depressing as hell.

TV Jane didn't look depressed, though. She looked delighted as she told us how we were going to wrap the bacon oh-so-care-fully around the heirloom carrots she'd picked up that morning at the market.

When it came time to cut the avocado, she said, "Opening these babies is an art." She halved the avocado deftly, pulled the sides apart, and whacked the pit with her knife. "Gotcha!" She pulled the knife away, the pit stuck to its blade, and smiled at the camera. "You have to either do things with force or not do them at all, people."

The episode was half an hour long, and it went by fast. Jane was mesmerizing onscreen, and real Jane next to me kept touching my arm. It excited me every time, so I pretended like it didn't.

Wrapping a strip of bacon around a maple-glazed carrot was

a novelty idea, one that had never occurred to me. Jane told the camera that she used to make bacon-wrapped carrots for her parents when she was young, because near where they lived in Arden was a farmer who'd give her carrots for free. "Giant bags of them. His name was Tay Tay." Her dad, especially, had loved this recipe because he was, in Jane's words, a "bacon-holic," and her mom had thought it was pretty good, too.

"Putting your bacon-wrapped carrots on a piece of avocado toast is my homestyle take on a modern favorite," Jane said. "Because we have to keep evolving, right?"

The finished product looked delicious, and Jane signed off by saying, "And remember, people, you don't need a lot of money to eat well."

"So what'd you think?" real Jane asked me.

"You were perfect," I said.

"Aww, thank you, sweetheart!" She curled her strong arms around me, then whispered in my ear, "You're the carrot right now, and I'm the bacon."

On Wednesday, it became clear that we'd finish our interviews soon, so I asked Jane about getting a ticket home.

"I could leave after the weekend?"

"After the weekend," she said as she opened a drawer.

We were in her closet because she'd just remembered she had a shirt she wanted to give me.

"Yeah," I said. "Maybe Monday?"

"Ah, here it is!" She pulled a plain white cotton T-shirt from the drawer. "I know it looks boring, but feel how soft it is."

She handed me the shirt, and I rubbed the fabric between my fingers. "So soft."

"The best T-shirt you'll ever wear," she said. "Try it on."

I waited for her to leave the room or at least turn around, but she didn't.

"What? You afraid I'm going to see your bra?" She laughed.

I laughed along with her, saying, "No, you've seen me in a swimsuit every single day. I think it's the same thing."

I lifted the shirt I was wearing up over my head, hoping my stomach looked toned enough from this angle, and quickly put the new shirt on. She watched me carefully, every move, and when I looked into the gigantic mirror she said, "That shirt is rightfully yours."

"I love it," I said. "It's simple and nice."

She walked up behind me and set her chin on my shoulder. Into the mirror, she said, "Simple and nice. That's all I'm trying to be. And don't worry about the ticket yet, hon. Let's finish first, and then we'll get you out of here. And I'm paying for your flight home. How's that?"

"Oh, you don't have—"

"I want to," she said, and gave me a quick peck on the cheek.

I watched this happen in the mirror. Jane was wearing the exact same T-shirt she'd just given me, but in black, and I thought, *We look like the same person.*

On Thursday, Jane stood behind me just like she had in the closet, with her chin nestled on my shoulder. We were in the kitchen, marinating salmon together, and her hands were over mine.

"You have to really rub it in," she said. "With love. You can fake the love, but real love is better."

Her breath was hot on my neck. The raw fish was slippery. I was trying to pay attention to the lesson, and I was saying things to prove that I was focused on the task at hand.

"How long do we do this for?" I asked.

"As long as it takes for the salmon to feel loved," she said.

I was also saying things to remind her and myself of the future. "I'll have to make this for Andie when I get home."

"Yes," Jane said, "you must."

"By the way, you haven't seen that package she sent, have you? According to FedEx, it got here."

"Nope," she said. "Haven't seen it."

Then she stepped away to wash her hands. "I think that salmon's good now."

As we ate the salmon outside on the patio, she told me she'd just gotten word from one of her spies that the filming of Bree's show was going well.

"I might need to make Bree my better friend," she said, gazing into the night. "Figure out what she wants."

"Good plan," I said.

"I know," Jane said. Then she tipped her head back and howled at the moon. "Fuck you, Bree Jones!"

I stayed up late making us a playlist, and on Friday morning, I sent it to her.

"This name! Honey! I love it!"

I'd named the playlist *Fuck you, Bree Jones!*

It contained ten angry songs and three were by Metallica. Jane thought it was the funniest thing I'd ever done.

That day, she had an extra-robust workout. Every time I looked over at her, her face was beet red, and she was pedaling faster than usual.

"Best workout I've had all week," she said afterward. "Anger is fuel."

On Friday night, I gave in to Jane's relentless offers to use her bathtub.

"Finally!" she said. "I'm going to make you the best bath you've ever had in your whole entire life."

I watched her add salts and bubbles to the steaming water. "And a bath bomb some company sent me that I adore," she said, dropping that in, too. Then she told me to enjoy myself and left the bathroom without closing the door all the way.

My first instinct was to close the door, but I didn't. I pretended not to notice that it was open instead. I heard the TV turn on in her bedroom. I glanced at the open slit between us and saw her bare legs on the bed. I was aware of what I was doing as I undressed. I was imagining her watching me. Every movement was part of a dance I was performing for her.

What would you do differently if you had an audience? How would you carry yourself? Would you not, in the act of making yourself more alluring for someone else, come to see yourself as more alluring?

Of course you would. And that was the thing about Jane. I liked myself more in her presence. I liked how she made me feel. I liked the tension between us, even if I still thought I might have been imagining it.

The closer I got to leaving, the more committed I became to memorizing the details: Jane's smooth back under my hands as I rubbed her sunscreen in, and the way she let her head fall forward, as if begging me to massage her neck longer. The way she groaned when I did. Her tiny diamond earrings catching the sun in flashes like a strobe light. Her uncallused feet. The freckle above her right eyebrow, the one that arched up alone sometimes, her signature move. The boyish way she walked. The pair of jeans that was so ripped you could see almost her entire legs. The other pair that was less ripped. Her faint southern accent. Her Dove soap.

I already knew that I'd be buying that soap when I got home, and I already knew that when I lathered up with it in the shower, I'd be imagining Jane in her shower in East Hampton, doing the same thing.

How long would it be until I forgot her?

I started wondering that a lot.

On Saturday night, we finished our interviews.

"We're done," I said, imagining the book in print already.

Jane sat up and looked at me. Her hair was all messy, and I thought it looked cute. "Really? We're done?"

"Really," I said.

She shot two fists into the air. "We have to celebrate! What should we do? Eat some fresh strawberries from the garden?"

"Sure."

"Strawberries because we're done, we're done, we're done," she sang as she trotted into the kitchen.

I texted Andie, *We're done!*

She wrote back immediately: *YES! Let me know when to pick you up from the airport!*

Then Jane returned with a bowl of gorgeous strawberries, and as she picked her phone up off the coffee table with her free hand, she was saying, "Jesus H, talking about yourself for hours on end—*days* on end—is exhausting! Although you know of course I liked it, too, because I'm very self—" She glanced at the screen. "Oh my god. Guess who's down at the gate right now?"

"Who?"

She handed me the phone, and then I was looking at Julian, pacing back and forth across the driveway. Head down, hands jammed into his pockets, a backpack on the ground. The aerial view showed the backpack. The view from the call box did not. For some reason, it was that backpack that creeped me out the most. What grown man with good intentions carries a backpack around at night?

The next time he walked toward the call box, he pressed the button and held it, and a red banner appeared at the top of Jane's screen: *gate*. Then Julian lowered his face, looked directly into the camera, and said, silently, *Jaaane*.

Jane winced. "He's so scary when he's like this."

"I don't like his backpack," I said.

"He's probably drinking again already." Jane buried her face in her hands and sighed. "And maybe it's my fault. If I had agreed to see him—"

"Jane, it's definitely not your fault."

Julian took his phone out of his pocket and started typing.

"He's probably texting you," I said to Jane.

But I was wrong. She checked and said, "No, he's probably calling an Uber."

Then Julian flicked off the camera and left.

I placed a hand on Jane's shoulder. Her bracelet's *J* charm flitted around in the firelight. That's what I was looking at when Jane covered it with her hand. She wrapped her fingers around my wrist, pressing the *J* into my skin with a trembling desperation that surprised me. I'd never seen her so fragile. And then in the tiniest voice, a voice that belonged to somebody younger and much less ferocious than the woman I understood her to be, she said, "Will you sleep in my bed tonight? I'm afraid."

She looked up at me, her eyes hopelessly dark like two empty wells.

A wiser version of me might have laughed and said, *I'll be just down the hall, don't worry.*

I was fully aware of that when I said yes.

18

That night in her bed, Jane coiled her arm around my stomach and fell asleep quickly. Her arm wasn't heavy, but to me it might as well have been made of stone. I fought off the urge to pee for an hour before delicately removing myself from our pose and going into the bathroom.

When I came back, she'd rolled to the other side of the bed. I lay awake reminding myself that this was innocent. Jane wanted comfort, and my presence was comforting her. We didn't touch for the rest of the night.

Early in the morning—total silence, the room filled with blue light—I awoke to find her propped on an elbow, her face hovering right over mine.

"Hi," she whispered.

And then her hand was stroking my hair, and she was lowering her face closer and closer and closer very slowly, giving me plenty of time to reject her. She smiled, and reflexively, I did, too. I hoped she thought I looked pretty. From this distance, I saw green flecks in her eyes that I'd never seen before.

And then she kissed me, first with her lips and then with her teeth.

I thought about saying, *Wait, no,* but my tongue was in her mouth already, and my hands were gripping her back as she climbed on top of me.

We kept kissing.

Jane was an expert, and I wanted to live up to her standards. I thought about Andie in Mill Valley waiting for me to text her my flight number, and for a second I might have felt guilty, but then I wondered if maybe Andie had kissed other women while I was gone. How well did I really know her, anyway?

The other thing was that Jane was a better kisser than Andie, or at least she was more exciting. Andie was thoughtful. But Jane was ravenous. And unpredictable. And her teeth were perfect veneers, whereas Andie's were a real yellow. My teeth were real and yellow-ish, too, so the comparison was unfair—unless you considered it from an aspirational point of view. I couldn't imagine Andie ever getting veneers, but I could imagine myself getting them.

When Jane bit me, I saw a vision of us in the future on a speedboat in Venice, going way too fast and loving it. I imagined all the times I'd walk through the front door, and she would yell, "Zara, you're home!" and then jump on me, expecting me to catch her. I thought about my stance. I'd have to place my feet in the right way so we wouldn't fall over.

She kissed my ear with tongue and said, "I thought you were going to make a move last night."

"I didn't know you wanted me to."

"What!" She pushed my shoulders down and sat up on me like she was riding a horse. "Are you kidding me, Zara?" She bounced a little, then stopped. "I have to tell you something," she said seriously.

I squeezed her thighs. "Tell me."

She rolled her lips together, thinking. It was unlike her not to know exactly what to say.

"What?"

She lowered her body over mine and smiled. "I think I'm in love with you."

I felt like I'd been punched.

I thought it was completely insane.

And then I thought it was the most logical thing that had ever happened.

In that moment, everything clicked, and suddenly the past looked different. I hadn't been imagining the tension between us. It was real. And some part of me had known that from the second I saw her that very first night in her driveway.

"What?" I repeated, because it still seemed too good to be true, or because I wanted her to say it again.

"I'm in love with you, Zara," she said, not taking her eyes off me. "I just am."

"I'm in love with you, too," I said, and I was so happy I wanted to cry.

Before she left for the day, Bijou made us a cheese plate with grapes, which Jane took to mean that she knew what was up.

"This is sex food," she said as she brought a grape to my lips. "Well, in movies, anyway, and ancient Greece. They're always eating grapes after they have sex."

We were lying on the same lounger outside by the pool, naked except for our sunglasses, and the grape tasted salty from her fingers.

"Mmm," I hummed, and kissed her neck.

We ate the cheese and grapes like animals and washed it down with fine sparkling water—the finest in the universe, according to Jane. It was Pellegrino, which she preferred to other brands because the bubbles were more *picante*.

We groped each other in the sunlight, hidden and free on all that land. We cannonballed into the pool together, and swam around aimlessly, and it felt like we'd become the younger, more carefree versions of ourselves.

In the shallow end, she said, "You can't leave me now, Zara," and I kissed her hard, our mouths slippery with water.

"No," I said. "I can't."

Then she dove down and grabbed my ankles and pulled me toward her until I was floating on my back. When she let go, I sprang off the bottom of the pool and dunked her, my hands firm on her shoulders, and then our playing turned to more kissing and the water and the sun and the tall green hedges and Jane's taut body all became a kaleidoscope spinning me deeper into a stupor, and it was wonderful.

In a quieter moment, she lifted my chin with her fingers and looked straight at me and asked, "What are you going to tell Andie?"

"I don't know yet."

She cocked her head and tugged lightly at my earlobe. "I have an idea."

"What is it?"

She draped her strong arms around my neck and said, "Just tell her you're staying here to write the book for now. I'm not exactly *out*, you know? So I think it's best to keep it between us. Just for a little while. Is that okay with you, sweet pea?"

In the evening, we watched the fireflies zipping around the great expanse of grass, and I told Jane their glow patterns looked like apostrophes to me.

"Oh my god," she said, "you're such a writer."

"I guess."

"When are you going to write your own book?"

"I don't know," I said. "Maybe never."

"Oh bullshit," she said. "You know I can tell when you're lying to me."

"I don't think I'm lying."

"Well, you're lying to yourself, then. You're not going to be a ghostwriter forever."

Her certainty enthralled me. "How do you know?"

"Zara, there's a monster inside of you that's just clawing to get out. Don't think I can't see that."

19

The next morning, I awoke to the sound of her voice.

"Come on, Julian," she was saying. *"Think."*

Phone pressed to her ear, she walked out of the room, and then five minutes later she returned with a smile on her face.

"Hey, sweet pea," she cooed.

"You're in a good mood," I said.

"That's because I have a way with words, hon," she said as she lowered her body on top of mine. "Julian was threatening to call Page Six, and I just talked him out of it. He's pissed I didn't let him in the other night. So he's retaliating."

"What would he have said to Page Six?"

"That I'm a bossy perfectionist. That I eat non–*30 Bucks Tops* meals pretty much every day. He could say anything to tarnish the brand. Hell, he could even make stuff up!"

"But wouldn't people figure out he was lying?"

"No, hon," she said flatly. "Nobody cares about the truth."

A few hours later, after I'd thought about it longer, I said, "Since Julian did what you wanted, does that mean you have to meet up with him now?"

"No," she said. "We actually had a heart-to-heart about how love means giving space sometimes."

For our workout that morning, I chose black spandex leggings and a sports bra that was similar to the one she was wearing, plus a blue top and some gray socks. For the first time, I wore a pair of her shoes, because it turned out that our feet were the same size.

"I like these better than mine," I told her. "They're bouncier."

"They're also more attractive, no offense," she said and pinched my ass.

From this day on, I would abandon my clothes and shoes and exclusively wear Jane's.

And from this day on, I would be the one to prepare breakfast. "Let me do it," I said one morning. "Show me how to make the coffee."

So she did. With a hand on her hip, she explained which burner to use for the kettle (the biggest one), how many scoops to add to the French press ("three, and make them heaping"), and where to find the energy bars that Bijou prepared three times a week (the lowest shelf of the fridge).

"Perfect," I said. "Now you relax while I do everything."

"You might be the best thing that's ever happened to me, Zara," she said as she slid onto the barstool and googled herself.

And I said, "You're definitely the best thing that's ever happened to me, Jane."

I placed the bars on small plates with love. I stirred the coffee with love. I poured Jane's cup with love. And then I said, "I did all of this with love. Can you tell?"

"I can," she whispered, her eyes twinkling in the low light.

We looked at each other in silence for a moment.

"Remember how you told me on my first day here that I was going to fall in love with you?" I asked.

She smiled. "I made a wish, and it came true. Didn't I tell you my life has been defined by luck?"

After our workout, we decided it would be fun to wear matching outfits.

Jane wore the very ripped jeans that exposed almost her entire legs, and I wore the jeans that were less ripped. I chose our shirts: black muscle tees. Jane chose our underwear: black thongs. We both wore Birks: her green, me yellow.

Once we were dressed, we stood side by side and looked into the gigantic mirror in her closet and, without speaking, she took a chunk of my hair and dragged her fingers all the way to the end. Before I could ask her what she was thinking, she grabbed my hand. "Come on, let's make sure you have everything you need in your office."

On the short walk there, we ran into Bijou, who took in our matching outfits and said, "You are twins today."

"We are *lovers* today," Jane corrected, and I felt happy when she said that, the kind of happy that's so big you tell yourself to make it smaller. Before Bijou had time to react, Jane pulled me farther down the hallway and through the office door, and it was right then that I realized Jane's concern about coming out to the public didn't include Bijou, so I said, "I'm surprised you told Bijou the truth about us. You must really trust her. And Tom?"

"Oh, hell no," Jane said. "I don't trust them at all. They signed an NDA."

Next, Jane started listing the contents of the office in the same way she listed her recipe ingredients. "You've got a desk, a printer, and an ergonomic chair so your back won't hurt."

"I like this anchor-shaped paperweight," I said as I picked it up off the desk.

"I don't know why I haven't thrown that away," Jane said. "I'm attached to it for some odd reason."

The desk was nice and big, made of wood, and the chair looked very comfortable, and two fresh reams of paper were stacked next to the printer, waiting to be used. And then there was the light in the room and the idea of Jane lounging naked by the pool while I wrote her book. When I said, "Could life possibly get any better than this?" I meant it as a literal question.

"Life can always get better," Jane said. "What else do you need? A whiteboard? Post-its?"

Our bodies were pressed together, and our faces were inches apart, and our voices were low and sweet and sexy.

"No," I said. "I'll just grab my laptop."

"And start *today*?"

"We need the Food TV people to read this book as soon as possible, right? So they'll renew your contract?"

"Thank *god* we're on the same page." She tugged at my belt loops. "How fast do you think you can be?"

"The last book I did took me two months."

"I bet you can write my book in half that time," she said.

After that, in my mind, I had a deadline: one month.

20

I already knew Jane's story, but going through it again delighted me. She was so charming. And wise. And eloquent. And funny. She was perfect.

And in the sections where she didn't appear perfect—I deleted those. The detail about how she changed the ingredients of her recipes before giving them to the cheerleader housewives so that they'd fail: I cut it. The description of the blood gushing out of Mark's head was a little dark for our audience, so I cut that, too. I was going to delete the part about how she'd paid the bouncer to lock that sleazeball Jed in the broom closet, but then decided not to. It would be read as an example of female empowerment.

One day, Bijou made us tuna fish tartines for lunch, and as we ate them outside by the pool, Jane said, "Have you texted Andie yet?"

"No, she's texted me a bunch of times, though."

Jane held out an open palm. "Can I see?"

I hesitated.

"Come on," she said.

"Fine." I gave her my phone, and she started reading Andie's messages out loud.

"'Hey, are you still coming home? . . . Hope you're okay? . . . Even if you never want to see me again, just let me know that you're okay, please.'" Jane frowned. "She's really into you."

"I need to write her back."

"I'll do it," Jane said, and before I could tell her no, she started typing. "'Hey, Andie, so sorry for the delay. I'm actually staying in East Hampton a little longer than expected. I'm writing the book here! In Jane's grand office! I really need to concentrate right now, so would you mind if I got in touch with you when I'm done?'"

"I feel bad," I said.

"Hon, she's going to get hurt no matter what."

It was true. So I didn't even reread the text. I just pressed send.

"Does anyone else know you're here?" Jane asked. "Besides Diego?"

"My agent."

"Hmmm. I wonder if it would be best to tell those two you went back home. Your agent might know something's up with us if you tell her you're here. And Diego will *definitely* know something's up. And he'll question you about it, is my guess."

I smiled, thinking about how Diego was going to freak out when I eventually told him about me and Jane.

"Just tell them you're back in California, hard at work." She set her hand on my thigh. "I know I'm asking a lot, but it's temporary. Soon we'll tell everyone about our love."

"Okay," I said. "I'll text them right now."

I narrated the texts as I was typing them out, just as she had done.

Afterward, she said, "Thanks, baby," and slid her hand up

my thigh. "Given today's cultural climate, I think being a little gay might actually be great for the brand."

"Definitely," I agreed, and then I was flashing forward to the part when Jane and I would do a fundraiser for queer youth while wearing cool leather jackets. If that was going to be my future, then keeping our love a secret for now was a tiny price to pay.

I worked until eight that night, and then Jane and I had a quick dinner at the kitchen counter and went to bed.

"Sorry, babe," she said. "I can't make love to you tonight. I'm fried."

"Same," I said, feeling suddenly fried, too.

"You can write in your journal in bed if you want," she said.

I was sure that I hadn't mentioned my journaling to her, but I asked anyway. "Did I tell you I usually write in my journal before I go to sleep?"

"Yes, silly."

Was that true?

"I'm not in the mood to write," I said. "I just want to lie here with you."

"Whatever you want," she said, stroking my hair, and her touch was so gentle that I started to second-guess myself.

By morning, I would believe that I'd told her I wrote in my journal at night, and that I'd forgotten.

21

Every morning for the next two weeks, I woke up happy to be lying next to her, and happy to kiss her cheek, and happy to make my way quietly across her bedroom to her closet, where I dressed myself in her clothes.

Every morning, when I looked into the mirror, a dumb smile was on my face.

Every morning, I made her breakfast with love.

One morning, I thought, *I have never felt this alive.*

My body continued to transform.

As the days went by, it looked more and more like her body. I ate what she ate. I exercised for the same amount of time that she did. I came to a new conclusion about why couples so often look the same. It's because they're living the same life.

I developed a new interest in my reflection. It might have been the same interest that Jane had in hers. Sometimes I was surprised that it was me in the mirror.

Were those *my* toned calves?

Was that *my* flat stomach?

I often recalled what Jane had said that very first day about her exercise regime: *I like to meet my potential. Know what I mean?*

Now that I was striving to meet my potential, I began to love myself more. There was nothing to feel bad about because I was no longer choosing to fail and then complaining about it. I was choosing to try, and the harder I tried, the stronger I felt.

I was still nowhere near as strong as Jane, though. One day, she invited me to arm-wrestle with her on the kitchen counter, and she won in two seconds.

"Gotcha," she said, and then she grabbed the back of my neck and squeezed until it almost hurt.

Once I started writing the book, we formed a new routine.

After working out, I went to the office. All the time that had been spent talking to Jane on the couch was now spent at the desk. I worked for a minimum of eight hours a day, but it didn't feel taxing. I fell into a trance writing Jane's story.

And I fell more deeply into Jane.

On the page, I became her. In life, I was becoming more like her.

I could feel the line between us disintegrating.

One day, Julian sent Jane an amends, which she read aloud to me:

"'I've been thinking about our relationship, and I realize I owe you an apology. I'm sorry for the atrocious things I said to you when I was drunk, and for pushing you into the wall, and for every other shitty choice I made.'" She laughed. "I wonder how many times I've been pushed into a wall. Mark used to do that, and my mom, too."

"Your mom?"

"Babe, my mother *killed* my father. It's not like the violence started there, you know what I mean?"

"But you never—"

"I didn't tell you because I don't want that in the book. Sorry, hon. It's not exactly my favorite subject. And you're prohibited from feeling sorry for me, okay? I'm not a victim. This house has *seven* bedrooms. Does that spell victim to you?"

I looked at her for a long time, long enough for her to understand that I was about to say something important.

"I'm honored you're telling me the whole story now, Jane."

I started writing in my journal first thing in the morning, before I got started on the book. After I filled up the second journal, I pushed it to the back of the desk drawer and started writing in the next one.

I wrote about the lull of Jane's voice and the silkiness of her legs and the dignified slope of her nose.

I wrote about my dreams of dying in the maze.

I wrote about how sometimes when I woke up in the middle of the night, she wasn't in the bed with me, and about how she'd explain this when I asked her about it later: "I'm a vampire, I told you."

Then she'd tell me she was downstairs answering emails and doing other miscellaneous admin stuff, or just walking around the house because that seemed to calm her for whatever reason.

Mostly what I wrote about were all the reasons I loved her. I loved her smell and her hair and her clothes and her hands and her mouth. I loved her entirely. I couldn't believe how much I loved her.

I wanted to tell Diego about us, but I knew I couldn't betray Jane.

Are you happy to be home? he wrote. *How's Andie?*

I kept making up excuses for why I couldn't talk, because lying when I wanted to be honest was exhausting.
Still in super-concentration mode. More soon!
Are you being weird? I feel like you're being weird.
I didn't respond.

Kim wrote: *How's the writing going?*
Me: *Great!*
And I meant that.
Between Jane's book and my journals, I'd never written so much so fast.

Andie was beyond accommodating.
I'm glad you're okay. Here to talk whenever you're not busy.
It made me feel worse to string her along, but Jane was worried that if I broke it off, Andie would figure out we were sleeping together and tell the press, or she'd tell someone who would tell the press, or whatever, the press would find out.
"I need a little more time, hon," she said. "Can you be patient with me?"
"Take as long as you need," I told her. "I'm not going anywhere."

Jane was getting antsy waiting for the book, so she started brainstorming ways to expand the brand.
What about a reality show? A line of cookware? A collab with Birkenstock?
Her agents had the same reaction to each of these ideas: "Let's put a pin in that and come back to it after your contract gets renewed."

We continued eating breakfast and dinner together, but we started skipping lunch.

One day, Jane walked into the office and said, "Do you want to eat lunch downstairs? Or would you rather I bring it to you up here so you can keep working? I don't want to interrupt your flow . . . unless *you* want to interrupt it?"

I'd been looking forward to my lunch break with her, but I realized then that it really wasn't necessary. I'd see her in a few hours for dinner instead.

"No," I said. "No need to stop."

She went to the kitchen and came back in with a beautiful tray of food: salad with veggies from the garden, a bottle of Pellegrino, and a cup of coffee.

"You know Hitler used to give his prisoners meth so they'd keep working," she said.

I laughed. "Too bad you don't have any meth."

She kissed me on the forehead. "You're such a good girl," she said.

Jane had read through every single factoid about Bree Jones on the internet because she needed to know exactly who she was dealing with. Bree was thirty-five years old, originally from Atlanta. She'd moved to New York in her twenties to marry a corporate lawyer. They had two kids, both boys, ages five and seven. She enjoyed power-walking and strawberry smoothies and welcoming her husband home from the office with a margarita or a martini, depending on the season. She'd written these details about herself on her very popular blog, which was how Food TV had discovered her.

Bree's blog also contained her recipes, which Jane described as stereotypical southern fare, the greatest hits. "She's a clone of Paula Deen, but younger." And her recipes weren't even trying to be inventive. In fact, they were anti-inventive. And high in cholesterol. Pecan pie with ice cream *and* whipped cream? Cheesy grits with three kinds of cheese?

"She's essentially schooling people on how to kill themselves early. If this woman ruins my career, I swear to God, Zara . . ."

"There's enough success for both of you, don't worry."

"I don't want a pep talk," Jane said. "I want you to hate her."

"Fine," I said. "I hate her."

After two weeks had passed, she said, "You need a break. Should we go to the beach?"

We wore her bikinis and her linen dresses and instead of bringing plastic water bottles, we brought the reusable ones I'd bought us online. "You're a genius," she'd told me when they arrived at the house.

But then at the beach, when she drank from hers, she didn't like it. "This top thing is awkward," she said.

"Sorry," I said reflexively.

"I'll get used to it."

As she rubbed sunscreen onto my back, she told me I was so sexy that she didn't even know what to do with me. The dumb smile on my face got bigger, and the yellow of the towel became a friendlier yellow, and I forgot that she didn't like the water bottle very much.

Whenever Jane touched me, and whenever she said nice things to me, I was filled with a sense of peace so great that it was almost like being sedated. If a volcano had erupted right in front of us, I wouldn't have even blinked.

We went swimming. Jane swam far into the distance, as she always did, and I returned to the towel first. Out of habit, I took out my phone. This was normally when I'd text Diego and Andie. I reread my most recent messages to both of them and thought, *I'm not being a very good person right now.* But just as soon as the unsettling thought arose, Jane was there to settle me again.

"Hey, babe." Her smile was bright white, and her perfect body was dripping with water.

"Hey."

She put her hand on my jaw and for a second I thought she was going to kiss me, but then she pushed me away. "Actually, I'm not sure we should do this in public," she whispered. "What if somebody takes a picture?"

Before I went back to work that day, we made love in the shower. She pushed me up against the glass so hard that I thought it might break. At the end, she melted her slippery body onto mine and said, "That was fun."

"So fun," I agreed.

Then she touched my hair as the water pounded down on her back. Sometimes, when Jane thought something could be improved, she squinted at it and pursed her lips. She was looking at the space above my head, so I thought she was going to make a comment about how the tiles needed to be cleaned more meticulously.

But then she said, "Your hair is so long, babe."

"I know," I said. "I need a trim."

"Me, too," she said. "Let's go see Johnny tomorrow."

———

Jane didn't feel like dealing with fans, so Johnny closed his salon for a few hours to cut our hair.

"Honey!"

"Jane!"

This was how they greeted each other, followed by a round of air kisses. Johnny was a flamboyant teddy bear of a man with a plentiful beard, and his work was la crème de la crème, Jane told me on the drive over.

When we got there, she introduced me to Johnny as her new best friend, which hurt my feelings, although it shouldn't have. What did I expect?

Johnny gave me an eye sweep and said, "You're hot."

"Isn't she?" Jane said, and I brimmed with pride. For Jane to acknowledge me as hot in public seemed like a definite step in the right direction.

A few minutes later, I was sitting in the chair next to Jane's, listening to Johnny talk about how he was considering a liquid diet.

"Absolutely not," Jane told him. "You need to chew. Chewing is a necessary part of the human experience."

After Jane's trim was done and Johnny had been convinced to abandon the liquid-diet idea, it was my turn. He buttoned a smock around my neck and examined my uneven ends. "Who did your last cut?"

"Me?"

"Zara!" Jane smacked my knee. "No!"

"No, no, no," Johnny agreed. He continued to comb his fingers through my damaged, self-cut hair. "How much should we take off?"

"I think you should give her The Jane," Jane said to Johnny.

"Ooh, do you want The Jane?" Johnny asked me.

"I think it would be really nice, hon." Jane grinned.

"That's a big change," I said.

"I think you should do it," Jane said.

"Me, too," Johnny said.

I looked at myself in the mirror. Jane was right there in the mirror with me, and her hair was flawless.

"When we look at each other, we'll see ourselves." She chuckled. "What could be better than that?"

I waited a beat before saying yes.

I didn't want her to know that getting her haircut was exactly what I'd hoped would happen.

22

For the next two weeks, I worked even more. I spent a minimum of ten hours at the desk, and most days it was twelve.

Once in a while, usually when I was staring at the ceiling trying to decide what to write next, Jane walked through the door and gave me a kiss.

I came to think of her kisses as buoys on a long-distance swim.

Somehow, despite all the time I spent looking at the ceiling, I noticed nothing out of the ordinary.

The line between us continued to blur.

But wasn't that the definition of love? A blurred line between two people?

"*Mon dieux*," Bijou said when she saw our matching hair for the first time.

Later, when she brought a glass of water to my office, she asked me if I was feeling okay. "You are not yourself," she said.

"Bij," I said. "I'm *fine*."

She was surprised. "You call me *Bij* now."

I raised my eyebrows. "So?"

———

The days blurred, too. From morning until night, I poured myself into the shape of Jane.

> *I was born in a place where everyone and their grandmother owned a rifle and a dirty baseball cap. In the summers, crawdads colonized the creek near my childhood home, and in the winters, the snow-coated mountains looked like pointy hats made of sugar. The beauty that surrounded our little house was a haven. It was also a source of confusion. Why weren't the bluebirds outside my window stressed that my mother was yelling?*

The clearest proof of our melding was that the iPhone didn't recognize us as separate people.

One day, Jane said, "Come here, I want to try something."

She held her phone up to my face—and it unlocked.

"Ha! It thinks you're me!"

"Because I did your mischievous smile."

When I showed her, she put her hand over her heart and said, "You know, when I was little, I used to tell the other girls at school to dress like me and talk like me. And I named all my dolls Jane."

"You were lonely," I said.

"I *was* lonely," she agreed. "And bossy."

"I'm sure your friends liked that."

"Do my smile again," she said.

So I did, and the delight on her face delighted me.

"In all my life," she said, "I don't think anyone has watched me as intently as you do now."

One day, she said, "What do you think about marriage?"

My heart leaped into my throat. "Are you asking me to marry you, Jane Bailey?"

"Not yet."

"It might be good for the brand. Especially if it's televised, you know?"

"Oh, baby, I like the way you think," she said. "You're thinking like me now."

The preparation for Bree's first season was continuing to go well, according to Jane's spies, and Jane had begun to wonder if she should go to the city sometime soon to congratulate Bree herself.

"You know, in the spirit of sisterhood," she said.

Diego wrote: *Are you mad at me?*

When I told Jane, she said, "That's annoying. Don't respond."

So I didn't.

Andie continued to be accommodating. *Still here to talk whenever you want,* she wrote.

When I read that, the idea of continuing to string her along seemed unbearable to me. *I'm so sorry to do this,* I wrote, *but I think we should stop talking.*

She didn't respond.

That night, I said to Jane, "Andie decided she wants to stop talking."

Jane set her hand on my cheek and said, "See? I told you to wait."

"My famous roast chicken with broccoli from the garden."
"Polenta with carrots from the garden."
"Swordfish with lettuces and baby tomatoes."
Jane always said the name of the dish as she brought it into my office. During the final week before the deadline, I started eating dinner in there, too.
"You done yet?" she kept asking.
You done yet? I asked myself.

I met her one-month deadline. As I watched the pages stream out of the printer, I felt satisfied. I'd never worked so fast. And I knew it was a good book, too. I had no doubts about that.

I carried the manuscript down the stairs like it was my baby. Jane was pacing in front of the fireplace, her phone to her ear. When she saw me, she said goodbye to whoever she was talking to. "I have to go. I'll be there tomorrow." Then she sauntered toward me, the smile on her face growing with every step. "Is that what I think it is?"

"I also emailed you a copy."

"Holy shit! I'm so grateful, honey." She kissed me as she took the manuscript from my hands and read the title, amazed. "*I Want You More* by Jane Bailey."

"Where are you going tomorrow?" I asked.

"The city." She sighed. "I'm taking a few meetings. And having lunch with Bree Jones. The town car's picking me up in the morning."

"Cool," I said. "Do you want me to go with you?"

"No! Stay here and go to the beach! Enjoy the fruits of

your labor! The city is disgusting in the summer, and I'll be so busy running around that I'll hardly have time to spend with you."

I was about to say, *I can hang out with Diego,* but then I remembered he thought I was in California. So I said "Great" instead and locked my eyes on the pool, which was a perfect pool, and a good reminder that I had nothing to complain about.

"Listen, I want to celebrate this with you," she said, "but do you mind if I read it first?"

"Of course!" I said. "I'm going swimming."

I was anxious as she read the draft. Even as I swam in our perfect pool, wearing our perfect bikini, looking up at the clear sky and knowing the book was good, I was anxious.

It took her three hours. Apparently, I was so tired that I fell asleep on a lounger outside after my swim. I awoke to her sweet voice saying my name.

"Zara?"

My eyes strained to blink open against the bright sun. It took me a second to see how puffy and pink her face was.

"Have you been crying?"

"I cried my fucking eyes out, baby. You did a great job."

I was so relieved.

"But, oh man, it was heavy. Reading about my childhood? And the stuff about Mark. You wrote that part so beautifully." She closed her eyes and took a deep breath. "I sent it along to the agents. And to the powers that be at Food TV." She lay down next to me, and said softly into my ear, "What you wrote is even better than what I said."

I knew she would like the improvements I made.

"The real story pales in comparison," she whispered.

"Jane," I whispered back, "this *is* the real story."

23

In the morning, she was gone. On her pillow was a note.

Couldn't sleep, left early. Love you.

I went through our routine without her. When she called at six fifteen to check on me, I was downstairs eating breakfast, and I'd just googled her name.

"No new updates," I said. "I just checked."

"I know, I checked, too," she said. "Sorry I left without saying goodbye. You're not upset, are you?"

"No," I said.

"I should be home tomorrow by sundown."

"Maybe I'll cook dinner for *you* for a change."

"You really are too good to me. And, hey, if you want to take the car to town to get groceries or whatever, go nuts."

"Really?"

"Yes, really! I've held you captive in the house for a month! Bijou can give you the keys."

After we hung up, I went to the gym and had a great workout. It sort of felt like since Jane was gone, I was stepping into the space she usually inhabited. I climbed onto the elliptical machine that she normally used and increased my resistance level from my usual eight to her usual ten.

As I pedaled with vigor, Metallica blasting into my ears, I imagined all the times I'd looked over at Jane while she was on this machine. I closed my eyes and saw the relentlessness on her sweaty face, and I knew my face looked just like that.

Bijou confused me for Jane that morning. I was ascending the staircase with buoyant energy when she walked through the front door and said, "Ah! Zara! I think you are Jane for a moment!"

"Hey, Bij."

She motioned to my head. "Jane's ponytail, too?"

I'd almost forgotten that I'd gathered my hair up in a ponytail that was a few inches higher than usual.

"It's just a ponytail, hon," I said sweetly. "Jane went to the city. And, hey, would you mind finding the car keys for me? I might want to go into town."

I turned and kept walking up the stairs. I told myself I could make my own lunch. Asking Bijou to make me lunch would be—

"Oh, and Bijou," I heard myself say. "Can you make me a picnic for lunch, please? I want to eat at the beach today. Thanks!"

I didn't wait for her to respond. I flashed her a smile and glided into the bedroom.

I spent extra time getting dressed that day.

More accurately, I spent extra time playing dress-up before actually getting dressed.

I locked the closet door, and then I tried on pants and shirts I'd never seen off the hanger before, because they didn't belong to the summer season. I swaddled myself in a wool coat, and then a down coat, and looked at my reflection from all angles in the expansive mirror.

I'd always been curious about what was in the drawers Jane never opened, so I opened every one of them. I found sweaters and scarves and socks made from cashmere. I found a collection of sunglasses and tried them all on. I tried on cropped slacks and army-green pants and silk blouses. I unzipped a hanging garment bag and found a sparkly silver gown inside. That was the last thing I tried on. I felt sexy wearing it, possibly sexier than I'd ever felt, and definitely more glamorous. I walked back and forth in front of the mirror for a while in the dress, mesmerized by its shimmer. Set delicately on the bridge of my nose were the largest pair of sunglasses from the collection, the ones that I equated with celebrity, the ones that said, *Please notice me but don't.*

In my mind, I heard Jane say, *You have to take about twenty shots to get one good one.* So I took about sixty shots of myself.

I was about to start trying on shoes when Bijou knocked. For a second, I was terrified that she'd see me in Jane's clothes, but then I remembered that I'd locked the door.

"Your picnic is ready," she said, and I responded cheerily, "Thanks, Bij!"

After that, I got dressed for the beach. I chose the black bikini, the green Birkenstocks, and the white linen dress with the vibrant floral embroidery that she usually wore. Then I surveyed the mess I'd made in the closet. I wondered how long it would take me to clean it up. *Too long* was the answer. So I started calculating how much it would matter if Bijou knew I'd tried on Jane's clothes. Was it really that big of a deal? Why did I care what Bijou thought about me? Also, wasn't she the house-keeper? Wasn't it her job to clean up? I knew that if Jane were me in this situation, she would have unapologetically left the mess, so that's what I decided to do.

On my way out of the closet, I had a last-second thought: *I should take the celebrity sunglasses.*

It wasn't really a last-second thought, though.

The sunglasses said everything I'd been trying to say my entire life.

Please notice me but don't.

At the beach, I spread my yellow towel out in a spot she would have liked, halfway between the dunes and the sand. I set the picnic basket on one corner and the Birks on the other and pulled my linen dress over my head with an ease that felt real. And then I followed the usual routine: sunscreen first. I lathered up my legs and arms, and when I got to my neck, I gave it a little massage, because that's what I was used to.

Without Jane there, I was more aware of the people surrounding me on the beach. Fifteen feet to my right, an old man sat in a striped chair reading a book. To my left, a group of teenage girls, all wearing what appeared to be the same bikini, lay face up to the sun, their long, still bodies like carrots roasting in the oven. In front of me, two parents were building a sandcastle with their two toddlers.

The mother of the toddlers was the first person whose gaze lingered on me for a few beats too long. I thought I might have been imagining it at first, but as I walked by her on my way into the ocean, her gaze followed me.

I swam out far beyond the waves that day, almost as far as Jane liked to go, but not quite. When I looked back at the shoreline, all the people and their umbrellas were tiny, and the dunes were one long wavy line, and the massive homes didn't seem that impressive to me anymore. I was operating from a mindset of abundance. If my dad was watching me now, then this was what I wanted him to see: me floating on my back in the water, my limbs outstretched in the shape of an X, taking up as much space as possible.

On the short walk back to the towel, and then while I was eating the salad Bijou had made, I felt more eyes on me. The old man put his book down and stared for a shameless amount of time. One of the teenage girls sat up, clocked me, and whispered something to her friend. The mother of the toddlers kept glancing.

I hid behind my giant sunglasses and pretended not to care.

Really, I was thrilled.

And I decided that tomorrow, I would definitely take that trip into town.

I spent the rest of the day writing in my journal.

At dusk, I moved from my office to the couch, and then I moved to the kitchen. I kept writing as I ate the simple dinner I'd prepared for myself: half a ham sandwich on rye. When I was done, I left the dishes in the sink for Bijou to wash the following morning and moved upstairs to the bedroom, where I wrote more.

I'm still trying to figure out if those people at the beach today thought I was Jane. So interesting to feel like you're being watched.

One second after the alarm had beeped and the soft mechanical sound filled the silence of the house, Jane texted me.

Sorry, hon, busiest day. What are you doing?

Writing in my journal.

What are you writing about?

The feeling of being watched.
Jane started texting back, but then she stopped.
I waited.
I waited longer.
And then I finally wrote, *Yes?*
Did Bijou tell you? Or did you figure it out yourself?
What was she talking about?
Technically, she wrote, *it's legal to film whatever you want within the confines of your own home.*
I stopped breathing.
Jane had cameras in her house. Why was this a revelation? It should have been obvious.
My mind started racing through all the images of me she could have possibly seen since I'd arrived. Were there cameras in my old room? In my office? Was this why she'd always known the right time to come in and kiss me while I'd been writing the book? Had she seen me trying on her clothes?
I figured it out myself, I wrote, then casually lifted my eyes and searched the upper corners of the room, where the tiny black dot of a camera eye was totally visible.
Good girl, Jane wrote. *Now spread your legs.*
I didn't hesitate. I just watched as my knees fall apart.
Now touch yourself.

24

After I learned about the cameras, I became the absolute best version of Zara.

Isn't this what everybody wants?

To become the best version of themselves?

Isn't being seen the same as being loved?

I thought the cameras were a good thing. Better than good. They were self-help gold. And they were sexy. Was Jane looking at my ass as I bent over to pick up the weights in the gym? Was she noticing how sensually I rubbed lotion on my legs in the bathroom? Was she watching as I went from room to room, blowing kisses at the camera eyes?

My real intention wasn't really to blow kisses. It was to see if cameras existed in every room.

They did, and yes, this included the closet. Apparently, though, I'd gotten lucky. Jane must not have been watching while I tried on all her clothes, because if she had been, she would have mentioned it. My guess was that she tuned in randomly, and since I would never know when, I'd have to be the best version of myself at all times. The last kiss I blew that morning was at the camera in the kitchen. I didn't realize that Bijou was standing right behind me until I heard her say, "You are crazy."

I whipped around. "Hey, Bij!"

"*Bonjour*," she said, and went to the sink to wet a rag.

I imagined Jane listening: *You are crazy. Hey, Bij! Bonjour.*

I followed Bijou to the sink and whispered, "Do the cameras have sound?"

"No." She wrung out her rag, then bent down to clean a scuff off the toe of her bright white shoe.

"You keep your shoes really clean," I said.

She stood back up and sighed heavily. "If my shoes are not white, then Jane says I must buy new shoes. And I don't want to buy new shoes. So I clean."

"That makes sense," I said, and honestly, I thought it was completely reasonable to ask Bijou to own clean shoes. She was, after all, walking around the house every day.

But some part of me must have also felt bad for her, because the next thing I said was, "You know what? I'm going to give you a break today and make my own lunch. And I'd love to take the car into town later. I'm making Jane her famous roast chicken!"

"Famous," Bijou scoffed.

"Would you mind giving me the car keys whenever it's convenient?"

Just then, Tom opened the sliding glass door wearing his usual enthusiastic smile. "Hi!" he said to me, and then he started speaking to Bijou in French, and so of course Bijou answered in French, and I had absolutely no idea what they were talking about because I didn't speak French. What I did know, however, was that the tone of the conversation went from pleasant to combative. I found myself in the middle of a marital fight. How had this happened? And why, as they spoke angrily, were they both still smiling?

It didn't take me long to answer my own question. They were smiling for the same reason I was leaning against the counter in a posture designed to captivate an audience: the cameras.

I flashbacked to the early days, when I'd seen Bijou looking sad. And remembered that Jane had been home then, sitting right next to me outside, and therefore clearly not watching the footage.

After their fight cooled down, I said, "Are you guys okay?"

Bijou, who now was removing the vacuum cleaner from the closet, barked, "Fine."

But neither of them seemed that fine.

"It's okay to not be fine." I knew I sounded like a lame school therapist, but I kept going anyway. "I don't think you have to be smiling every second, right?"

"Ha!" Bijou said.

"What?"

Then she lost it. While marching around like an angry robot, she yelled, "We must be happy all the time! We must be happy all the time!" Then she grabbed the vacuum cleaner by the neck and stomped off.

I looked at Tom, who gave me this explanation: "She's just stressed."

"Did Jane tell you guys she wants you to be smiling while you work?"

Tom shrugged his big shoulders. "Jane likes us to act like her family."

After I learned this, I realized I'd been wrong to think that Tom had a crush on Jane. He'd just been doing his job. Jane had requested a performance from him and he had complied.

When I imagined Jane making the request, I felt sorry for her. She'd never had a loving family, and now she was trying to create a pseudo version. I imagined her lying awake in the middle of the night, which is when the whispers of truth get loud, feeling an emptiness that no amount of money or creativity would ever fill.

A few hours later, I was sitting by the pool, studying Jane's cookbook, when Bijou came outside. She handed me the car keys and said, "I made your lunch. It is in the fridge."

"Oh, you didn't have to do that!"

Bijou crossed her arms over her chest. "The chicken must be cooked at three hundred and fifty degrees in this oven."

"Really? The recipe says three seventy-five."

"Three hundred and fifty in this oven," she said again.

"Are you sure?"

"I am sure!" she yelled, but then she was regretful. "Sorry."

"It's okay."

"Zara, I will tell you something now. Because I think you are a nice girl even though you are a very stupid girl."

I waited.

"You cannot tell Jane."

Just then, my phone rang.

JANE.

I picked up. "Hi!"

"Hey, hon, would you mind telling Bijou that I'm not paying her to chitty chat?"

I was staring at Bijou's face, thinking, *She looks exhausted.*

"Sure," I said.

After we hung up, I told Bijou. "Jane doesn't want us to be talking while you work."

Bijou turned to leave.

"Wait! What were you going to tell me?"

"That you are the stupidest girl I've ever met," she said, and walked back into the house.

Maybe I would have followed her if Jane hadn't just asked us to stop talking. But then again maybe not, because I assumed that whatever she wanted to tell me had no real weight.

25

At four o'clock, I descended the driveway wearing the very ripped jeans, the ones that exposed almost my entire legs, and the simple white cotton T-shirt she'd given me. On my feet were the green Birks. On my face were the enormous sunglasses. On the radio, country music played at low volume.

At the end of the driveway, the gate slid open, revealing the pristine street like a theater curtain reveals a set. The tall hedges. The black pavement. The fruit basket left by a fan near the call box. And me in the driver's seat, spotlighted by the sun.

As I pulled out onto smooth road, I remembered why I liked this car so much.

Because in it, I was bigger than everyone else.

As I loaded my cart at Citarella, I pretended not to notice that people were noticing me. It was kind of like being at home with the cameras, but more exhilarating, because my audience was larger, and the audience was full of strangers, and the strangers were often standing so close to me that I could have reached out and touched them.

People had different reactions. The locals saw me and went back to shopping, the honest tourists stared, and the dishonest tourists tried to act like I was nothing.

I probably don't need to explain that I was my best self at the store, or that every movement I made was full of grace and thoughtfulness, or that it was hard to pay attention to the quality of the sweet potatoes I picked from the pile because I was more focused on the ballerina-esque quality of my hand as it extended through space to pick them up.

I was comparing the labels on two chickens when I heard a woman say, "Jane Bailey?"

I turned. The woman was petite and blond, with round features.

"Oh, sorry," she said, laughing at herself. "I thought you were someone else."

"No worries," I said, and I felt silly for thinking that anybody would confuse me for Jane.

But then it happened again.

As I walked out of the store, I put my enormous sunglasses on. I rolled the cart toward the Range Rover, thinking that later, over dinner, I'd tell Jane that somebody had almost confused me for her. I was imagining her laughing at that when I looked up and saw a man in a convertible waving at me.

"Jane Bailey, I love you!" he yelled across the parking lot.

I didn't hesitate.

"Thanks, hon!" I yelled back.

The convertible exited the lot, so the man never got a closer look at me. I assumed the distance was why he'd confused me for Jane.

As I was loading the trunk, though, I realized it could have also been the sunglasses, which covered so much of my face.

Again, I started imagining telling Jane the story later.

I yelled back, "Thanks, hon!" Hilarious, right?

And then I thought the story would be better if there was

more of a story. So instead of getting back into the car and driving straight home, I decided that I would walk to Carissa's to get a croissant.

It was crowded that day, so there were many opportunities to be confused for Jane.

First, a middle-aged woman in a pink hat said, "I *love* that ricotta-on-a-waffle thing."

Then another woman—younger and wearing socks up to her knees—said "Dig your food" in monotone as she walked past me.

Somebody cried "Jane!" and one second later, a guy was handing me a copy of a newspaper and a pen and saying, "Would you mind signing this for my wife? Her name's Patty."

"Sure!" I uncapped the pen. As the man went on about his life—he and Patty were from Cleveland; she was a teacher—I scribbled Jane's name with a steady hand.

Then I gave the guy a big old smile, and he thanked me effusively.

"My pleasure," I said with a southern lilt.

When my phone rang, I was so startled that I basically jumped off the sidewalk for a second. I turned away from the guy with the newspaper abruptly, and by the time I said "Hey, babe," I was already speed-walking back toward the car with my head down, hoping that nobody else would recognize me. What was I doing? Had I really just signed her name on a newspaper? I realized that I could never tell Jane about any of this.

"Honey, I'm so fucked." She was frantic and talking fast. "I am so beyond fucked. I lost control. That's the truth. Lunch did not end well, to put it mildly."

I was barreling down the crowded sidewalk, trying to keep my breath even as I asked, "What happened?"

She exhaled loudly. "I've been on damage control for the last two hours. I've called the lawyer, I've called the PR gal, I've called Bree to apologize directly. She didn't answer, of course. Oh, honey, I'm so fucked."

I'd almost made it back to the parking lot when a man screamed, "Jaaaaane!"

"Where are you?" Jane asked.

"The grocery store," I said. "Getting stuff for dinner."

"Why the hell is somebody yelling my name?"

"I don't know. People are crazy."

"That's what they're going to say about me. 'Jane Bailey, she's crazy.' Zara, I need you to promise me something."

I unlocked the car. "Anything."

"No matter what happens, you can't leave me."

"Jane, I would never leave you."

"Fuck, the lawyer's calling again. I gotta go. I'll see you in an hour."

"An *hour*?" I said.

But she had hung up.

26

I zipped home, and twenty minutes later, there I was, careening through my dinner preparations at a reckless speed. Given what had just happened in town, the least I could do was have food ready for her.

I jammed the chicken into the oven, threw the potatoes into boiling water without washing them, and ripped the kale with my hands and tossed it in a sauté pan for a few minutes before rushing upstairs to take a shower that didn't last long. I dressed, I sped back downstairs, I set the table, I told the chicken to hurry the fuck up.

Exactly an hour after she'd called me, Jane walked through the front door. "Babe?"

Half of me was terrified of her finding out what I'd done, and the other half of me was already planning to do it again the next time she went out of town.

"I'm so happy to see you!" I said, and gave her a comforting hug while thinking, *Jane doesn't look like herself.*

"Oh, honey." She sighed, relaxing in my arms. "I'm so happy to be home."

"Dinner will be ready soon," I said.

"I don't give a shit about dinner," she said. "Come sit."

We sat on the couch, which we hadn't done in weeks. To me, it was a return to normalcy. So when Jane said, "Everything's about to change," I didn't really believe her.

"Tell me what happened, sweetheart."

She groaned. Then she told me about the ill-fated lunch with Bree Jones.

"As you know, my goal was to get closer to her, find out what her weaknesses are. Because she's on my territory. So I suggested southern food. You know, as a hint. 'Here we are eating southern comfort food together because that's what we both cook on TV because you're on my fucking territory!'"

They went to Sweet Chick. Wasn't that funny? A frenemy lunch at Sweet Chick. Jesus. Bree arrived early, which annoyed Jane. "It's like she wanted to one-up me." When Jane walked into the restaurant, Bree popped up from her seat like a champagne cork shooting out of a bottle.

"I'm a *huge* fan!" she yelled. "I just *love* you!"

"Oh, thank you, doll," Jane said, and didn't return the compliment.

Bree was better-looking in person, which aggravated Jane. Her face was just annoyingly symmetrical. And her hair—Jane was hoping it would be hair-sprayed to death, the consistency of straw, but no, it was silky as hell.

They ordered sweet teas, and Jane asked for hers without sugar, because, you know, she wasn't only a Food TV personality. She was also a fitness personality. And Bree Jones, who was as chunky as a clog, said, "There's this sugar company that wants me to do a commercial."

"Which company?" Jane asked.

"Domino?"

That really pissed Jane off. But of course she concealed her irritation. She told Bree in the sweetest sweet-tea voice, "Wow, girl, I'm so proud of you!"

"Thanks," Bree said. "I really want to be a body positivity role model."

Jane did not share her true reaction to that statement. No, instead she played it nice and asked Bree all sorts of questions about her family and her neighborhood and where she'd gotten her sweater—it was the most hideous crocheted sweater Jane had ever seen—and, finally, her show, *Little Money, Lotta Love.* How had Bree come up with that miraculous name and concept?

As Bree explained her inane reasoning, which just double-proved how contrived she was as a person, Jane was trying not to vomit in her mouth.

Eventually, the food came. They ate. Bree told Jane how fun it was to film and that she couldn't wait to see the finished product. She hoped her show would turn out to be half as good as Jane's.

And Jane said, "Yeah, well, it's most likely going to resemble my show because our concepts are pretty similar, don't you think?"

And Bree said—had the *gall* to say—"Oh, does that bother you?"

Jane laughed. That was all she could do. Laugh and say "Of course not, sweetie pie."

The rest of the lunch was a wee bit tense, you could say. Or, no, that wasn't it. Jane was tense. Bree seemed thoroughly unencumbered by her status as an unoriginal moron. She had not a care in the world as she waxed on about the wonders of being a plus-size woman while sucking down three sweet teas.

Which of course meant that she had to pee at the end of the meal. Jane paid the check while Bree was in the bathroom. And considered abandoning her at the restaurant, but didn't. She waited. And then the two frenemies walked out together, with Jane feeling like she hadn't accomplished her mission at all.

What were Bree's weaknesses? Besides a love of sugar, Jane had no clue. Because Bree was guarded. "One of those women who pretends to be much stupider than she is," Jane explained. "That's the most cunning kind of woman. And the most misogynistic. The women who play deep into the stereotype of the helpless female, you know what I mean?"

This type of woman drove Jane *nuts*. Because it was the opposite of everything Jane was: anti-stereotype, anti-bullshit, anti-helplessness. Hell, if somebody cut off Jane's *leg*, she'd still make it to work. Jane was a warrior. Bree was manipulative! Jane had an edge. And a vision! Bree had nothing. She was filled with nothingness. Yes, Jane was Rinds 'n Cream. And Bree was plain vanilla fucking ice cream—the generic brand—with no toppings. And this was the problem. *Acutely* the problem! Because the Brees of the world were widely appealing. They offended no one. And therefore, they were always—*always*—the most popular.

And where did that leave the Janes of the world?

In a ditch, potentially.

Jane and Bree had actually already said goodbye out on the street when everything went wrong. So the lunch had *almost* ended okay.

But then Bree, as an afterthought, looked at a hot dog cart across the street and said, "Ooh, street food."

And Jane said, "Nasty."

And Bree said, "I can't believe I forgot to tell you. The network offered me a spin-off show about street food!"

This was when Jane boiled over with rage.

Or not *rage*, but, you know, she was certainly upset.

So she pushed Bree. Not that hard, mind you. But yes, she pushed her. A playful push. And she said, "Are you fucking serious? Fuck off!"

Well—no surprise—Bree was not a woman who knew how to take a joke. Or a little push. And she totally freaked out. And started crying like a helpless woman. And she'd fallen down, too, which was ridiculous. The histrionics!

Jane, if she was being honest, wanted to smash a hot dog into Bree's face. But no, she didn't do that. She was too mature for that. And like a mature adult, she apologized. And helped Bree up. And told her she was so sorry and that she had been *joking*! And that she was sorry, too, for being so strong! She hadn't meant for Bree to fall over. Jesus!

Jane rubbed her face and looked straight at me. Her eyes, which normally twinkled, were bloodshot.

"Do you see, Zara?" she said. "Do you see why everything's about to change? Soon she's going to go to the press with this. The lawyer says there's nothing we can do. Except hope and pray that no one took a picture."

27

When I woke up the next morning, Jane was already on her phone, checking the news.

"Nothing yet," she said.

I kissed her cheek. "Did you sleep?"

"Not a wink."

"Oh, sweetheart, I'm sorry. This is stressful."

"Thanks," she said, her eyes locked on the screen.

We ate breakfast downstairs, same as always. Her face was paler somehow, and her vitality was gone. She only took one bite of her energy bar, then sighed and said, "I feel like the world's about to end."

We worked out that morning, but not to *Fuck You, Bree Jones!*

"I deleted it," she said.

"Do you want me to make us another playlist?" I asked.

"No, thanks," she said, not looking up at me.

She was slow on the elliptical that morning, and she couldn't take her eyes off the phone. Over and over, she kept refreshing the search of her name.

I deleted the *Fuck You, Bree Jones!* playlist because she had, but then I listened to the same Metallica songs that were on it because they'd become part of my routine.

After our workout, we took a shower together as usual.

Normally, Jane was meticulous with the soap. She lathered every crevice. But that morning, she lathered her body haphazardly, in patches, then rinsed off fast. She was anxious to get back to her phone.

I stayed in the shower after she got out. I felt a new distance from her, and I didn't know what to do with it. Jane was on her own island, unreachable, and I knew that nothing I said or did could fix what had happened.

I chose an outfit from our closet as usual. I walked down the stairs as usual. From the hallway, I heard her weeping and broke into a jog.

"Jane?"

I found her on the couch, doubled over herself, crying the kind of cry that makes your body heave.

Bijou was sitting right next to her, patting her back with one hand. In her other hand was Jane's phone. It was playing a video.

You're on my land!

"Oh god, turn that off," Jane begged.

Bijou muted the sound and kept watching.

I kneeled in front of Jane and put my hands on her shoulders. "Oh, Jane" was all I could think to say.

"It's over," she said and groaned. "It's over."

Bijou winced in reaction to whatever she was seeing on the screen, then took her hand off Jane's back and covered her mouth.

Without speaking, she gave me the phone, then went into the kitchen to do the dishes.

I took her place on the couch. I rubbed Jane's back with one hand. With the other, I pressed play.

The video was two minutes long. It had obviously been shot

by a curious pedestrian, one who happened to have a steady hand and a clear view, which was unfortunate for Jane.

I watched without sound the first time, so I didn't hear what Jane and Bree were saying to each other. What I did hear was Jane right next to me, crying until it hurt. That must have colored my view. She felt remorseful about what had happened. And that made sense. Because the video wasn't good.

It began with Bree and Jane having what appeared to be a banal conversation on the street—until Jane's hands shot into the air.

Bree, terrified, stepped back.

And Jane stepped forward and slapped Bree in the face. With force. Twice. Which was not what I'd imagined when Jane, the night before, had said, "I pushed her."

Bree lost her footing, fell back, and landed in the street.

I waited for Jane to help Bree up. But that's not what happened.

Jane stared at Bree for a beat, then stormed out of the frame.

The last few seconds: a stranger helping Bree stand up.

I looked at my hand on Jane's back. For a second, I felt disembodied. *Whose hand? Whose back? What house in East Hampton?*

Then Jane wrapped herself around me and the warmth of our bodies pressed together anchored me to her, and that's when I started building a case on her behalf.

If Jane had been the victim of not one but *two* men, and also of her mother—her *mother*!—wouldn't it only make sense that she'd be lashing out now?

Who, really, was the victim here? Was it Bree, who'd gotten slapped a few times? Or was it Jane, who'd suffered through a lifetime of abuse?

28

Jane was right. Everything did change, and fast.

The video spawned dozens of headlines:

"Jane Bailey Assaults Food TV Newbie"
"*30 Bucks Top* Star Lashes Out"
"I Want to Attack You More"

Throughout the course of the day, Jane's emotions were unpredictable. She was in tears, and then she was screaming "Fuck these people!" into the phone at her lawyer, and then she was desperate again. "Tell me what to do. Please. I'll do anything."

There was nothing to do except issue a public apology, which she did—Candice the PR gal helped her with the wording—and then wait out the storm.

She was on the phone for hours, yelling and crying. Everyone on her team thought the next best thing to do would be to hire someone to help her start fixing her public image, but she wasn't convinced. "I can fix my own image," she said. "I just need some time."

She kept checking Google to find her good name slandered in more malicious ways. She kept making frantic phone calls. She was trying to get ahold of Peter, the president of the network, to explain her side of the story. And maybe to ask if he'd read her book yet. But Peter was on vacation. Well, allegedly.

I followed her as she moved from the living room to her office and then back to the living room. I brought her tissues. I tried to get her to eat lunch, because she'd eaten almost nothing since her return from the city, but she refused.

"I can't even think about food right now, Zara! Stop!"

I looked at Bijou then, who said, "You eat," to me in a motherly way, and then made me a salad.

I knew it was wrong to enjoy food while Jane was starving herself, but I felt better when I reframed the situation like this: I had to be nourished enough for the both of us.

As I ate, I practiced what I would say when she needed me again.

Nothing is for nothing. You said that. Remember?

A few hours later, a circus had formed down at the gate. Fans, journalists, the dreaded paparazzi.

"Look at this shit." Jane held up her phone to show me.

I couldn't believe how many people were milling around in the driveway. Twenty? Thirty?

"Great," she said, "so now we're on house arrest."

Bijou picked up her bag and was about to leave.

"You can't go out the main gate," Jane said to her. "Have Tom collect you at the secret door."

Then her phone rang. She picked it up—"Hello?"—and walked down the hall.

Bijou pointed to the closet where her vacuum lived and whispered, "There is something for you there. A box. Jane asked me to throw it away, but I did not."

I thought that sounded cryptic.

"Later you look."

"Is this what you were going to tell me before?"

She shook her head, then motioned for me to follow her outside.

Once we were there, she put her hands on my shoulders and said in a grave tone, "Zara, I am not permitted to tell you this, but I will tell you, because you are very stupid."

I laughed.

"It's not funny."

"Okay, sorry," I said. "I'm listening."

Bijou tightened her grip on my shoulders and whispered, "Jane's recipes are *my* recipes. Almost all."

"Are you serious?" I asked, although I'm not sure why. The second she said it, I realized that of course it was true. When Jane saw an opportunity, she took it. That was why she'd succeeded in life.

"I am serious," Bijou said, and then she was gazing off into the distance with a distressed look on her face, but her hands were still on my shoulders. "This video," she said. "I knew it."

"Zara?" Jane called from inside.

Bijou leaned in so that her face was very close to mine and said, "Jane is dangerous. And I knew this before. When—"

"Wait. It's probably better if you don't tell me. Since you signed an NDA, right?"

Bijou's eyes widened like Jane's famous sunny-side-up eggs, and then there was Jane standing in the doorway, asking a question she already knew the answer to.

"Are you two talking about me?"

29

That evening, Jane's worst fear came true. She got fired. Peter called her from the Bahamas to let her know himself.

"He said he had no choice," Jane told me. "And that maybe one day, if I get my *issues* under control, I can come back. He actually said that to me. My *issues*. *Fuck* Food TV. I'm never going back. I asked him if he'd read any of the memoir yet and he said he hadn't even seen the email!" She rubbed her tired face. "He's going to talk to Bree and try to convince her not to press charges. I hope that works, because I can't handle legal shit right now."

"Oh, Jane," I said. "You're going to be okay. Nothing is for nothing."

"No platitudes, hon. Jesus!"

After the phone call with Peter, Jane became lifeless. She stared blankly at the walls. She didn't want to get off the couch. And she didn't want to eat, either, but she had to, because she hadn't eaten all day.

"Please?" I said. "I'll make you a sandwich."

Eventually she relented. "Fine."

I made her a sandwich with so much love. I toasted the bread and washed the lettuce and sliced the tomato as meticulously as she would have if she'd been making this meal on TV. As

always, I was glad to feel useful to her, and glad to have something to do with my hands. It was a lot easier than comforting
her with my words, which apparently were the wrong ones. I
told myself that moving forward, I would say less and listen
more. That was the kind thing to do.

When I focused on the distant future, I felt better. Years from
now, when we told this story to our friends, Jane would talk
about how strong I had been, and how she couldn't have done
it without me. I would smile and pretend to be humble, even
though really I would feel proud.

I plated our sandwiches and added chips on the side. I poured
our glasses of Pellegrino. I brought everything to the living
room on a tray.

"Thanks, hon," she said.

I kissed her cheek. "Of course."

With a limp hand, she ferried the sandwich to her mouth and
took a tentative bite. I'd made her an entire sandwich, not just
a half, because she hadn't eaten in so long. I assumed she'd take
a few bites and then put it down. I knew she had no appetite.

This turned out to be wrong.

Jane was hungry now. Astonishingly hungry. I'd never seen
her eat so fast, or so messily. A tomato fell onto the couch, and
she didn't seem to mind. She picked it up and sucked it off her
fingers and said nothing about the light red stain on the fabric,
so I didn't, either.

"I'm so glad you're eating," I told her.

"I'm so glad you're here," she said. "I'm bad at taking care of
myself when I'm upset. This is going to be like after Mark died.
I can feel it. I didn't get out of bed for months."

I wanted to say, *You didn't tell me any of that during our
interviews.*

What I said instead was "If you need to stay in bed, I'll take care of you."

"I know," she said, and stuck more chips in her mouth, and then more chips in her mouth, and then more chips in her mouth, and then they were gone, along with the entire sandwich, and all the Pellegrino. After she took the last sip, she burped.

"That was good." She patted my knee.

"I made it with love," I told her.

She didn't respond to that. She said, "Let's see who's still here," and opened the camera app on her phone. The crowd down by the gate had dwindled, but not by much.

"Are they going to stay overnight?"

"I don't know." She laughed. "Do vultures sleep outside?"

"Maybe?"

She yawned. "I'm exhausted. Let's go to sleep."

"Do you want me to do the dishes?" I asked, possibly only so that I could look for the mysterious box in the closet while she was upstairs.

"No, we can do them tomorrow."

Yes, I did notice that she said "we" rather than "Bijou," but I guess I assumed it was a mistake.

30

That night in bed, she held me like I was her life raft.

"I love you," she said. Her breath smelled like chips.

"I love you, too, Jane."

It didn't take her long to fall asleep. She started to snore, but very lightly, and it made her seem so harmless and unguarded and young, and the warmth of her body pressed against mine reassured me, as it always did. Everything was going to be okay. Whenever Jane and I held each other like this, with neither of us speaking, I was completely at peace and I think she was, too.

Time passed.

Then more time.

I couldn't sleep. I was going back over the video in my mind. Had the slaps really been that forceful? Maybe they hadn't been. Maybe Bree had overreacted.

More time passed.

I counted sheep, I counted clouds, I thought about my dad.

Finally, Jane rolled over to her side of the bed, which was probably what I'd been waiting for, even though I didn't want to admit that to myself, because sneaking downstairs in the middle of the night to look for a mysterious box seemed creepy.

But that's what I did. I snuck out of the bed. I was slow and careful. The floors didn't creak as I moved down the stairs in slow motion. The handle on the closet door stayed quiet as I pulled it down.

There was no box in the closet. It was a small, tidy closet, so it didn't take me long to find this out. It just wasn't there.

I closed the closet door and started back up the stairs.

"Where you going, hon?"

I looked up and there was Jane, standing at the top of the staircase. My heart was beating in my ears as I said, very calmly, "Back to bed."

She laughed. "Walking like that? Like a robber? Try again."

"I couldn't sleep."

"Nope," she said. "Try again."

I stared at her. She stared at me.

I thought: *She already knows.*

"Bijou—"

"Yep, that's the one!"

For a moment I couldn't speak.

"Bijou told you about that box in the closet," she said.

My face was tingling.

"And about my *borrowed* recipes. She called and confessed to everything, because she no longer cares about the NDA she signed. She said, 'If you sue me, I will reveal all your secrets!' It was a bold move. I'm kind of proud of her."

I reminded myself to keep breathing.

"I want you to know that I didn't steal anything. I paid her a lot of money. And it made sense for both of us. It's not like Bijou was going to get a cooking show, you know what I mean?"

I thought about moving, but my legs felt numb. Sweat beads prickled at my hairline.

"Bijou and Tom are funny people. One day they love me, and the next day, after many years of loyal service, they're traitors."

"What do you mean?"

"They quit, babe. According to Bijou, I'm a bad woman. A bad woman!" She disappeared behind the wall for a second, and then she was descending the stairs.

"They *quit*?" I wiped the sweat off my forehead.

Then she was right there, coiling her powerful arms around me. "It's just you and me now, Zara."

"Why didn't you tell me earlier?"

She cocked her head. In a voice that was dripping with sweetness, she said, "Because then I wouldn't have gotten to witness your sexy tiptoe, silly."

What I thought: *I deserve this. Jane wanted to see if I'd tell her what Bijou had told me, and I hadn't. So I'd betrayed her, too.*

"Also I was kind of busy getting fired this afternoon, remember?"

"I'm sorry."

She took my hand. "Come," she said, and then she was pulling me up the stairs and into our room, and I saw it immediately: a box on the bed.

I looked at Jane. She grabbed my shoulders and turned my body to face hers. I remember thinking, *Her hands are so heavy, her hands are holding me down,* as she said, with authority, "I hid this from you, but Zara, I swear on my life: I will *never* hide anything from you again."

Then she lifted her hands off me, which I took as a signal that I was free to go, and I moved toward the box.

I checked for Andie's name first, and there it was. I'd forgotten her street was called Shadow Lane.

I watched my hands open the box, feeling detached.

Whose hands?

What box?

What house in East Hampton?

I was hoping that whatever Andie had sent me was trite. Like bath products, maybe, or one of those stupid hats that says LIFE IS GOOD. I think I was only hoping that because I suspected I would be wrong. And I was. Andie was a thoughtful person, and her gift—a framed photo of us on the first hike we'd ever taken—was proof of that.

The frame was nice, made of dark wood. And within the frame, there we were, grinning like two happy women who'd just slept together for the first time. I remembered how gentle the weather had been that day, and how Andie and I had discovered we walked at the same pace. I remembered, too, how I'd felt about her then, which was insanely hopeful that we'd end up together.

"I knew I was in love with you already," Jane said, "and when this arrived at the house, I was jealous. I worried that if you saw it, you wouldn't love me back."

"Why are you showing this to me?"

"Because, Zara, I want our relationship to be honest. I'm confessing my sins to you. I made a mistake. Like I said, I was filled with jealousy, a jealousy that I've never felt before. Which tells me that I've never loved anyone as much as I love you."

She set her strong hands on my hips. "Are you upset?" she asked. Then her hands were roaming up my back and grabbing the nape of my neck and squeezing and I wasn't thinking clearly anymore.

"I'm not upset," I said. "I'm just surprised."

"Love makes people do crazy things." She leaned in and bit my lip. "I think you should be flattered."

I can't explain this, because it doesn't make sense, but I felt flattered even before she'd said that.

31

The next morning, I woke up to find Jane standing by the window, gazing out.

"Hey," I said groggily.

She looked at me for a flash—"Hey, hon"—then returned to her original position.

"What are you doing over there?"

"Making sure I have no trespassing paparazzi on my property. If I do, I'm going to shoot 'em down." She chuckled to herself. "Country style."

"That's funny."

"I'm serious," she said, but I didn't believe her. And when she pulled a gun—a *gun?*—out of the pocket of her robe, I somehow didn't believe that it was real.

"Anybody who doesn't own a firearm is incompetent, as far as I'm concerned," she said. "I know that probably doesn't go along with your liberal values, but there it is."

I was staring at the gun, and then Jane was bringing it closer to me, saying, "Here, feel. It's heavy."

I'd never held a gun before, and I wasn't sure I wanted to.

"Oh, come on, don't be a weenie," she said, and pressed it into my palm, and I watched my fingers curl around its shape.

I remember looking at my hand and thinking, *This isn't supposed to be happening.*

I imagined dropping the gun. I imagined it falling onto the bed. But in reality, I was testing its weight in little pulses, saying, "Yeah, it is heavy."

"And less frightening than you thought."

I wasn't sure what to say to that. "Have you ever shot it?"

"No." She laughed. "I prefer to assault people with my bare hands."

Then: "Zara! That was a joke. Jesus."

While I was pulling on my leggings that morning, she walked into the closet and pushed her winter coats to the sides, then opened a little wooden door on the wall I'd never seen before, revealing a safe that was small and gray like the ones in hotel rooms. "Look away for a sec?" she said. "I can't have you knowing the code."

When I looked away, my eyes landed on the garment bag that contained the sparkly silver gown, and I thought, *She still doesn't know I tried that on.* It made me feel better about the fact that she'd failed to mention she owned a firearm. We'd both kept secrets.

I watched her put the gun into the safe, and then she said, "I need coffee."

"Are you going to get dressed?" I asked.

She stuck out her tongue. "What's the point? I'm not going to be on TV anytime soon."

Downstairs, I prepared breakfast while Jane sat at the counter, reacting to the Google search of her name.

"Oh god."

"Oh shit."

"Oh no."

As I added the coffee and then the water to the French press, I was thinking about the very first morning we'd worked out together. I'd arrived downstairs without a hair tie and without my phone, totally unprepared, and Jane, whose energy had been as perky as her ponytail, had given me a coffee and asked, "You want cream with that, hon?" And I had said no, even though before I met her, I took cream.

Now I had no desire for cream, and I was the one making the coffee.

And now Jane was the one with her morning hair falling all over her face.

"I'm beyond canceled," she was saying. "Bury me now. Ugh."

"Ugh," I echoed as I opened the fridge. And then I meant the *ugh* even more because I was looking at the fridge with new eyes—the eyes of a person who knew that Bijou wouldn't be arriving to replenish our groceries ever again.

"Hey, Jane?"

"What, hon?"

"We don't have that much food."

"I'll order some later."

"Thanks," I said. "And maybe later you can teach me how to make your energy bars?"

She sighed. "Just read the recipe."

It stung when she said that. I wanted her to teach me to make the energy bars herself. Maybe I'd imagined her measuring out the ingredients and me stirring them together with love and efficiency. She'd be impressed with how quickly I'd become an excellent cook, and when she gave me a compliment, I'd pretend to disagree, then kiss her hard.

Halfway through my workout, I decided that Andie deserved an explanation.

I thanked her for the gift, apologized profusely, and wrote, *I fell in love with Jane. She's not really out yet so don't tell anyone, please.*

After that, I wrote to Diego, who'd texted me thousands of times and left several voicemails.

Sorry for massive delay! I'm not mad at you. I've just been busy!

He responded quickly. *Zara, that's bullshit.*

A minute later: *No one is too busy to return a text. It takes two seconds.*

A minute later: *I'm mad at you now.*

I knew that if I'd told Jane about it, she would have said Diego was behaving like a child, and I would have agreed. The more I considered his immature behavior, the more annoyed I became. Actually, I was on fire with annoyance, which translated into a robust workout. I pedaled faster, remembering how hard Jane had worked out the day I sent her the *Fuck you, Bree Jones!* playlist. I made it look easy, too. I raised the weights like they were air while thinking, *Anger is fuel.*

And yes, the entire time, I was imagining Jane watching me on the cameras.

But she wasn't watching. When I walked down the hall, I found her in her office, replaying the video.

"Hey," I said from the doorway.

"Hey." She didn't turn around.

On the computer screen, Jane slapped Bree in the face. The real Jane in front of me shook her head, almost imperceptibly, or at least I thought she was shaking her head. It might have been me, though. I was shaking my head. It took me a second to notice that.

"I'm going to shower," I said.

She still didn't turn around. She just said, "Yup."

Upstairs, I decided I didn't want to shower. I wanted to go swimming. Swimming would relax me.

This is what I was thinking as I tugged on a bikini. On the way out of the bedroom, I grabbed Andie's box, and when I got downstairs, I tore it into pieces and chucked it, along with the photo of us, into the trash. Like so many of the things I did at Jane's house, this was a performance, designed to be seen by her. Later, I thought, when she went to throw something away, she'd notice the photo and the shredded box and be reminded not only of how much I loved her, but also of how much I had sacrificed.

Jane had pressed play on the video again. I knew this because I could hear it as I walked to the row of sliding glass doors and tried to pull one of them open. But I couldn't. The door was stuck.

I toggled the lock back and forth. I pulled harder. Then I tried another door. And another. There were six sliding glass doors in total. I tried them all.

I really didn't want to bother Jane to tell her that her doors were malfunctioning, so I decided I'd just go out the front door and around the house to the pool. But the front door wouldn't open, either.

As I walked down the hall toward Jane's office, the sound of the video got louder. How many times was she going to replay it? If I suggested she stop, would she hear me?

Just then, Jane in the video screamed, "Eat shit and die, you fucking cunt!"

And I stopped walking. What had I imagined Jane was saying when I'd watched the video without sound? Her use of the word *cunt* surprised me. I'd never heard her say that before.

I took the last few steps, and then I was standing in the doorway of her office again, saying, "Jane?"

On the screen, Jane smacked Bree Jones, and Bree screamed as she fell into the street. I hadn't heard Bree's scream before, either.

"Jane?" I said again.

"What is it?" she said, not trying to hide her agitation.

"The doors aren't working."

At that, she paused the video and turned to face me. Her expression was cold, and suddenly, I felt too vulnerable standing there in nothing but a bikini and a towel.

"The alarm's on," she said.

I let a long beat go by, a beat during which I wanted to say, *Can you turn it off?* But I couldn't make myself do it.

"If you go out there, I can't protect you."

"I'm sure I'll be fine."

Her eyebrow arched up. "All righty, then," she said, and swiped her phone off the desk. "There are still tons of vultures down at the gate, just so you're aware, and I wouldn't be surprised if they band together and find a way onto this property soon."

"Don't worry," I said. "If I see anyone, I'll sprint back inside." At the word *sprint* I broke into a dorky impersonation of a runner. I wanted to make her laugh.

She didn't. She gave me a detached stare—her eyes hopelessly dark like two empty wells—and then pressed some buttons on her phone. The alarm beeped, followed by the mechanical sound I had never been able to place exactly.

Now I understood why. It was coming from every door in the house.

"The alarm locks all the doors," I said.

"And the windows," she said. "Double deadbolts on each pane."

I heard myself repeat "Double deadbolts on each pane."

Then my body, without me, was moving toward her. Or it was sauntering. I think I was trying to remind her that we were on the same team and sex was one way to do that. I leaned over her and kissed her mouth. She smiled faintly, which I took as a sign that it was safe to say, "So you've been locking me in every night, Jane Bailey?" I was an inch from her face and my voice was low, almost a whisper.

"Oh, don't be dramatic." She set her hand on my cheek, then patted it just once.

All I could think about when she did that was her slapping Bree Jones's cheek. I wondered if she was thinking the same thing.

"I'm turning the alarm on again in two minutes," she said. "Text me when you want to come back in."

Then she turned around and pressed play.

I didn't have to ask Jane to let me back inside because an hour later, she opened the door and yelled, "Zara!"

My first thought: *I did something wrong.*

I turned around. I was in the deep end, and for the last half hour, I'd been contemplatively staring at blades of grass, wondering how long it would take Jane to go back to being the Jane I knew.

"Hey!" I called.

My tone was carefree, curious, content. It was a subconscious attempt to offset the severity of hers. I remember thinking, *It's interesting how naturally I did that,* as I pushed myself off the wall and swam toward her.

She trudged to the edge of the shallow end, her eyes on her phone. She hadn't changed out of her robe yet, or tied it up, and the way the fabric belt drooped asymmetrically down the length of her legs seemed unbearably sad to me.

When I reached her side of the pool, she said, "You're not going to believe this email from my editor."

"What does it say?"

She sat down and dropped her legs into the water. The belt of the robe fell in, so I plucked it out and set it on the concrete. Jane didn't react. I'm not even sure if she noticed.

"Ready for this bullshit?"

I kissed her knee. "Yup."

She started reading. "'In order for this book to meet its potential, I think it's necessary that you cover recent events and how you're healing from them. I would need an additional chapter or two in about a month. Does that work?'"

"I can do that," I said. "No problem."

"*Yes* problem! I'm not writing about recent events and how I've healed from them! I already apologized!" She flopped back onto the ground. "My life is a junkyard."

"No." I set my hands on her knees. "Your life is dazzling. So many people would kill to be you."

"Well, they're welcome to kill me," she said. "Because I'm already dead."

I moved her knees apart. "You are *not*."

She lifted her head and looked at me. "Hey," she said. "Keep doing what you're doing down there, okay? I just need to feel something."

She set her head back down on the ground and widened her legs.

And without hesitation, I pulled her underwear down, grateful to be needed.

32

For the rest of that morning, things were better.

After her orgasm by the pool, she wanted another one in the shower, so I gave it to her. It was fine with me that she didn't return the favor. I was just happy to hear her moan and feel her writhe around, not only because these were signs that I was doing something right, but because they were signs of life. Her body, which was so sullen before, became wild and unencumbered. For about ten minutes, we forgot about the sense of doom that now clouded the locked-up house, and we forgot about our regrets.

But then we remembered them.

"I can't believe I hit her," Jane said as she tied the belt of her robe.

It was a different robe than the one she'd been wearing earlier, and the fact that she was tying the belt made me feel somewhat relieved, but I still didn't like that she hadn't put on real clothes.

"You got caught up in the moment and you made a mistake," I said. "The public will forgive you eventually."

"Eventually?" She was gazing at her face in the closet mirror as if it was foreign to her. "I might be dead by then."

"You're not going to die anytime soon," I said. "You're healthy."

"Anything could happen, hon. That's the best and the worst thing about life. At any moment, anything could happen."

She stared at me blankly as I pulled on her jeans, the ones that were so ripped they exposed almost her entire legs. "You look cute in those," she said. "You should keep them."

"Really? Thanks, babe."

She threaded her arms around me. "If I die, you can have all my clothes, okay?"

"Stop talking about how you're going to die," I said. "It doesn't go with your brand."

"I don't know what my brand is right now. Angry lady. Violent lady. Sad, angry, violent lady."

I rubbed my hands up and down her back. "What does my sad, angry, violent lady want for lunch?"

"You're making me lunch?"

"Of course," I said. "What else would I be doing?"

She let her head fall back like a rag doll's and then started swaying a little, and in a high-pitched voice, one I'd never heard her use before—it sounded like the impersonation of a child— she said, "I would like chips. And a peanut-butter-and-jelly sandwich. With extra, extra jelly, please."

She had a big smile on her face, and I thought, *Jane is happier after sex. If we just keep having sex a lot, then we're going to be fine.*

I considered making myself a peanut-butter-and-jelly sandwich, too, but then I realized that what I really wanted was a salad. My desire for a bountiful bowl full of greens grew as I opened the fridge, and when I saw that we barely had any lettuce left, my desire grew even more.

While I prepared the food, she ordered groceries. "Normally, I don't allow myself to eat Cinnamon Toast Crunch," she called from the couch, "but now I'm eating whatever I want!"

She didn't want to go to the table outside. She wanted to stay on the couch, so I joined her there. I ate my salad thoughtfully while she wolfed down her peanut-butter-and-jelly sandwich. Out of nowhere she said, "You haven't told anyone about us, have you?"

"You asked me not to."

Technically, I hadn't answered the question, and therefore, it wasn't a lie. I still thought there was a good chance Jane would know that I was leaving something out, but if she did, then she said nothing about it. She looked at me innocently as she handed me her empty plate and said, "I'd love some more chips, please."

"Of course," I said, and brought her more chips in a bowl.

"No, I want the whole bag," she said in her new childlike voice.

So I brought her the bag, then went to clean the kitchen. While I was doing that, I threw some paper towels into the trash can. They covered the photo of me and Andie, which meant that the scene I'd imagined of Jane going to throw something away and seeing the rejected gift would never happen.

Once I was done cleaning, I lay down next to Jane on the cloudlike couch and rested my head on her shoulder. She was still eating chips, and I was wondering if her new hunger was a form of self-destruction or a form of self-love. After her comment about how she didn't usually let herself have Cinnamon Toast Crunch, I thought, *Jane isn't eating too much because she's out of control. She's eating too much because she was too controlling before, and now she's making up for it.*

But when she wiped her greasy hand on her robe, it worried me how much she'd stopped caring.

Her life exploded, I reminded myself. *This is temporary.*

"This is temporary" became a constant internal refrain in the days after the scandal. It helped. Touching her helped, too. The closer my body was to hers, the less I worried.

She finished the bag of chips, and then she decided that it would be a good idea to issue a public apology on Instagram.

"You don't mind writing it, do you, sweet pea?"

"Of course not."

She stroked my hair while I wrote, and it was tender. It was the opposite of violence. I think that's what made it easy to separate Jane from the violent act I was writing about.

The sun slanted through the row of sliding glass doors, bathing us in warm light. Her hand moved sweetly over the dome of my head. My eyes were on the screen, and in my periphery, I could see the cheerful blue of the pool and brilliant green of the high hedge.

In other words, everything around me was reminding me to be happy as I wrote:

Hey there, people. I messed up. I know that no apology can make right what I did wrong, but I do hope that in time, you'll come to see that I'm just like you: a person who makes mistakes sometimes. Bree Jones, if you're out there, I love you, girl. And I am so, so sorry.

Jane thought it was perfect. "You're talented," she said, and for some reason I thought of how her mother had told her the same thing about her cooking and cleaning when she was a kid. The compliment made me feel incredibly full, and I imagined young Jane feeling the same way.

She decided to pair what I'd written with an old picture she had on her phone of some flowers, "because flowers are unhate-able." As she posted it, she murmured, "Please, Baby Jesus in the manger, let this help."

Then she refreshed the Google search of her name.

"Jane Bailey Out on the Town Post-Assault"

A wave of terror crashed into my chest.

She was confused at first. "What *is* this?"

"I'm so sorry."

She clicked on the headline and an image of me and that guy with the newspaper appeared on the screen. My head was down, which obscured a lot of my face. The enormous sun-glasses obscured the rest.

"Is this *you*?" Her eyes were wide open and so was her mouth. *"Zara!"*

She read the caption: "Jane Bailey in East Hampton signing autographs hours after assaulting Bree Jones." Then she read the entire article. These are the parts I remember most vividly:

"She seemed nervous."

"She bought groceries at Citarella."

"After the assault on Bree Jones, she changed into a more casual outfit."

When Jane was done reading, she looked at me with pure shock on her face and said, "The monster inside of you has come out."

"I didn't mean for any of that to happen! People just assumed I was you." I could feel the tears forming in the corners of my eyes. I told myself not to blink so that my eyes would suck them back up. "Do you want me to leave?"

"You're not going anywhere," she snapped, and yes, her tone

was harsh, but I was so relieved she wasn't kicking me out that I didn't care.

"So let me get this straight," she said. "Some people confused you for me, and you went with it?"

"Yes."

"Why?"

"I don't know."

She raised an eyebrow. "Did you like it?"

"No."

"You didn't like being famous?"

I didn't answer.

She clapped once. "I want to hear about every minute of this trip to town. Start at the very beginning, please."

So I told her all the details: How inside Citarella, a woman had called me Jane Bailey, but when I turned around, the woman realized she'd made a mistake. How in the parking lot, when I put the sunglasses on—which I'd found in a drawer in the closet; I hoped that was okay?—someone confused me for her again.

"And then you went for a walk? Why didn't you just drive home?"

"I wanted to go to Carissa's for a croissant," I said.

She looked disappointed. "Oh, please."

"But I never got there because all these people started screaming my name—your name, sorry, *your* name—and then you called me. Jane, it was an accident."

"An accident! That's how I feel about hitting Bree Jones." Just then, her phone buzzed. "Groceries are here."

She narrated the text as she was typing it: "Leave at gate, please. Sorry for crowd."

Then to me she said, "Goddammit, I look like absolute shit. I don't want to go down there."

"Want me to go?"

"No! Sending my ghostwriter to fetch my groceries for me? I see the headline already. 'Bossy Narcissist Has No Basic Skills.' Or 'Jane Bailey's Sleeping with Her Ghostwriter!' Which I'm not ready to divulge."

She stared at me for a long, pensive beat, and then her eyes shot open. "Oh my god."

"What?"

"You're going to be me again."

"Jane—"

A slow smile spread across her face. "What a fun game, am I right?"

"I—"

"What? You don't want to be famous anymore?"

"Well—"

"Get the sunglasses," she said sternly. "Now."

"Jane."

"And grab a hat. And a shirt with a high collar. Something summery."

"Jane, please."

"Chop chop! Our ice cream is melting."

A few minutes later, I was sitting next to her on the couch, wearing all the articles of clothing she'd assigned to me, and she was styling my hair with her fingers. Her movements were brusque. I felt like her doll. She pulled the brim of the hat down, "because your forehead's less wrinkled than mine," she said, and upturned the collar of the shirt to hide my jawline, which was slightly more pronounced than hers.

When she was done, she leaned back and gave me a once-over, and then she said, "You're my clone! Go look at yourself in the mirror."

So I did. The sunglasses and the hat and the collar had totally erased our minor differences.

"See what I mean?" she called from the couch. "Uncanny!"

As I walked toward her again—her sad robe, her neglected hair, the empty bag of chips beside her—I thought, *I look more like the public version of Jane Bailey than Jane Bailey does right now.*

"When you get down there, open the door and let them take some shots, okay? Be sincere and humble. Keep your head down. Say *nothing*. Got it?"

"Got it."

"Good. I'll be watching."

As I walked across the grassy slope, I adopted her gait—shoulders forward, heavy footfalls; had I done this in town, too?—and felt the sadness that went along with being fired tugging every part of my face downward.

Once I'd reached the gate, I stopped and listened to the voices of the paparazzi on the other side.

"Yeah, man, I got these at that outlet mall," one said.

"Cool," another one answered.

I put my hand on the knob and took a deep breath. I'd never left the property from this door before, so the knob felt foreign to me, and I didn't have a sense of how hard I would need to push.

I pushed too hard. The door swung open fast.

Flash.

"Jane!"

Flash.

"Jane!"

The bright lights made me dizzy. Sweat prickled everywhere. I watched my hands pick up the grocery bags. I was there, but I also wasn't.

"Jane!" they screamed.

I was nobody.

"Jane!"

I was a ghost.

"Jane!"

I was Jane.

33

The new photos of me pretending to be Jane appeared online the following morning and nobody questioned them.

"We've fooled the masses!" she said. "And good job with the sad face, hon. You do look 'positively haunted.'"

That was a line from one of the articles: *Jane Bailey looks positively haunted.*

Jane stuck another spoonful of Cinnamon Toast Crunch into her mouth. It was six thirty in the morning and she was halfway through her first box. I, meanwhile, had finished my energy bar ten minutes earlier. I'd made my first batch the night before. It was easy, as easy as Jane's recipe had promised. When I showed her my work, she said, "Nice, although Bijou's are a little nicer. No offense, hon."

This was the second time in the last twelve hours that Jane had compared me to Bijou. After I'd put the groceries away, she told me I'd stowed various items in the wrong places. "The ice cream lives on the top shelf of the freezer, not the bottom, and the pickles live in the side door of the fridge, labels face-out," she said. "It took Bijou a while to learn, too."

Along with peanut butter, jelly, bread, chips, Goldfish, ice cream, pickles, and the ingredients for her energy bars, Jane had ordered prosciutto, bacon, salami, eggs, many types of cheese, many chocolate bars, some grapes, and only one box of lettuce.

I wanted to say, *You didn't get enough lettuce.* Instead, I silently marveled at how drastically our lives had changed. A week earlier, we'd been salad eaters. We'd been gym rats. We'd been a stylish couple.

Now Jane was unemployed and shoveling Cinnamon Toast Crunch into her mouth with the largest spoon she owned. She was still in her robe, her hair in a wild tangle.

I kissed her cheek. "Are you sure you don't want to work out with me?"

"Nah," she said. "I'm waiting to hear if Bree Jones is going to press charges or not."

On the one hand, I felt bad for deserting her in the kitchen.

On the other hand, I hoped I was setting a good example and that eventually she would follow, just the way I had once followed her.

Over the course of the next week, I continued to set a good example and Jane continued not to follow it.

Or, as she put it, she continued to live like she was going to die any day now.

"Carpe diem," she said one evening as she carved herself another spoonful of ice cream, which she'd taken to eating straight from the tub.

The second time we ordered groceries, I asked if we could maybe get more lettuce. "And some purple cabbage might be nice?"

"I have an idea," she said. "Why don't you take over the groceries? You know what I want."

So I downloaded the app on my phone, and she entered her credit card number. I could have been thinking about how I wasn't going to get paid now that her memoir probably wouldn't be published, but since living together essentially meant that our property was communal, I knew I didn't need to worry about it.

"Order me three boxes of Cinnamon Toast Crunch, will you? And some macaroni. Kraft."

I got really good at making macaroni and peanut-butter-and-jelly sandwiches. For the first few days, I gave her the sandwiches with crust, but then she told me she wanted them crustless.

"My mom used to make sandwiches just like this. Sometimes, she was so nice." Jane laughed. "And then she'd lock me in my room again for no reason."

I continued to not eat the sandwiches. I made myself beautiful salads instead and enjoyed them next to her on the couch in the hope that one day, she'd look over and say, "Can I have a bite?"

I didn't expect this to happen the first time, but I did start expecting it the second time, and definitely the third.

"Want a bite?" I would ask. "Want a bite?"

"Nope," she'd say, without looking over.

And then one day she said, "Stop asking. It's irritating."

I stopped asking her to work out with me, too.

The guilt that I'd felt about abandoning her with her less healthy choices diminished as the days went by, because Jane didn't seem to feel abandoned. She didn't seem interested in what I was doing at all. She was glued to her phone, and she was glued to her spot on the couch, which she'd started calling her Command Post. She was watching reruns of her show while eating chips.

One day, during the "Stew That Almost Makes Itself" episode, she muttered, "Damn, I used to be so good."

Right after that, Jane on TV said, "The point is to live well and be *healthy*, people!"

Real Jane sighed. "I'm never going to be that good again."

I was happy to take over all of Bijou's old jobs, because it made me feel indispensable.

Along with placing the grocery order and going down to the gate in my costume to pick it up, I made the food, I made the bed, I vacuumed the floors, I wiped down the counters, I did the laundry, I fetched the mail, I took out the trash.

For all the tasks that required me to go beyond the gates of the property—the trash, the mail, the groceries—I dressed as Jane. This meant that I was making an appearance as her almost every day. It quickly became second nature to me. My nervousness wore off. I got used to wearing the hat and the shirt with the upturned collar and the sunglasses. I became accustomed to the flashing lights, and to the familiar shoes of the paparazzi: the faded New Balance sneakers, the pair of Chucks that were always untied. I came to expect their screaming.

"Jane! Jane, look over here!"

I had never received so much attention, and even though it was for her, it made me feel powerful.

Now that the alarm was on all the time, I no longer had the power to go outside by myself. I needed to ask her first.

"Hey, do you mind if I go swimming?"

She was always nice about it. "Sure," she'd say, and then she'd turn off the alarm for me. "Text me when you want to come back inside."

I had assumed that Jane was only watching me on the cameras when I went down to the gate, but this turned out to be wrong.

After I did the laundry for the first time, I walked into the living room and she said, "Does my washer confuse you? You stared at the knobs for three minutes!"

The back of my neck was suddenly on fire. "You were watching me?"

"I was checking to see that nobody's snuck in here!" she said. "What if someone was hiding in the laundry room? I'm trying to protect you."

"Thanks," I said slowly. "But the alarm's on, right?"

"Yup."

"So I don't think anyone could sneak in."

"That's what we *think*," she said. "But it's not what we *know*."

We started sleeping with the lights on in every room except for the bedroom.

"So if I wake up in the middle of the night, I can see on the cameras that nobody's in here."

She was often gone in the middle of the night when I got up to use the bathroom. I never went to look for her. I assumed that she was grabbing a snack or down in her office doing miscellaneous admin stuff.

I assumed she was doing something innocent.

I noticed that I kept imagining this scene over and over:

I'm walking across a stage in my Jane clothes with my Jane attitude. I'm not overcaffeinated or underslept. I've never felt better. I bring the microphone to my mouth and say, *Thank you so much for coming,* and right after that, I see my dad in the audience. He's looking at me in a new way, a way that says, *Oh, now I understand who you are.*

Even though I'd given up on asking her to work out with me, I apparently couldn't let go of my desire for her to be physically active.

I tried to get her to go outside for a walk, but she refused. "I know my legs still work," she said. "I don't need to test them."

I tried to get her to go swimming with me, but she said it was too sunny.

She wore one of three robes every day. There was the gray one, the cream one, and the black one.

Underneath, she wore nothing, which made it easier to go down on her. I was always happy when she wanted an orgasm, because I knew it meant she'd be in a better mood for at least two hours.

One day, while my face was buried between her legs, I heard the crunch of a chip. "You are *not* eating chips right now, Jane!"

"Sorry," she said. "Sorry, you're right."

I hoped that things would change when she received the news that Bree Jones was not pressing charges, but they didn't.

"Lawsuit or no lawsuit," Jane said. "I'm roadkill either way."

In some moments, she did seem to think the future could be salvaged.

One day, a pair of unhateable red oven mitts arrived, and she decided to post them. "We'll take the temperature of the public," she said. "See how I'm doing now."

She asked me to take a close-up of her hands in the oven

mitts. But then she decided that no, they should be my hands. "Because then we can include your cute flannel sleeves. *My* cute flannel sleeves."

I put the mitts on. "Should I just open the oven?"

"Actually," she said, "we need food in this pic. Would you mind baking something? My potatoes! I could eat those."

"Sure," I said. "Do you want to do it together?"

Jane scrunched her face. "Not really, hon, sorry. I'm depressed." She gave me a quick kiss, and because this was more affection than I'd received from her in a while, it felt like a colossal amount.

Luckily, we had a bunch of potatoes in the pantry. While they were cooking, I sat with Jane on the couch, and we watched an episode of her old show, the one in which she made the Jell-O with fancy berries hiding at the bottom.

At some point, I took her hand, because I wanted to feel close to her, and said, "You're so pretty, Jane."

"Ha," she said, glancing at the screen. "Which one? Her or me?"

"Both," I said, because I refused to believe that she was diverging from her previous self, or at least I refused to believe that it would last.

An hour later, when the potatoes were ready, she took pictures of me holding them in the oven mitts. We picked the best one. But then Jane had second thoughts.

"What am I doing?" she said. "Nobody's going to want my endorsement now."

"But aren't you more famous now than you were before?" I asked. "We don't know what's going to happen."

"Fine," she said, and sent the photo to Candice with this note: *Tell them I'll do it for free.*

The following morning, Candice wrote back:

> *Toasty Mitts is appreciative of your desire to*
> *endorse their product but is no longer interested in*
> *a collaboration. I'm sorry, Jane. :(*

"Fuck 'em," Jane said. "I'm posting it anyway."
The comments were mixed.

> *Queen Jane forever!*
> *If you slap someone while wearing oven mitts, it*
> *will hurt less.*
> *I love these potatoes!*

Diego didn't write to me all week and I didn't write to him, either.

Sometimes, when Jane was in a bad mood, I'd imagine him giving me advice:
She just got fired. Let her grieve.

I knew that in the future, Diego and I would sit at a café in the city for hours and I'd recount every detail. Jane and I would be out to the public as a couple by then, and everything that was happening now would be a distant memory.

As I cleaned the house and worked out and swam in the pool and walked down the grassy slope in my Jane costume, I was thinking about the future.

I was thinking about the future a lot.

One day, while I was sweeping the floors, I remembered something an old therapist had said to me once: "Your vivid imagination is your greatest strength and your greatest weakness."

———

Many nights, I had the same nightmare about the maze, and that night it happened again.

At first, I felt happy. Then I got lost. The hedges grew to skyscraper heights. I panicked. I knew I would never escape. I was going to die in the maze.

I kept hoping for a better ending, one in which I emerged unscathed, but my subconscious was either too smart or too dumb to agree with my waking story, so the ending didn't change.

I always woke up right before I was about to die.

At the end of the week, right before we went to bed, Jane lifted the couch cushion and pulled out the gun. I watched her slip it into the pocket of her robe.

"Just in case," she said.

Upstairs, I watched her slide the gun into the drawer of her night table.

Her movements seemed habitual. How many days had she been carrying the gun around the house and I had failed to notice?

"You're looking at me like you're scared of me," she said.

"Sorry."

"*Are* you scared of me?"

"No." I laughed. "Why would I be scared of you?"

She sighed. "I don't know."

We lay down on the bed. She smelled like chips and hadn't showered in three days, but I still thought she was beautiful.

34

How things deteriorated over the course of the next week could not have been drawn in one straight down-sloping line. It was more confusing than that. Our downfall was a disorienting series of peaks and valleys. Every time the line plummeted, I thought the world was ending. And every time it rose again, I thought I was crazy for thinking the world was ending. I was reinfused with hope.

Jane's unwillingness to be anything other than sedentary persisted. I stopped asking her to go swimming with me. I stopped asking her if she wanted to get dressed. The only time I asked for anything was when I wanted to go outside.

"Hey, would you mind if . . ."

I always started my requests like that.

What I remember most about that week is how the air in the house changed. Her ceilings were very high, but the rooms started to feel claustrophobic anyway, and the silence in the early morning and late at night when she wasn't watching reruns of her show was stark and deep. I became more aware of my breath in that silence and of the pounding of my heart inside my chest.

———

"I want breakfast in bed."

That's how the week started.

I didn't skip a beat. "Cinnamon Toast Crunch?"

"Hmm." She stretched her neck to one side and then the other. In the corners of her eyes were crusted bits of sleep that I was waiting for her to rub away.

Eventually I just did it for her.

She laughed. "Thanks, Mom."

"You're welcome."

"Ooh, I know what I want."

"What?"

"French toast. With powdered sugar. And maple syrup. And a fat hunk of butter. And berries from the garden."

"Great."

"Actually, never mind about the berries. I don't want you going outside anymore unless I'm downstairs. If a vulture attacks, I won't be able to get to you fast enough from up here."

"I'm sure I can protect myself, don't worry."

"No," she said sharply.

"Okay," I said in a chipper way. My body language was saying the same thing: *I'm peppy, I'm happy to be here with you, I understand you're going through a hard time right now.* I was effervescent in my movements, just like the old Jane had been. And I was funny like her, too.

"You know, I didn't want to get your berries from the garden anyway! Who gives a shit about fresh air!"

She laughed in one syllable while looking at her phone. "Ha."

Then: "Seven vultures down at the gate already."

"Great!" I sang. "See you in a minute with your French toast!"

The long row of sliding glass doors taunted me as I made the French toast. I could feel the grass underneath my feet every time I looked outside. It pissed me off.

Or I was fine.

Yeah, I was fine. Later, I'd ask to go swimming. And for now, I had a beautiful house with a state-of-the-art kitchen to cook in. What more could I possibly want?

I brought the French toast to her on a tray along with a cup of coffee and a glass of water because I wanted to make sure she was hydrated.

"Thanks, doll."

"My pleasure."

I watched her cut a substantial chunk of French toast. She chewed like she enjoyed it, but she didn't give me any compliments.

"I'm going to go work out," I said.

"I'll be watching you," she said, her mouth still full.

She didn't come downstairs that day, so I couldn't swim.

"My back hurts," she said. "Can't you go swimming tomorrow? It's just a day."

There was no point in arguing with her fear, because I knew that to her, it was real.

"Turn around," I said. "I'll give you a massage."

Thursday

I haven't been outside for two days now. Jane doesn't want me out there unless she's downstairs, and she's been too tired to move. Hopefully she'll have enough energy tomorrow.

———

"Hey, would you mind if I jumped in the pool after I grabbed the groceries? Since you'll be downstairs anyway?"

"Fine," she said. "But I don't want to stay down there long."

After two full days stuck in the house, going outside to pick up the groceries felt miraculous to me. I walked slowly, feeling the plush grass under my shoes and inhaling the fresh air as extravagantly as possible. When the paparazzi surrounded me with their flashing lights, I was strangely comforted. Besides Jane, these men were the only people I had physical access to now.

After putting away the groceries—"Labels face-out, don't forget!" Jane called from the couch, because apparently she did still care about neatness, but only when she wasn't responsible for creating it—I went swimming. I was so delighted to float on my back and look up at the cloudless sky. It was a blue that went on forever. I noticed every chirp of every bird and every rustle of every leaf, and I thought, *This is the bright side of being locked in a soundproof house. I'm so much more grateful for nature now.*

Ten minutes into my swim, I saw Jane get off the couch. I knew she was coming outside, so I plunged to the bottom of the pool and stayed down there until I had to breathe again.

"I was calling your name!" she yelled when I emerged.

"Sorry, I didn't hear you."

"Liar." She clenched her fists. "Come back inside."

I looked at her for a long moment, unsure of how to respond.

"*Please,*" she pleaded. "My back hurts."

———

Friday

I'm crying in the office right now, and I hope Jane's watching.

The more time Diego and I went without talking, the less I needed him.

But on Friday night, after Jane called my peanut-butter-and-jelly sandwich inedible and asked me to remake it, I thought, *I miss Diego.*

Also: *How has he not noticed that the pictures of Jane are actually me?*

How has nobody noticed that?

"I've gained four pounds, and I don't give a shit!" Jane announced. "I'm free!"

She was also breaking out. She wasn't concerned about that, either.

"What *is* skin, anyway?" she said. "Just a thin encasement that gives us the illusion that we've got it 'together.'"

She stopped showering completely.

"Will you just wash me with a rag on the bed?" She laughed. "Like I'm a little baby."

I was happy to do this because she'd started to smell. I put lavender oil on a wet rag and moved it gently across the landscape of her body. When I got to her crotch, she said, "Oh yeah, that feels good."

Maybe I saw Jane's orgasms as a gateway to her former self, the self who was still excited to be alive. And maybe I saw my job as a sort of facilitator, the one who was diligently ushering her through the gate, whispering, *See? You* do *still care.*

The paparazzi headcount was falling. There were seven and then there were five and then there were four.

"They're losing interest," Jane said, disappointed. "Soon I'll be obsolete, nothing more than an answer on a game show nobody watches."

A company sent Jane a Taser to promote. She thought it was hilarious.

"Take a video of just the Taser, Zara," she said as she held it away from her body.

This was what I filmed her saying: "The next time someone like me attacks you on the street, use this, people!"

The end of the video was her pressing the button to demonstrate how it zapped.

This time, she didn't bother sending Candice an email. "I don't want to get rejected again," she said. "I *hate* getting rejected. Plus, this is the perfect thing for the public to see right now: my ability to make fun of myself. People love that."

But she received so many negative comments that she deleted her Instagram page.

"This is the first step to nonexistence," she said.

On Saturday afternoon, I asked her if I could go outside to pick some veggies from the garden and she said, "Again? You went outside yesterday."

"I know, but—"

"Just order whatever you want from the store."

I opened the grocery app on my phone, feeling excited about my walk down to the gate.

Then Jane said, "But set up the delivery for Monday, when you do the trash. My back hurts so much, baby. I can't get out of bed today."

On Saturday night, I had a dream that I was drowning.

Then I woke up and realized why.

Jane was pinching my nose.

I gasped for air. My instinct was to start crying, but I forced myself not to.

"Why did you do that, Jane? That was mean!"

"Sorry!" she said. "You were snoring *so* loud, honey."

Upset, I turned away from her in the bed. She curled her body around mine. She enveloped me in her warmth.

I tried to stay angry. But as the minutes ticked by, my anger dissolved into sadness, and my sadness dissolved into compassion, and my compassion dissolved back into love.

Sunday

I've started going to the gym twice a day because there's not very much to do in here. But it's great. My ass looks ten years younger now.

On Monday, there were only three paparazzi at the gate, and one of them was a new guy. His name was Bill.

"Jane, remember me? Bill! From the Little Bear days!"

I kept my head down as I dragged the trash bins to the curb.

"I hear Julian's doing well now. *Really* well. Fancy dinners every night. A new car. Have you seen each other lately?"

When I got back up to the house, I said, "Jane, this guy *knows* you. And he probably expects you to talk to him. At some point, we're going to get caught."

She laughed me off. "People are idiots, hon. That's the part that you're forgetting. Also, *look* at you! You're *me*!"

"According to your friend Bill—"

"He's not my friend."

"According to Bill, Julian's doing really well now," I said. "I guess he got a new car?"

Jane laughed. "A midlife-crisis car, I know. I saw it online."

While I was downstairs waiting for her macaroni water to boil, I googled Julian.

He looked great. Allegedly, he hadn't been drinking. He'd quit his job at the Clam Bar and now he was spending money like he was very rich. Recent photos showed him shopping, and driving his midlife-crisis Porsche convertible, and handing the valet his keys outside a waterfront restaurant.

Monday

It's only going to take one mistake.
What if the hat falls off?
What if the shirt collar isn't high enough to cover my jawline?
The sunglasses are the main thing . . .

———

Tuesday

I've only been outside two times this week. Maybe today, I'll ask Jane if

"Zara?" she called.

I put my pen down. I closed my journal. I put on my happy face and walked into the bedroom. It was ten o'clock in the morning. I'd already worked out and was now wearing my signature outfit, which had once been her signature outfit: ripped jeans, a flannel top, Birks.

Jane was in the cream robe. I disliked that one the most because it got dirty faster than the others. On her chest was a yellow splotch left from the macaroni she'd eaten in bed the night before.

"What can I get you, hon?" I said. "Are you hungry?"

"No, I'd like you to mop the floors, please." She flashed me a smile. "I'm just lying here looking at that lint in the corner." She pointed. "And that dot over there. It's driving me nuts."

"No problem," I said. What else was I going to say?

"Great," she said. "Do the whole house, please."

My first reaction: *The whole house?*

My second reaction: *It's not like you're busy.*

"No problem. I'll go grab the supplies from Bijou's closet."

"Oh god." Jane brought her palm to her forehead. "Don't say her name."

"Sorry."

She stuck her tongue out, then grabbed the remote and pressed play. A rerun of her show started playing.

As I walked out of the room, Jane on TV said, "Today on *30*

Bucks Tops, can you guess what we're doing, people? We're grilling lettuce!"

Downstairs, I found the mop. I filled the water bucket. I added soap. I went back upstairs and walked straight to the far corner of the bedroom and picked up the piece of lint she'd pointed to and put it in my pocket. And then I started mopping. I held the mop like Bijou used to hold it, with her hands far apart, and gripped firmly. When I arrived at the space between Jane and the TV, I worked faster so I wouldn't block her view for too long.

Still, she said, "I can't see."

I apologized, then mopped the rest of that area in a ducked position.

Jane's house was ten thousand square feet, so it took a long time. I had to keep refilling the bucket with water, and then I needed more soap, and when I found areas I'd mopped imperfectly, I remopped them. I was really trying. I was working with all the vigor that Jane no longer had.

By the time I got downstairs, I was tired. I decided I needed some musical encouragement, so I put my earbuds in and kept mopping to Metallica.

An hour later, I found a chip underneath the couch and was about to throw it away when I looked up and—

Jane was standing at the foot of the staircase, and she didn't look happy. I pulled my earbuds out.

"I've texted you *twelve* times," she said. "I was screaming your name."

"Sorry," I said. "I was listening to music."

"Why is this taking you so long? I'm hungry!"

She barreled toward me, and fast. She was full of her old energy, and her back seemed fine. Then, right in front of me, she stopped. Her face was an inch away from mine. Her nostrils flared. I took a step back. And Jane, her eyes alive and spinning, took a step forward, but said nothing.

"I was almost done," I said.

"Bijou was faster," she said. "And better. What is *that*?" She pointed at a fleck of something on the ground, one I hadn't seen yet.

"I was about to pick it up."

She mocked me. "No problem, Jane! I'll grab the supplies, Jane!" I was shocked into silence. "It's been *hours*!"

I'd contained myself so perfectly until then, and suddenly it was too much.

"Did you pay Julian not to talk to the press?"

Her jaw clenched. And then—so fast, I didn't have time to move—she slapped me. And everything slowed after that. My hand moved to my cheek like it was moving through honey.

"Oh baby, oh sweetheart, oh Zara, I'm so sorry. Come here. I can't believe I did that. I don't know what's gotten into me. I'm so sorry."

These were the things Jane said to me as she held my head in her hands, as she rocked me back and forth like a mother, as she kissed every part of my face like it was the most precious face she'd ever seen, as she started crying, as I started crying, as our tears washed away the past, as the line on the graph rose sharply, as I was flooded, again, impossibly, with hope.

35

The next day was the best day we'd had since the Bree incident.

Jane took a shower. She brushed her teeth. She got dressed in real clothes. Sweatpants. A T-shirt. No bra underneath, but still, it was better than the robe. She came downstairs for breakfast and didn't bring the gun. Her back was feeling a little better. She ate only one bowl of Cinnamon Toast Crunch. She told me I looked nice in her leggings, and I said, "Thanks, baby." There were no new headlines that morning when she googled herself. Down at the gate, there was only one vulture left, and it wasn't Bill. It was someone else.

"Nobody cares about me anymore," she murmured.

"Maybe it's a good thing," I said. "Things can go back to normal now."

She laughed. "Things will never be normal again."

After breakfast, she went to the couch instead of the bed, which delighted me. She turned on her old show, which delighted me less, but what did I expect? That things would do a 180 in a day?

Since she wasn't in the bed, I could finally wash the sheets. It was only as I was stripping them off that I was able to admit to myself how sour they smelled. I'd been ignoring it before, or trying to.

After I put the laundry in, I went to the gym. As I pedaled, I went over my plan: at some point today, I would bring up what happened last night.

Wouldn't I?

Her slap had left no mark on my face, which made the problem invisible. Jane hadn't asked me how I was feeling that morning, which made it more invisible. I didn't want to bring it up and ruin the peacefulness of the day. But I was also getting sick of being invisible.

I googled Julian again while I was on the elliptical machine. A few new shots appeared. One of them showed him walking into the lobby of The Maidstone.

I checked the map. It was only one mile from the house.

By the time I was making her lunch, I still hadn't brought it up.

As I added the peanut butter and then the jelly, I looked at her several times, imagining what I would say.

Hey, I was wondering if we could talk about what happened last night.

Hey, I was wondering if you could answer my question about Julian?

Hey, do you see me?

I put the sandwich on a plate; I cut off the crust; I put the plate on a tray. I poured her a glass of milk and walked into the living room. My hands were calm as I set the tray down next to her, because I forced them to be calm. I didn't want her to know I was scared.

Hey, I was wondering if we could talk about what happened last night.

"Here's your sandwich, sweetheart," I said.

"Thank you." She touched my arm. "Sit down a minute, will you?"

I sat. I placed my hand on her leg. "Hey, I was wondering if we could—"

"I need to make a confession."

"What is it?"

"You're right about Julian."

I waited.

"I did compensate him for his silence."

The reason why was obvious. Jane had hit Bree Jones, and now she'd hit me, which suggested that it was a pattern.

"Is it because you hit him?" I asked.

She skirted the question. "He would have said I was controlling, manipulative . . . He would have gone on and on!"

"Okay, but—"

"Let's stop fighting, baby. It hurts my heart." She kissed me, then gazed at me sadly. "I'm starting to think I might have an anger problem."

It was a relief to hear her say that. "I agree."

She let her head flop to the side. "I'm defective."

"You're not defective."

"I'm defective."

I resituated myself on the couch and took her hands, and then somehow—*how?*—I found myself taking her side of the argument.

"Listen. With Bree, you were upset about the book and feeling vulnerable. You lost control. And last night . . . I mean, you've been under so much stress lately, so I understand—*almost* understand—why you lost control again. So, as I see it, you've lost control two times recently, which is not an indication of what's going to happen in the future."

"I hope not," she said.

"I *know* not," I said. "Have you ever thought about talking to someone?"

"A shrink, you mean?"

"Yeah."

She sighed. "No. But maybe I should."

We spent the next few hours looking up therapists together. It felt like we were making incredible progress.

"This one looks dumb."

"This one looks like a wise owl, but she's way too young."

We snuggled on the couch as we assessed the options. The sound of her show playing in the background was an annoying distraction, and eventually I worked up the courage to say, "Hey, would it be okay to mute the TV?"

I was relieved when she said, simply, "Sure."

My cheek was resting on her shoulder, the same cheek she'd slapped the night before. "I love you, Jane," I said.

"I love you, too, doll." She kissed the top of my head.

I squeezed her hip. "And I'm *so* happy that you got out of bed today."

"Well, yeah," she said. "I figured it was time for you to wash the sheets."

She let me swim for as long as I wanted to that day, which felt like a win.

On my way out the door, I said, "Maybe soon we can go to the beach? After the last vulture leaves?"

She said, "Maybe," which felt like another win.

I swam for an hour. I luxuriated in the sounds of nature. I got kind of silly, too, and did some handstands in the shallow end. The pool had become very familiar to me, and so had the house. I'd now been at Jane's long enough to feel like I officially lived there, and I thought, *It's like we're married already.*

In the future, I saw us appearing on a talk show together. The host would ask us how we'd fallen in love, and I would say, *The first time my agent mentioned the name Jane Bailey, I didn't even know who she was.*

No.

I'd start by saying, *I was her ghostwriter.*

"Zara?"

I popped my head up. I'd been floating on my back, looking up at the cloudless sky, which promised everything.

"I'm ordering some groceries," she said. "Want anything?"

Another win. She was asking me what I wanted.

"I'd love some tofu, please."

"You never eat tofu."

"I used to eat it all the time! Before I met you."

In the voice of a commentator, she said, "She's striking out on her own, folks!"

As usual, she styled me in my costume before I went to pick up my groceries an hour later. While her hands were smoothing my upturned collar to make sure it stayed in position, she said, "Oh, and by the way, hon, I need you to be me in town tomorrow."

"In town?" I asked, because by then, town seemed like a faraway dream.

"I'll tell you about it when you get back. Now go."

On the walk down to the gate, I went over my visions of the future. The speedboat in Venice. The almost-matching leather jackets. The red carpet. I had zero doubts that all of this would happen, but when? When was Jane going to tell the world about us? When was the world going to know that I existed?

Just before I opened the door, I stopped to scratch my neck, which accidentally turned down the collar of my shirt.

That's what I wanted her to see on the cameras: an innocent accident.

I pushed the door open.

"Jane!"

Flash. Flash. Flash.

I let the single paparazzo take a few shots of me standing there in the light, and then I reached down to grab the grocery bags, which were much heavier than usual.

Sorry, I must have accidentally pushed it down while I was scratching my neck.

I practiced what I was going to say about the collar on my way back up to the house.

Why were the bags so heavy? I could have stopped to inspect them, but I was so in my head that I didn't.

When I looked up, I saw Jane in the doorway, waiting. She never opened the door for me, so I knew this meant that she was upset about the collar. But when I arrived at the door, she didn't seem angry at all.

"Good job," she said, and started walking toward the garage. "Follow me."

"Where are we going?"

"We're putting the cans in the car."

Along with my tofu and a new loaf of bread for her sandwiches, Jane had ordered twenty cans of black beans and twenty cans of corn.

"For the food bank," she explained as she rounded the Aphrodite fountain. "We're staging an act of goodwill. I know what you're thinking. It's pathetic. But it's also wonderfully simple. What better way to convey that I'm a nice person? Am I right? If the public doesn't warm to me after this, then I'm done. I can't keep begging for love. It's just not my style."

We deposited the cans in the trunk, and a few minutes later, while I was toasting the bread for the second peanut-butter-and-jelly sandwich she'd ordered that day, she explained my itinerary in more detail.

"You'll drive into town. If our last vulture's at the gate, he'll follow you. If not, I'll tip someone off. The food bank's easy to get to. It's right off 27. All you have to do is pull up at the back, unload the cans, and let them take some shots. Then drive home. Okay? I would do this myself, but you're so much more beautiful than I am right now."

We made love that night, slowly and thoughtfully. Jane's body was pudgier than before. I kind of liked her new softness.

Who was stronger now?

That's what I was thinking as she took off my underwear.

"I'm rewarding you for tomorrow," she said. "I know you're going to do such a good job."

When I came—for the first time in weeks—all the thoughts in my head disappeared, and it was perfect.

Jane came quickly, as usual.

We held each other afterward. We closed our eyes and let ourselves buy into the sweetness of the moment. We talked about what tomorrow was going to be like. Jane would call the therapists we'd chosen while I did my errand in town. She wanted me to go early in the morning, right after my workout. She'd already chosen my outfit in her head. A white shirt, a pair of jeans, the green Birks.

"Green," she said, "is the color of hope."

36

The next morning, our single vulture was not at the gate, so Jane called someone at Page Six to tip them off.

"I told them I'd be there at nine thirty sharp," she said as she buttoned my shirt.

It was nine o'clock. We were standing in the closet, and she was back in the cream-colored robe, the one with the Kraft cheese stain on it, which hadn't come out in the wash. Or at least I didn't think it had. I could still see yellow. But Jane, when I'd mentioned it at breakfast, had said, "I don't see anything."

I was staring at the faint splotch of yellow, wondering if it was real or not, as she told me how to act at the food bank.

"You have to be gracious. Elegant. *Repentant*."

"Jane?"

"Zara?"

"After this, I want to stop pretending to be you."

She reangled the tilt of my hat and didn't answer.

"Jane, I'm serious."

"I know you are, sweet pea." She stepped back to examine her work. "This is good," she said. "You're ready." And then she walked out of the closet.

I didn't follow her.

My knees locked. My expression stopped hiding its anger.

My mouth felt like it was full of cement. The fact that Jane had dismissed my request, and so flippantly, made me feel more invisible than I already did, and it was right then that I reached the tipping point I'd been approaching for a while.

All my previous selves—the child, the teenager, the younger adult—were silently shrieking inside of me.

Are you blind? Are you deaf? Are you ever going to see me? Are you ever going to listen?

"Come on!" she yelled from the hallway. "I need you to be on time!"

In that moment, something shifted inside me. I made a decision: I was done being invisible.

Downstairs, she opened the front door, gave me a quick peck, and repeated the word *Repentant*.

As I descended the driveway, I noted the ways in which the landscape had evolved since the day I'd arrived at Jane's house. The grass hadn't been mowed in weeks. The hedges hadn't been trimmed. Jane's property looked as unkempt as she now did.

At the end of the driveway, I watched the gate slide open soundlessly. I knew there were no paparazzi, but I expected one to jump out of the bushes anyway, even though there were no bushes, either. There were no fans and no gifts.

I drove onto the empty street, and then there were no cameras on me. I was completely alone. I checked the time: 9:10.

The food pantry was ten minutes down the road.

The Maidstone was three minutes down the same road.

As I drove, I took off my hat. I turned my collar down. In two minutes, I would arrive at The Maidstone. And then it was one minute. And then I was there, pulling into the parking lot. I found a spot easily, took my sunglasses off, and jogged inside.

"Hi, I'm meeting Julian Wright here," I said to the woman at the front desk.

"Your name?" the woman asked.

"Zara Pines."

The woman picked up the phone and I stuffed my clammy hands into my pockets. A man who wasn't Julian walked down a nearby staircase and out the door. I pretended to admire the lobby. There were walls painted dark colors, a staggered book-shelf underneath the staircase, and some photographs that seemed important, or at least old, although maybe they weren't.

"Mr. Wright?" the woman said into the phone.

I couldn't believe Julian had picked up. And that she was talking to him—"Yes, I have a Zara Pines here"—and then I couldn't believe that he'd agreed to come downstairs.

"He's on his way," the woman told me. "Feel free to take a seat." She motioned to a patterned chair.

"Great, thanks." I stuffed my hands deeper into my pockets and went to the chair and sat down. I told my leg to stop bounc-ing. I felt like I was going to explode.

And then, a minute later, there was Julian walking down the stairs, and I was standing up to greet him, and my neck was on fire.

Understandably, he was surprised to see me. "What are you doing here?"

"I—"

"If it's about Jane, I can't answer."

I glanced at the woman, who was staring at us.

Julian smiled at her. "Let's go in here," he said, and I fol-lowed him around the corner into a room that contained a black leather couch and a coffee table with a wooden duck perched on top of it.

"Where's Jane right now?" he asked.

"At home."

"Did she send you here? Is this a test or something?"

"No."

"Are you sure?"

"I'm worried about her."

He seemed conflicted about how to respond. Then he said, "You should be."

"I know she paid—"

"Which is why I can't talk to you."

Julian looked clear-eyed. And not menacing at all.

"Are you wearing her shirt?" He gave me a once-over. "And her pants? Oh, man."

"What?"

"She used to dress me, too," he said.

I defended her. "She has great taste." And then I was singing her praises. "Didn't she pay for your rehab?"

He scoffed. "After I threw a baked potato at somebody's head?"

"She told me that story."

"That never happened," he said. "And I never went to rehab. I'm not even an alcoholic. I got a little too drunk *one* time, and Jane ran with it."

I was about to say, *But aren't there stories about this online?*

Then I realized: "She's the one who planted those stories."

"Yeah, you might have noticed there's only one picture of me drunk, from the *one* time I got drunk with her, that gets reprinted everywhere."

It was true that besides the single photo of Julian vomiting into his hand on the street, I hadn't seen any evidence of him drunk.

"But haven't you been texting her every day about how you're still sober?"

"No."

"You weren't begging her to meet up with you?"

He laughed. "You know, when we were together, she used to tell me all these guys were calling her and texting her, and then I found out she was just trying to make me jealous."

I imagined Jane writing Julian's fake texts with a grin on her face. "Wait," I said, "but then why did you show up at the house that one night and ring the bell a bunch of times?"

"Because she begged me to come over. She said she had to tell me something. And then she wouldn't open the gate."

I flashed back to Julian putting his face right in front of the camera and saying her name. At the time it had seemed so sinister.

"Why would Jane want to shut me up *now*?" he asked. "Have you thought about that?"

I had thought about it, yes.

"You haven't been a threat to her until now," I said. "You've been the crazy drunk boyfriend with no credibility. Nobody would have believed anything you said about her."

He didn't speak, but the look on his face was telling me, *Yes, exactly.*

"But what would you have said?"

He looked at the floor. "After that video came out . . ."

I waited for him to look up.

Then he did.

"She told me she used to hit you," I said.

He took a deep breath. "I suggest you leave before it gets worse."

SWAN HUNTLEY   239

"She's going to a therapist soon," I said. "So maybe it won't get worse."

He looked at me like I was a total dumbass, and then he brought up the subject I'd been trying to ignore.

"I bet that's what Mark thought, too."

I got back into the car at nine twenty-two and sped to the food bank. On the way, I turned my collar back up and put on the hat and the sunglasses. I arrived at nine thirty exactly. The paparazzo was already there waiting for me.

Gracious. Elegant. Repentant.

I turned the engine off. I lowered the brim of my hat. I got out of the car with repentance on my face, or at least the tiny portion of my face that was visible.

Flash.

"Hey, Jane!"

Flash.

"How's it going today, Jane?"

The paparazzo took shots of me opening the trunk.

Flash flash flash. The camera shutter sounded like chattering teeth.

"Donations, huh?"

There were three grocery bags filled with cans. I dropped the first two into the crates underneath the sign on the wall that said *DONATIONS HERE.*

As I walked back to the trunk, I was thinking about how much I was doing for Jane, and how little credit I was getting. She had inspired me to become more like her, but now she was drowning me in her shadow. Did I have a purpose beyond fulfilling her needs?

Wasn't I just as invisible now as I had been to my dad?

When the fuck was it going to be my turn?

I dropped the last bag into a crate, and then my hand was scratching my neck, and then it was flipping my collar down.

I turned. The paparazzo was standing five feet in front of me. Flash flash flash.

Slowly, I took off my hat. I stared straight at the eye of the camera as I took off my sunglasses.

"Whoa! Whoa! What!"

The paparazzo was excited already about how much money he was about to make.

I let him take plenty of shots before I got back into the car.

37

At first, I felt exhilarated.

Finally, I had stepped out of the dark. Finally, I had asserted myself. How brave of me! How independent! I suspected that I would look good in the photos, and yes, of course I was imagining people from my past seeing them, ideally people who'd been assholes to me in high school. I wanted them to be impressed that I'd made it into the news cycle.

The closer I got to the house, though, the slower I drove, because my doubts were growing. Jane had a gun and I'd just done something she wasn't going to like. I knew that if I were watching this moment in the movie of my life, I would have screamed at the character who was me, "Escape!"

But I kept driving forward. I turned onto our street, and then I was taking the clicker out of the center console and opening the gate, and then I was ascending the driveway. I imagined myself saying, *Jane, I have to tell you something.*

I parked in the garage. I walked toward the door. In front of the Aphrodite fountain, I stopped. I was making calculations. Had she noticed that I was back on the property already? Was she watching me on the cameras?

Then, suddenly, without fully making the decision to, I was

sprinting across the great expanse of grass toward the secret door, thinking, *This makes no sense. I just drove back here willingly, and now I'm running away?*

At the secret door, I didn't wait for a lull between cars. I yanked it open and ran into the middle of the street and started waving my arms.

I was thinking, *I'll never come back.*

A car stopped. It was black, a hatchback. The driver inside was a man with a beard. I walked around to the passenger side. He rolled down the window and asked, "Are you okay?"

"I—"

I couldn't catch my breath. *Never* come back? The *never* seemed like too long.

"Can I give you a ride?" the man asked.

My phone rang. Of course it was Jane. Everyone else had stopped calling me. Because I had no one else. I needed her. Eventually, I told myself, she would have to forgive me. What other choice did she have? She needed me, too.

My phone kept ringing as I left the man and went back in through the secret door. I hadn't closed it all the way, and now I realized why. On some level, I had known I wasn't going to leave. As I jogged toward the house, I said a bunch of things into the phone that may or may not have made sense.

"Hey, sorry, I thought I saw a rabbit eating our grass. I'm headed back up now. Do you want any peaches—"

"Zara! Just get back here."

When I walked into the house, the entryway seemed tiny, even though it wasn't. The walls tightened around me, the ceilings lowered. I imagined the chandelier smashing me into the floor.

But I ignored all of this. I pulled it together. In the grand scheme of things, what I'd done wasn't actually that big of a deal. It was amazing how quickly I talked myself into a new mindset. Or maybe it wasn't that amazing. We are designed to protect ourselves. This is what I was thinking as I walked confidently into the living room and said, "Hey!"

Jane was sitting on the couch. "Hey, babe! I made you lunch!"

Suddenly, I regretted everything I'd done.

"Peanut butter and jelly!" She patted the cushion beside her. "Come," she said. "Tell me. Was it great? Did you look humble?"

"I really did," I said, and kissed her. Then I stuffed the sandwich into my mouth in the hope that it would prevent her from knowing that I was lying.

"Mmm-hmm," I said, "very humble."

"You must have gotten there early." She put her hand on my leg. "Was he there or did you have to wait?"

"I waited a few minutes." I took another bite. She'd burned the bread, so the sandwich tasted like char with a hint of peanut butter and jelly.

"Good girl," she said, rubbing my leg.

I just couldn't bring myself to tell her.

After I was done eating, we snuggled on the couch and whispered things to each other in low voices. We sounded like purring cats.

"Your hair looks nice."

"Yours, too."

We petted each other. We kissed. Sun poured through the sliding glass doors, drowning us in light. Jane's cheeks were soft and glowing. Her eyes twinkled. The rhythm of her voice was hypnotic.

Remember this, I told myself. *Because it's about to change.*

When Jane got up to use the bathroom, I checked my phone. Diego had written:

HOLY SHIT! And why are you back in New York without telling me?

Jane, cozy in her robe, wandered back into the living room and yawned as she took her phone out of her pocket.

"Jane, I have to tell you something."

She looked at the screen.

"I'm sorry," I said. "I didn't want to hide anymore."

Eyes still on the screen, she was calm, calm, calm—and then she flinched. "What is this?"

"I'm sorry."

"What *is* this?"

She looked up at me.

"I'm so sorry, Jane."

Her face darkened. Full of venom, she lunged at me. Her arm pulled back.

I could have shielded my face with my hands, but I didn't.

38

I spent the rest of that day locked in the downstairs bathroom, which wasn't very big.

She'd hit me a few times, or a dozen times. I lost count. Then she confiscated my phone for being untrustworthy. After that, she went through my messages and deemed me more untrustworthy than she'd originally thought.

"I asked you not to tell anyone about us and you wrote to Andie, 'I fell in love with Jane'?"

"You took a picture of me at the beach when I wasn't looking?"

"What the fuck is this one of me sleeping?"

"And of you trying on all my clothes while I was away? Oh my god, you in my dress." She laughed. "You're *obsessed* with me."

She said all of this from the other side of the bathroom door as I sobbed. The sobbing made everything hurt more, but I couldn't stop.

"Oh, Diego's writing again. 'You need to text me back,' he says. *Need* is in all caps, in case you were wondering." She laughed. "Let's write him back. 'Hey! Yes, I'm in New York and Jane Bailey is the best thing that's ever happened to me.' Send!"

A few seconds later, she said, "Who's Kim?"

I kept crying. The pressure in my head intensified. I told myself to breathe.

"Jane," I said, "I think I need some ice."

She ignored me. "Oh, Kim's the agent! She wrote, 'What the fuuuuuck! Are you with Jane?'"

Jane narrated her response. "'Yes, I'm obsessed with Jane!'"

"Jane," I said. "Please stop."

"Honestly, hon, you brought this on yourself."

Then she left. I listened to her walk down the hall and then the sound of her footsteps disappeared.

She was gone for awhile. There was no clock in the bathroom, so I didn't know what time it was, but it felt like hours. I found some Advil and washed it down with water I poured into the toothbrush holder. Then I put all the towels on the floor and made myself a nest.

The light outside brightened in the midafternoon, then dimmed. I wondered if she'd called those therapists while I was in town. I'd forgotten to ask about that while we were on the couch because I felt so bad about what I'd done.

Night fell. I was in pain every time I moved. My left shoulder was especially bad. My swollen face in the mirror made me feel sorry for myself. I took more Advil. I drank more water. I wondered, *Will we ever recover from this?*

That's the last thing I remember thinking before I fell asleep on the floor.

When I woke up and saw Jane looming over me, my head jolted back and smacked into the side of the tub.

I stayed very still, letting the impact reverberate through me, and then I started to cry. I couldn't help it.

"Oh, sweetheart." She was sitting on the floor, an ice pack in her hands. "I'm sorry I lost my temper." She placed the ice against my face. "Oh, honey, I'm so sorry."

Like before, she apologized thousands of times. And like before, she started crying with me, so it was confusing.

Or it wasn't confusing. We'd both made mistakes, and we were crying about them. After a while, she pulled me off the floor and led me up the stairs with her arm around my waist.

"I drew you a bath," she said.

"What time is it?"

"Nine."

"You left me in there all day."

"I know, sweet pea."

In the bathroom, she helped me undress. I could have done it myself, but I wanted her to show me she cared.

She seemed happy to take my clothes off, and then she helped me into the tub and asked me if I was hungry. "What can I make you?"

"Peanut butter and jelly," I heard myself say.

After she left, I closed my eyes. I saw Mark getting out of this tub. I saw him falling to the floor. I saw the blood gushing out of his head.

I replayed this vision of Mark falling over and over. A sadness was flooding my heart. I touched my face to see if it would hurt. It did. And then I touched it again, and it hurt again. Why did I keep doing that?

A few minutes later, she reappeared, singing, "Peanut butter and jelly! And a glass of milk for my baby."

I was in too much pain to smile, and there was something I liked about that. The inability to fake it felt good.

She sat on the side of the tub and handed me the sandwich,

and I stuffed it into my mouth. I was starving. I thought it was the best peanut-butter-and-jelly sandwich I'd ever eaten. It hurt to chew—something was wrong with my jaw—but I pushed through the pain, grateful that my mouth still worked. When she handed me the chilly glass of milk, I was in heaven.

"Yum," she said. "Dinner in the tub. Why not enjoy some decadence while I update you about what's happened since your little outburst?"

She crossed her legs and took her phone out of her robe pocket.

"For starters, the vultures have stormed the gate. Back in hordes!" She laughed. "Oh, and you've been identified! Sorry, I should have led with that. Somebody has identified you. Correctly. As my ghostwriter. For the book that will never come out. How do you like that? And here's the best part. You ready?"

I kept stuffing the sandwich into my mouth, because what if she took it away before I was done?

"Our internet friends dug up some old photos of you, and now they're asking questions. Why would Jane Bailey's ghostwriter also be her doppelgänger? Why would Jane Bailey have a doppelgänger to begin with? How long have we been falling for the charade? All those pictures of her at the gate weren't really her! So *where* is Jane Bailey? Nobody has seen her since that ill-fated lunch with Bree Jones. Is she dead? Did the ghostwriter kill her? Killed by her ghostwriter! That's a real headline, hon. You're a suspect!"

I was choking on my sandwich.

She handed me the glass of milk. "Why are you eating so fast, murderer?"

I patted my chest. My eyes were watering. "Can I get out of the bath, please?"

"Why are you asking? Do whatever you want, honey!"

She stood up. She held out a hand. As I took it, and as I stepped out of the tub and onto the slippery floor, I imagined falling.

Half an hour later, we were snuggling in bed. My head was resting peacefully on her chest, and I told myself that the softness of her body was the truth. Her heartbeat under my ear was the truth. The sound of her voice was the truth. When we were close like that, the actual words she spoke became secondary. When she said, "You've ruined our lives, baby," it somehow didn't seem that bad.

"Can I have my phone back?"

"No. And I put your laptop in the safe. That's off-limits now, too."

Somehow, this didn't seem that bad, either.

"Your punishment's not over," she said.

Jane needed help. I needed compassion. Silently, I forgave her.

"The world's closing in on us, Zara," she said as her hand enveloped the back of my neck.

I decided that for one last night, I would believe that the warmth of her body was the only truth. Because it's not like I was stupid. Along with *I forgive you,* I was also silently saying goodbye.

39

"Hey!"

Jane was shaking me awake.

"Hey!"

She was kissing my brow.

I opened my eyes.

"Hello," she said.

Then she laid out the details of my punishment with such articulation and gusto that for a second, I almost believed they made sense. She was, after all, a performer.

"You were a bad girl, and you know that. And now you will cook and clean all day, every day, until your debt to me is paid."

She didn't say this harshly. She said it like she was reading a verdict in a courtroom.

"These are just the facts, honey. How are you ever going to learn if I don't teach you?"

I opened my mouth as little as possible to ask, "What do you want me to clean?" Something was definitely wrong with my jaw.

"Everything. And when you're done, you'll start over." She set her hands on her hips. "You wanna know the real reason why I told you I hid Andie's gift from you?"

"Why?"

"To see if you'd stick with me." She caressed my swollen cheek. "And you did. Do you regret it?"

"No."

"I told you that if you ever lied to me, I'd know," she whispered.

I said nothing.

"I want breakfast in bed, please. Cinnamon Toast Crunch. Bring the whole box."

I kissed her. "Okay, sweet pea."

She was suspicious. "Yes. Play nice. That's a good idea."

Playing nice wasn't a good idea. It was the only option. If I obeyed her, then she'd be less likely to hit me again. If I cooked and cleaned for days without complaint, then maybe she'd let me go outside—"Hey, would you mind if . . ."—and then, the second the door opened, I would start running.

Or I could take her phone when she wasn't looking—or when she was asleep?—and open the door with whatever app she used to do that and start running.

Somehow, I would run.

And at the gate, there would be a group of men ready to take my picture.

But what if I wasn't fast enough? And what if she had the gun? Would she shoot me? How fast could I run in this state?

My legs felt okay as I walked into the bathroom. That was good. But my arms hurt. Especially the left one. That wasn't good. I needed more Advil. I went to the medicine cabinet.

At the sight of my face in the mirror, I went into a state of shock that blurred my reflection for about ten seconds. After that, my pain increased. When a kid scrapes a knee, they're often fine until they see the wound. The sight of the wound is what makes the kid cry. I remembered reading that once.

I'd seen my wounds already, but in the morning, they looked worse. The bruises had darkened. My face was a puzzle of distorted shapes. How could Jane be giving me chores when I looked like this? That scared me. It also answered my question. If I ran, then, yes, she would shoot.

I took two Advil. I brushed my teeth. In the closet, I pulled on my workout gear. Then I walked back into the bedroom.

Jane looked up from her phone. "No gym today."

"Okay."

I went downstairs. The pool laughed at me. And the high hedge. Everything outside was cackling and teeming with life and doing cartwheels. Inside, it was as stifling as a coffin.

I set the kettle on the stove. I took an ice pack out of the freezer and pressed it against my jaw and held it there while looking at the sink, which was filled with dirty dishes. The counter was littered with breadcrumbs and gobs of jelly.

I opened the fridge. She'd eaten almost all of our food. In one day? My energy bars were completely gone. Only one box of Cinnamon Toast Crunch was left in the pantry. I grabbed it, along with an old, half-empty bag of muesli. I stuck a handful in my mouth and winced. The camera eye in the kitchen was watching me, so I might have winced for longer than necessary.

I poured two coffees. I added cool water to mine and chugged it, because I didn't want to keep her waiting. I put her breakfast on a tray: the coffee, the box of cereal, the carton of milk. The weight of it sent a splintering pain into my shoulders and up through my skull and all I could think about was death.

When would I die?

Would it be in this house?

Or on the lawn when she shot me?

Or in a rocking chair fifty years from now?

Where would Jane be then?

When I walked into the bedroom, she was on the phone.

"No," she was saying. "Absolutely not."

I set the tray on the bed.

"Stop asking me the same questions! No comment!" She hung up, let out a long sigh, and ripped open the box of Cinnamon Toast Crunch. "They want me to make a statement. But I'd rather keep everyone confused for now."

She filled the bowl to the brim, then poured in an overwhelming amount of milk, which splashed across the sheets.

"Meanwhile, there are twenty-two guys down at the gate. Twenty-two! People just *love* misery. Fallen stars, in particular. Oh, look, she fell off the gilded mountaintop! It makes the peons of this world feel less alone."

She took a big bite. A square of Cinnamon Toast Crunch landed on her chest, right on top of the old macaroni stain. With her mouth full, she kept talking.

"Look at the mess you've made of our lives, Zara. Messy girl who's going to clean all day." She chewed, swallowed, considered. "I don't see a way out of this."

"I'm sure—"

"It's a rigged game." She took another bite. "Unwinnable."

"That's the last box of cereal," I said. "We don't have very much food left."

She laughed. "What do you think I should do, hon? Order some? Who's going to the gate to pick it up? Not me. And not you looking the way you do."

"Do you want me to go see what we have in the garden? I could at least grab some peaches."

"Ha! You think I'm an idiot."

"No, I don't."

"If I were you, I'd be devising ways to get out of here."

"That's not what I'm doing."

"*Don't* lie to me!"

I stared at her—her pink cheeks, her pretty eyes, her tangled hair, her desperation, her wisdom, her as a child, her as the woman I'd met, her as who she was now.

How would I die? Would it be in her arms?

40

As I cleaned the house, I was caught between heart-palpitating anxiety and a strange state of surrender that felt like being in the deepest part of the ocean, where everything is calm.

Where was the gun?

How many days would the food last?

What were they saying about us in the news now?

When would I steal her phone?

I asked the same questions over and over. I looped and looped and looped. The repetition mirrored what I was doing with my hands: sweeping, vacuuming, wiping, rinsing, wringing.

The pain in my shoulder was so intense that it became something beyond pain. I lost myself. I had no shoulders. I had no body. Adrenaline coursed through me. Hours passed. The changing light annoyed me, and the view of the yard continued to mock me.

Could I break a window? A door? How much longer would I pretend to be her servant?

Jane didn't leave the bed all day. She stopped answering her calls. She kept watching reruns of her old show. At lunchtime, she called for me.

"Zara!"

She ordered two peanut-butter-and-jelly sandwiches with two glasses of milk.

"We're out of milk," I told her.

"Seltzer, then."

An hour later, she called for me again.

"Zara!"

She wanted a snack. "Something sweet. Ice cream. Rocky road! The whole tub!"

So I brought it to her.

"Hey, I have a question," she said as she peeled off the lid. Her eyes stayed on the screen.

"What?"

"Would you come to my funeral?"

"What?"

"If I died, would you come to my funeral?"

"Jane."

"Answer the question!"

"Yes."

"Do you think Bijou and Tom would come?"

"I don't know."

She sighed. "How's your cleaning going?"

"Fine."

She took a long look at me. Her tub of ice cream was in one hand. Her spoon was in the other. "You're such a good girl," she said sadly.

More hours passed. Every molecule in the house was both frantic and horribly still. I cleaned the kitchen. I cleaned the gym. I cleaned the living room. I cleaned the hallways. I cleaned the stairs. In my old room, I opened the dresser drawer and thought, *Who bought these clothes?* I could barely remember the person I'd been before Jane.

While I was cleaning my office, I opened my journal and quickly wrote:

If I'm dead, Jane Bailey killed me.

I pushed the journal to the back of the desk drawer with the others, and then she called for me again.

"Zara!"

Had she seen me?

Apparently not. She just wanted more food. "Macaroni," she said. "And a massage. My toes hurt."

I brought her macaroni and rubbed her feet while she ate it.

"Yeah, right there," she said. "Oh yeah, baby."

I liked her feet in my hands better than I liked the broom. And I liked her feet because they hadn't changed. They weren't heavier or sadder or meaner or more complicated than before. I'd had this same thought about my dad's feet when he was dying.

After she finished eating, she said, "You can be done for the day. Take a bath."

I imagined stepping out of the tub and falling.

"I think I'll take a shower."

"Suit yourself."

I brought her dishes downstairs. I ate another few handfuls of muesli for dinner and an expired yogurt. I took more Advil.

In the shower, I lathered myself in her soap. The hot water on my shoulders felt good. For a few blissful moments, I lost myself in the sensation.

Then I put on my pajamas and was reminded of my pain. I slipped under the covers next to Jane. She took my arm and wrapped it around her stomach.

"I need you close," she said. "I need to know where you are at all times."

An hour later, I was pretending to sleep, and she was still awake, scrolling on her phone. I could feel her muscles tensing as she typed. Every so often, she let out a small sigh.

Go to sleep!

That's what I was thinking.

I kept envisioning how it would unfold: somehow I would find her phone, somehow I would get outside, somehow I would dodge her bullets.

But I was so tired from cleaning all day that I fell asleep before she did.

41

Hours later, I woke up and she was gone.

Slowly, I moved myself to her side of the bed and started searching for her phone, mostly with my hands, because my eyes hadn't adjusted to the dark yet. I checked the night table, the floor, underneath her pillow. Her phone wasn't there.

I walked carefully across the room and peeked into the hallway, and that's when I saw that the door to my office was open.

Blood rushed to my head. My stomach turned violently. For some reason, I already knew exactly what she was doing. I rushed down the hall. And then I stood for a moment outside my office door, just watching her—her ankles crossed on the desk, the back of her head, that tangle of hair, that disgusting cream robe, the careless movement of her hand as it flipped the page.

On the floor—oh shit—was her phone. It must have fallen out of her pocket.

I got down on all fours. I had to be fast, but patient. I crawled forward. And forward. And then—*No noise, please, no noise*—I picked up the phone, stuck it in the waistband of my boxer shorts, and pulled my shirt down over it.

Somehow, she still hadn't noticed me. But then, as I crept back out of the room, the floor creaked and she yelled, "Whoa!"

And then she whipped around, bringing her legs with her. I took a quick step back so they wouldn't hit my shins. She still possessed the agility of an acrobat even though she'd become a sloth.

"How long have you been doing this?"

"Awhile," she said, her eyes trained on me. "I know! Let me read you some of my favorite passages!"

Then she started reading.

"'If I'm dead, Jane Bailey killed me.' Do you think I'm going to *kill* you, Zara?"

I said nothing.

"I'm not going to *kill* you, silly. Who would feed me then? Who would clean the house?"

She pulled another journal out of the drawer, flipped to a page, and read, "'It doesn't feel like a choice to love Jane this much. I just do.' Aw."

She flipped to a new page.

"'Jane's voice is a lullaby. It's a field of tall grass you want to lie down in forever. It's a'—oh, and here, you crossed out 'willow tree.' Good move. That would have been a little cheesy."

She flipped again.

"Please stop."

She ignored me.

"'I love Jane's smell and her hair and her hands and her mouth. I love her entirely. I can't believe how much I love her.' Wow," she said. "That's so sweet."

"Jane," I said with more force.

"'I can't believe how shapeless I felt before I met Jane. I was a soup. She became my container.'"

An impossible amount of anger was speeding through every

one of my veins, a series of rivers pounding at a series of dams. Jane turned to take another journal out of the drawer.

And that's when I lost it.

I grabbed a chunk of her hair and pulled hard, and harder than that, and harder than I'd ever pulled anything. I pulled down so hard that her neck folded over the back of the chair and she screamed.

I let go of her hair, and right then, she punched me in the stomach, and I was coughing, catching my breath, and then she was grabbing a fistful of my hair and yanking harder than I'd yanked hers.

And I was sticking my hand in her face, clutching at all the crevices. With my other hand, I pushed her, then I swiped the humungous anchor-shaped paperweight off the desk and spun around and held it high over my head.

She was squinting, wiping her eye.

And then she was screaming a rattling scream that went on forever and rushing at me with her fists, and I was giving her my back and she was pounding me like the water that breaks the dam. Her phone fell out of my waistband and onto the floor and we both went for it, but I was faster.

She was crouched on the floor, looking up at me with terror and respect. And then she tried to stand, but the belt of her robe, caught under her foot, yanked her downward.

That's when I smashed the anchor into the back of her head.

As she softened to the ground, she let out a high-pitched sound.

I ran downstairs. I held her phone up to my swollen face. I prayed that it would recognize me. And it worked! I couldn't believe it worked.

I searched for the alarm app on her phone. My hands were trembling. She had so many apps. I scrolled through. I scrolled through again. How was it not here? Was it an app within a folder? How many folders did she have? I had to pay attention. I started over. I opened the first folder. The second folder.

I sensed movement and looked up and saw her running down the hall toward the bedroom.

The third folder. The fourth. Finally, I found the app.

"Stop whatever you're doing."

The command in her voice alerted me to what I was about to see: the gun in her hand.

I sprinted to the kitchen.

She ran down the stairs.

I ran right up to the sliding glass doors and—*no!* The phone had gone to sleep.

I showed it my face again.

Her feet were getting closer.

The phone unlocked. I opened the app again.

"Stop!"

She shot the gun, and I screamed, and the phone dropped from my hands.

And then she was walking toward me, saying, "Look what you made me do to my knife rack."

I looked. The knife rack had exploded into wood chips, and the knives had scattered all over the counter.

She leaned down and took her phone off the floor—and then she sprang up and smashed the side of the gun into my head.

I moaned.

She stared at me. I watched a line of blood trickle from her hairline down to her eyelid. She smeared it away with the sleeve of her robe.

"Come on," she said, "we're going back upstairs."

I didn't move.

"Let's go!" She grabbed my arm and twisted it hard and I had no choice but to start walking.

The stairs. The hallway. The bedroom. It took forever.

"Go to the closet."

"Why?"

"Don't ask me questions! Just do it!"

She let go of my arm, but kept the gun trained on me. I went to the closet. She opened the drawer that contained her scarves.

"Take four of those out," she said.

So I did.

"Now go to the bed and pull the covers all the way down to the bottom."

Once I'd done that, she said, "Lie down. And make your arms and legs into a T." She laughed. "Like Jesus Christ."

She started tying me to the bed. When she got to my left wrist, she said, "Who gave you this nice bracelet? Somebody wonderful?"

I closed my eyes.

Her knots were tight, but they should have been tighter.

When she was done, she said, "Be right back," and went into the bathroom.

I heard the faucet. Then the shower. I stared at the ceiling. I could have screamed, but no one would have heard me. I was going to die here, in this soundproofed house, with all those men standing just outside the gate, having accomplished nothing in my life.

I started making promises. *If I ever get out of here . . .*

Ten minutes later, she appeared in clean pajamas. Her hair was wet. She sauntered toward the bed. "There's something I love about physical violence. It's so . . . clarifying. Reminds you that you're made of nothing more than stardust."

She pulled the covers up to my chin. She didn't plug her phone into the charger. It was still in the pocket of her robe. When she took a sip of water, I turned to see the blood dripping down the back of her neck, and I started to cry.

How could I have been so cruel? Who had I become?

"Don't cry, baby."

She kissed me, and I cried harder.

She turned off the lights. She coiled her warm arms around me and whispered in my ear, "I can hear your heart beating. It's talking to me. What is it saying?"

I kept crying. And with every exhale, I yanked my left hand away from the knot.

Jane was on my right side. I could see the bulge of her phone on her hip.

The knot got looser. And looser.

But then I realized that it wasn't going to get loose enough to free my hand, so I conceded to my fate.

I was going to die in Jane's arms.

42

Imagine the beauty of East Hampton in summer. Imagine its long lines of fine sand and its pristine roads and its meticulous lawns. Imagine the decadent shades of green, and the swimming pools reflecting the sky like paintings in pretty tiled frames. Imagine how the salty air tastes like a dream.

The last morning Jane Bailey and I spent together was the most beautiful morning you could imagine. I looked out the window at the bright sun and closed my eyes to imagine the rest of what I knew was there. All you really need in order to tell a story are a few details.

Jane was curled around me, her head resting on my chest. I looked down the length of her and saw the phone, peeking out from the pocket of her robe. I knew it would be a waste of time to try to yank my hand out of the knot again, but I tried anyway, and—was it the angle? Was it a miracle?—it worked. I couldn't believe my hand was free. And Jane was snoring, still fast asleep. Very carefully, I pulled the phone out of her pocket. She kept snoring. I wasn't breathing as I held it up to my face. It unlocked.

I turned the volume all the way down and dialed 911. I couldn't hear the voice of the operator, so I imagined them saying the things I'd heard them say in movies.

911. What's your emergency?

I left a long enough silence for the dispatcher to figure out that I was in danger and unable to speak. I imagined them tracking the call to Jane's address, and then calling a cop who was patrolling the streets nearby and saying, "You need to go check on this."

I could see the cop turning on the sirens and picking up speed as I slid the phone back into Jane's pocket and returned my hand to the prison of the knot.

I could feel my heart beat faster, and I thought that if she'd woken up right then, she would have said, "Your heartbeat is telling me you're scared."

But she didn't wake up.

Time passed. It must have been minutes, but it felt like much longer. Then my stomach made a noise and her head lifted off my chest, and my immediate reaction was to miss its warmth.

I watched her lean her head back and yawn, and then she looked in the direction of my left wrist, the one that was falsely tied up, and I expected her to see the lie immediately, because I thought that Jane, like god, knew everything.

In reality, though, Jane was a tired woman with a puffy morning face looking down at me with sad recognition, as if to say, *Oh yeah, this is where we left off, with you tied to a bed.*

"Morning, sweet pea," she said.

"Morning."

She sat up and checked her phone.

"A throng of vultures at the gate," she reported. "Let's count them. You ready?"

She angled the screen so I could see it and counted with her finger. "One, two, three, four, five, six, seven, that's a leg right there, so I'm counting that as eight, nine, ten, eleven. Oh! And we got more coming! Twelve, thirteen . . ."

I think we saw it at the same time: two cops.

"Are those *pigs*?"

The cops cut straight through the crowd and went to the intercom.

"Shit!"

One pressed the call button, and the red banner at the top of Jane's screen blinked the alert: *gate.*

"This is how every tragedy ends," she said. "With pigs."

Then she cleared her throat and said into the phone, "Hello?"

"Jane Bailey?"

"Yes?"

"Can we come in, please?"

"What do you want?"

The cop leaned closer to the intercom. "I'm not sure how much more you want us to say with all these people down here."

"Who called you?"

"We can't—"

"Was it Julian Wright?"

The cops exchanged a look, and Jane whispered under her breath, "That's a yes."

"Ma'am, is there anyone in there with you?"

She looked at me. Into the phone, she said, "Give me five minutes."

"We need you to open this gate right now."

She hung up.

I imagined the first cop saying to the second, "Should we look for another entrance?"

And the second cop saying, "Yeah."

Jane was staring at me blankly. "What am I going to do?"

Slowly, she closed her eyes. Every muscle in her face relaxed and turned to stone. I think that was the moment she settled on her plan, because she was nodding just slightly.

Or maybe it was me nodding.

"You're going to go answer the door for us, okay?" She reached up to untie the first scarf.

"What do you want me to say?"

"Anything your little heart desires."

She looked at my mangled face. "Your poor sweet thing." She sighed, then went back to her untying. "This is what happens when you grow up in the country. You're basically born dead." She laughed. "Born dead, with a Cheeto hanging out of your mouth and a future that looks like a future for a while, but really, it's just the past in an elaborate headdress, fooling you into thinking that hope will be enough."

She stared at me for a long moment. "The empty look in your eyes," she said. "That's why I chose you, you know. I saw a vacancy I could fill. I thought, *If I can get this ghostwriter to fall in love with me, then my book will be perfect.*"

She finished untying my wrists and moved down to my ankles. I was imagining the cops had found another way onto the property and now they were almost at the house, about to break through the door.

"I didn't like you that much at first, so I thought there was no chance in hell I'd develop real feelings for you . . . but I guess we don't get to choose who we love." She set her hands on my cheeks and kissed my forehead. "You know I love you, right?"

"Yes," I said, and I believed her.

"That's the one true thing, maybe the only true thing." She

sighed. "Of course you know that a lot of what I told you during our interviews was fiction."

"Memory is faulty," I said. "Every memoir is fiction to some degree."

As she kept untying her knots, she told me more. "I only taught that class in Harlem once. And Claire. Claire was the kindest person you could ever hope to meet. But if I hadn't painted her as a villain, I would have had less to overcome. I wanted the arc of my hero's journey to be really pronounced, you know?"

When I said, "I understand," I wasn't really thinking about her story arc. I was wondering what was taking the cops so long. Why hadn't they broken through the door yet?

"I have something else to tell you." She pulled a scarf through the air, then looked right at me. "Mark didn't slip in the bathroom."

Why did my heart sink when she said that? I guess I still somehow wanted to believe that she was good.

"I should have done a murder-suicide, just like my mom. She really did shoot herself right after she shot my dad, by the way. That's a true story."

"I'm sorry."

"Thanks, sweetheart," she said. "And, listen, I do feel guilty for the things I've done. But not enough to make me want to change the past. Everything I did was necessary."

She finished untying the last knot, and then she was pulling the last scarf through the air.

Why wasn't I happy to be free?

Why wasn't I sprinting out the door?

Why did I love Jane?

"Come here," she said. She pulled me up with her hands, and

then we were sitting side by side at the edge of the bed, our bodies pressed together like peanut butter and jelly.

I was thinking, *I've never loved anyone this much.*

Then: *Is she going to kill me?*

How was it possible to hold so much desire and so much fear in the same body?

"Sweetheart, don't cry," she said, and then she started crying, too.

I wrapped my tired arms around her little body. I set my hand on the back of her head. I could feel the sticky patch of blood in her hair. I wanted to hold her forever and forget everything that had happened and start over, maybe somewhere new. I wanted to go back to the very beginning of the story.

When she pulled away from me, I thought I was dying. Her face was radiant in the light. She pressed her lips against mine. My eyes were wide open and so were hers, and it felt like looking at the most beautiful version of myself.

She picked up her phone and opened the gate.

"Go," she whispered.

I kissed her again and again and again.

"Go."

I knew that if she was going to shoot me in the back, it would have been right then. As I walked across the room, I could feel her eyes on me, and I could feel her considering her options. But when I got to the doorway and turned around, I saw she hadn't moved at all. I gazed at her for a moment. I blew her one last kiss.

My final image of Jane: she's sitting on the side of the bed in that gorgeous bedroom, the one that's like an ad for the life you want to be yours, and she's looking up at me with that mischievous smile on her face, and at the very last second, she winks.

Did I know what was coming as I walked down the stairs?

How could I not have known?

I kept walking. I watched my hand open the door, but it didn't feel like my hand.

The cops started talking.

My eyes fell on the fountain in the driveway.

That's what I was looking at when the single gunshot roared through the beautiful morning: Aphrodite, the goddess of love, her eyes closed to the sun.

Two Years Later

"You could have escaped," the journalist said, "after you went to the food bank, but you didn't. Why?"

We were sitting at a restaurant in San Francisco, the type of place that would have impressed my dad. The sky outside was thick with fog, and I was trying not to fidget.

"When you went back to the house after everything that had already happened, what were you thinking?"

I laughed, because I knew that's what she would have done, and then I said, "I guess I was thinking that history wouldn't repeat itself."

The journalist squinted at me. "You know, it sounds like you have a slight southern accent. But you grew up here, right?"

"In Bolinas, yeah, with my dad."

"And your mom left when you were young, as you say in the book."

"Right, she moved to Rome to live with a woman—a sculptor, actually—and then she died."

"And what about the woman who currently lives in Rome and claims to be your mother?"

The journalist was referring to the random-ass lady who'd told the internet she'd given birth to me. Apparently, she'd seen my book and read it and now wanted to reveal "the truth."

"I don't even know her," I told the journalist. "I think she just wants money."

A teenager in bell-bottoms walked by our table just then. She did a double take, then stopped. "Wait, are you Zara Pines? I loved your book! Will you sign my arm?"

"Of course, doll."

I flashed a wide smile—a flawless, wide smile, because I'd invested in veneers—and took the Sharpie out of my purse. I always carried a Sharpie for occasions like this.

The teenager held out her forearm. I made my signature big enough for Instagram to see it clearly.

After the teenager had thanked me and left, the journalist said, "You still have Jane's haircut. Do you think that makes you more recognizable?"

"Maybe," I said.

"And the title of your book. *I Want You More*. That was the title she was going to use."

I was unapologetic. "Yes."

The journalist tapped her pen against her cheek. "Would you say that the pain you endured was worth the recognition you're receiving now?"

I raised my eyebrows. "Nothing is for nothing."

"Isn't that Jane's line?"

Again, I was unapologetic. "Yes, and what a great line it is."

Next the journalist brought up the secondary characters in my story. I've been interviewed many times now about what happened in East Hampton, so I've come to expect this part.

Yes, I told her, Diego and I are still friends, and we still love each other a lot.

I didn't mention that he's taken some space from me recently, or that he wasn't thrilled about how I'd portrayed him as a sycophant in the book, or that he wasn't surprised I'd done that because, according to him, I have a habit of bending the facts.

In my defense, is everything not subjective?

Yes, I told the journalist, I still talk to Bijou and Tom every so often, and I'm delighted that they opened a restaurant. It was the next natural step after everyone learned that Jane's recipes were actually Bijou's.

Yes, I apologized to Andie for my atrocious behavior, and I wish her the best!

What I didn't tell the journalist was that Andie refused to speak to me and blocked me on all her social media accounts.

Had I talked to Julian?

No, but I thought he was a great guy.

I left out that he'd called a few times wanting details about Jane's death—apparently, he couldn't envision her killing herself—and I never returned his calls.

When asked about the lies in Jane's memoir—which was never published, but somehow got leaked to the press—I made a vague statement: "There are a lot of ways to remember the past."

And there are, dear reader. There are so many ways.

Imagine, for example, that when the journalist asked me why I didn't escape, I'd said, "If I had, then this story would have been missing its dramatic ending."

Imagine that when the journalist mentioned the woman in Rome, I had said, "So what if she's my mom? Maybe my dad decided to tell me she was dead when I was a kid, because he thought it would disappoint me less. And maybe by the time he told me she was still alive, I was eighteen years old and no longer interested in seeing her again. I was also uninterested in changing the story I'd been telling all my life about a mother who'd abandoned me in the middle of the night carrying a checked suitcase and bracing herself against the furious winds of Bolinas."

Or, dear reader, imagine this:

What if there's a different version of my final moments with Jane?

What if, as we sat on the edge of her bed, our bodies pressed together like peanut butter and jelly, she had said, *Nothing can save me now, right?* And I had echoed, *Nothing.*

Imagine her tiny gasp.

I'd never said anything like that to her before.

What if I'd put my hand over hers, and together, we'd curled our fingers around the gun?

What if we'd brought the gun to her temple, and I'd whispered, *There's only one way out of this, but I think you know that already.*

Can you see me getting up and walking to the door?

Can you see me turning to take one last look at her?

What if instead of smiling at me, she had just stared, her eyes hopelessly dark like two empty wells, and after I blew her one last kiss, I had said, *If your brand is more real than reality, then the truth is you're already dead.*

ACKNOWLEDGMENTS

Thank you

Nora Gonzalez
Bridie Loverro
Maddie Woda
Danielle Christopher
Zibby Owens
and everyone at Zibby Publishing.

I'm endlessly grateful.

ABOUT THE AUTHOR

Swan Huntley's novels include *Getting Clean With Stevie Green, The Goddesses*, and *We Could Be Beautiful*. She's also the writer/illustrator of the darkly humorous *The Bad Mood Book* and *You're Grounded: An Anti-Self-Help Book to Calm You the F*ck Down*. Swan earned an MFA at Columbia University and has received fellowships from MacDowell and Yaddo. She lives in Los Angeles.

@swanhuntley
www.swanhuntley.com